Deadly Odds 2.0

Allen Wyler

Deadly Odds 2.0

Other books by Allen Wyler (fiction)

Changes
Deadly Odds
Dead Ringer
Dead End Deal
Dead Wrong
Deadly Errors
Dead Head
Cutter's Trial

Other books by Allen Wyler (nonfiction)

The Surgical Management of Epilepsy

Deadly Odds 2.0 ©2019 Allen Wyler, All Rights Reserved

Print ISBN 978-1-949267-22-8
ebook ISBN 978-1-949267-23-5

Visit Allen online at www.allenwyler.com

Cover design by Guy D. Corp
www.grafixCORP.com

STAIRWAY≡PRESS

STAIRWAY PRESS—APACHE JUNCTION

www.stairwaypress.com
1000 West Apache Trail, Suite 126
Apache Junction, AZ 85120 USA

Chapter 1

"CLAIMS IT'S IMPORTANT...something about a death threat on one of your clients."

"Which client?"

"That makes a difference?"

"Perhaps."

"Seriously?"

"You know Fisher...and his tendency for drama."

Davidson sighed, flipped to a new page of the legal pad and jotted down the time. He habitually took notes during conversations, especially if there was the slightest whiff of a case.

"Have a seat." Davidson ushered Special Agent Gary Fisher into his office. "Joyce, please hold any calls until Agent Fisher leaves," hoping the not-so-subtle hint would sink in, as doubtful as that might be.

Fisher struck him as impervious to hints, blatant or otherwise.

Davidson's office—in Seattle's iconic Smith Tower—was best described as straight out of a 1930s Hollywood noir: Art Deco furniture, dark stained mahogany wall paneling, wood-slat venetian blinds in perfect concert with the building's time-warp interior. He even carried the theme one step further with a wall of original black and white photography of Seattle's Pioneer Square in the early 1900s during the period when the building held the brief distinction as the West Coast's first skyscraper. The two Persian carpets on the polished hardwood added another nice touch.

"Thanks for seeing me on such short notice."

After a quick handshake, Fisher folded himself into one of the two leather armchairs and shot the sleeves of his crisp white dress shirt.

Davidson shut the office door, settled into his leather desk-chair and steepled his fingers under his chin.

"Joyce said you wanted to talk about a client. Who might that be?"

"Arnold Gold."

Arnold?

The name caught Davidson completely off guard, at a loss for words.

"Where is he?" Fisher pressed.

"Are you kidding...the lad is dead."

He studied the FBI agent's serious-as-hell expression.

No, this didn't appear to be a joke.

"We have evidence that he's alive. I want to know where he's hiding."

"Really!" Again, momentarily stunned. "What makes you think that?"

Fisher sucked a tooth, as if weighing exactly how much to divulge.

"What I'm about to disclose can't leave this room. We clear?"

Davidson nodded. "Understood."

"SFD's investigation," referring to the Seattle Fire Department, "indicated an initial explosion in the basement. They never determined the exact cause but suspect it involved the gas line. That detail was never released to the press."

Interesting.

"Because?"

"Two reasons. The investigation took two months to finish up and by then was the news outlets could care less."

"But—"

"We never disclosed the terrorist angle. Those details were—and still are—classified."

Makes sense.

Davidson studied Fisher's smug body language. "What are you

not telling me?"

Fisher smiled. "We believe Gold detonated it. Intentionally."

Wow!

Davidson recoiled.

"Are you saying he blew up his own house? Why on earth would he do such a thing?"

"Could be several reasons. Maybe it was an accident. Or, just maybe—and this is what I believe—he intended to kill Karim."

Davidson chewed on that one a moment.

Was it possible? Perhaps. But was it likely? Hmmm....

Several questions came to mind.

"Back to my original question; why do you believe he is alive?"

"From very clever deduction, Counselor. Only one body was recovered from the debris."

Silence...then, "I assume it was not Arnold?"

"Correct assumption. It was Karim Farhad."

"Huh!"

News to Davidson. The local media—his only source for post-fire facts—reported that the homeowner, Arnold Gold, perished in the fire. He now understood why the terrorism link wasn't mentioned; the press wasn't informed of it. Nor had any news sources provided a follow-up story. Which now made complete sense. Without the terrorist angle, the story had no legs. After all, no one of consequence owned the house. No babies or lovable pets perished, eliminating any tear-jerking angle. And, because he simply assumed Arnold died in the fire, he had no reason to follow-up with the police, fire department, or Fisher. Instead, he simply turned his attention to his next client. Realizing this left him feeling unsettled and irritated at himself.

"I want to be absolutely clear on one point," Davidson said. "Are you alleging that Arnold willfully triggered an explosion with the specific intent of killing Karim Farhad?"

Well, why not? A move like that would be pure Arnold Gold.

He fought to curb the faint smile tugging the corners of his mouth.

By God, he did do it! Blew up his goddamn house, then vanished. Bravo!

"I'm convinced of it. And that part doesn't leave this room under any circumstance. Understood?"

"Understood. However, if your assertion *is* correct, Arnold is vulnerable to a possible charge of premeditated murder."

Fisher signaled Time Out.

"Whoa...before you go getting yourself wrapped around the axle, let me be the first to say that if Gold *did* turn that asshole into charcoal, hey, more power to him. Chalk one up for the good guys. Let me also say that when I do see him—and I will—I plan on shaking his hand. Then I want to sit him down and ask how the hell he pulled off a stunt like that. Got it?"

The lawyer in Davidson didn't completely buy it, but nodded agreement anyway. "Go on."

"Reason I'm here is I want your help with finding him."

Fisher's tone certainly came across as sincere....

"I would, but have no idea where he might be...assuming, of course, he *is* alive and his body wasn't completely consumed in the fire."

He found himself amused by the image of Arnold kicking back somewhere—the coast of France perhaps—enjoying the good life while siphoning money from crooks.

"Think back to your conversations with him...he say *any*thing, anything at all, that might give a hint where to look?"

"Not a word." Pause. "I assume you have exhausted your usual due diligence?"

"Obviously. And I can't find a goddamn trace. The kid simply vanished."

Davidson leaned back, closed his eyes, and worked on recalling events now warped by the vagaries of memory.

"I gave a statement last year...what did I say then?"

"I reviewed it again before walking over, but want to hear

what you remember *now*. We both know how tricky memory can be. There may be some things you remember now."

Davidson massaged the bridge of his nose and thought hard. A name popped out of nowhere. He snapped his fingers.

"Nawzer. Did I mention him last year?"

"Who?"

"Nawzer…he was trying to steal Arnold's system. Did I include him in the report?"

Fisher appeared to think about it.

"Name doesn't ring a bell…" and made a note on his laptop. "Anything else?"

Davidson shook his head. "Nothing at all."

Neither man spoke for several moments, Fisher making more notes while Davidson mulled over the shocking news.

"Back up and tell me why you believe his life is in danger?"

"Good question. The answer's very interesting. Last week a story popped up in Al Jazeera. The reporter claimed to be in possession of our case file and that Gold is presently in the W-P-P."

Witness Protection Program? Al Jazeera? Wow, another bombshell right out of left field.

"Hold on…I want to be absolutely clear on this…an *Al Jazeera* reporter got his hands on a copy of Arnold's *FBI file*? How the hell does that happen?"

Fisher glanced at the door, before lowering his voice.

"We're actively working that up before we entirely buy it. Some of the story's true, but some's pure bullshit. We *do* believe Gold's alive, but the W-P-P? Hey, that's total bullshit. Yes, he was offered that option early on, but the kid flat-out refused."

"How did the reporter get his hands on his case file?"

"*If* they did."

"But—"

"Believe me, OPR," meaning the Office of Public Responsibility, "is crawling up everyone's ass over this looking for a leak, but if they they've found the source, it's way above my pay grade."

"Huh!" Davidson looked at his notes. "Which brings up another point...how were you made aware of the story? I do not see you reading Al Jazeera over your morning coffee."

"Another great question. The story was picked up by one of our intelligence agencies and immediately passed on to OPR. And because Gold was my investigation, OPR sat me down to ask a few, ah, let's say probing questions."

Davidson suspected he knew the next answer, but wanted to hear it from Fisher.

"Where does the life or death issue come into play?"

"Ever since the article's release, CIA's been hearing increased chatter that Farhad's cell is determined to hunt down Gold to cut his fucking head off. Seriously. Actually behead the kid."

Davidson made another note.

"Just out of curiosity, is this an official Bureau investigation?"

He believed Fisher had a soft spot for Arnold in spite of trying not to show it.

"It is and it isn't. It is from the OPR standpoint, but it isn't from the aspect of focusing any major effort on doing anything about Farhad's group."

"Why would they ignore a threat from a terrorist group like that?"

"Very simple; the Bureau's tapped out with other priorities at the moment. *But*...if you did find him and gave us actionable information, that priority would jump the list immediately."

"What qualifies as actionable information?"

Fisher grinned.

"If we were to unequivocally verify he *is* alive, and *if* I can persuade him to assist in an investigation, well..." with a shrug.

"In other words, you want me to find him so you can use him as bait." Then added, "Good luck with your hunt."

"Look, Davidson...I'm out of leads. I'm asking you, as his lawyer, to find him."

And there it was.

"No. I do not have time even if I was inclined to assist, which I am not."

"Let me get this straight; you're saying you don't give a damn about the kid?"

"No, that is not what I said. I thought I was extremely clear. My case load is full and I have no idea where he might be...or if he is alive. Most importantly, I do not wish to see the lad used as terrorist bait."

Fisher shook his head.

"I'm not buying it. Look, we both want to help Gold. Yes, he's a hacker and gambler, but you have to admit, he's a damn good hacker and gambler...so, if he turned that fucker into a crispy critter, hell, more power to him."

Fisher applauded.

"My answer is still no. But, for the sake of argument, if I were to consider working on this, and say I *did* to locate him, what would be the legal repercussions?"

"Thought we covered that. Our goal is to protect, not prosecute him."

"But the death remains under investigation."

"True. But I have to tell you in all honesty, there's not a shred of evidence against him. Far as the Bureau's concerned, there is no case. We now clear on this?"

"Fine, but we both know the Bureau does not speak for the DA."

"True again, but if Gold is alive, this case becomes Federal. Because at that point, it becomes a Homeland Security issue."

Davidson considered that a moment.

"And the Bureau will agree to sign the appropriate documents attesting to your assurances?"

Fisher laughed.

"Absolutely." Pause. "You'll give it some thought? And call me if you remember anything?"

"I will consider what you said. But, you need to understand that any participation on my part is *extremely* unlikely." Davidson pushed back from the desk, stood, extended his hand. "Nice to see you again, Agent Fisher."

After escorting him to the elevator, Davidson returned to his office, shut the door and sat at his desk to reread the notes he was working on before the interruption. Hard as he tried to reconstruct his train of thought, he couldn't stop worrying about Arnold. Hmmm…why become involved in what might end up to be a difficult, time-consuming, fruitless search? After all, the lad chose to disappear for a reason and was undoubtedly well hidden. What might be the unintended consequences if he did find him?

Assuming I could.

After all, Naseem knew he was Arnold's lawyer last year. Meaning, if she was seriously searching for him, would she already have eyes on him?

He leaned back in the chair, hands clasped behind his head and stared at the ceiling.

Chapter 2

DAVIDSON POKED HIS head back out the office door, said, "Please hold any calls for the rest of the day."

Joyce turned, "You got it, Mr. Davidson."

She was his only full-time employee for ten years now and thrived on the solitude, sitting for hours, ear buds in place, fingers flying in a noiseless blur over the keyboard. Most importantly, she could be trusted to not blab sensitive information. For her loyalty and excellent work ethic, he rewarded her each Christmas with a generous cash (read, tax-free) bonus.

Back in his desk chair, swiveling side to side, tapping steepled fingertips against his chin, he mulled over Fisher's words. It seemed likely—no, absolutely certain—that Arnold *was* alive. The pivotal question was: is he truly in danger?

Perhaps. But only if Naseem could find him.

How likely was that?

No way to know. Arnie was a very canny, resourceful young man and, no doubt, difficult to track down. But how could he be sure of this? The only way to answer that was to try finding him. Because if he could, then...

Well, that wasn't entirely true. He wasn't on a level playing field with Naseem. She held a decided advantage by knowing whatever personal information she gleaned during their nights together. He wasn't privy to their pillow talk. Who knew what they discussed?

Which left him only one option: he needed to warn Arnold before she could locate and annihilate him.

Fine, with that issue resolved, he was faced with where to begin. When taking on any new case, his first step was to personally verify each fact rather than accept hearsay. Why should Fisher's word be any different?

Because he was an FBI agent?

He knew law enforcement lied when it suited them.

He Googled Al Jazeera, found the English edition, entered a search for Arnold Gold, and in return was left with a full screen of irrelevant hits for the Arnold P. Gold foundation and the commodities index. He refined the search parameters to Arnold Gold, Seattle, Washington, and voila, there was the article. Fisher was correct.

Davidson phoned a contact in the Seattle Fire Department, a friend he frequently used when fact-checking such issues.

"I need a favor," he said.

"Don't we all." Pause. "What?"

"Last year a house near Greenlake burned to the ground." Davidson gave him the address and date. "I need to know how many bodies were recovered in the investigation."

"I assume this is for a client?"

Davidson didn't answer.

After a short pause, "How soon you need it?"

Davidson hated to ask for a rush job, but knew the information would probably not otherwise arrive for a week or two because his busy friend tended to let such requests slide.

"Soon as possible. It is critical."

"I'll see what I can find out."

Chapter 3

DAVIDSON GLANCED AT the manila folder on the desk; the police report for a case he'd been asked to represent. The defendant, a petty career criminal had been yo-yoing in and out of detention since age twelve without ever holding down a real job. Exactly the type of case that was his bread and butter. When graduating law school, he'd wanted to make sure each of his accused clients received a fair and vigorous defense. But after years of dealing with clowns like this one, serious doubts began to undermine that resolve. Plus, the redundancy and futility of representing his dirtball clients was now excoriating his spirit.

What was the point of investing such effort to defend criminals who never wanted, nor seem able to change their antisocial behavior? Was he doing it simply for the money now? He craved a change of pace, a distraction from the knee-jerk defensive machinations required to defend his enlarging circle of dirt-bags. This was precisely why Arnold had been such a refreshing client. Instead of a petty criminal, here was a brilliant young man who, ironically, supported himself by living off of society's piranhas; an image that possessed karmic symmetry. This thought brought a chuckle.

The phone rang; his friend at the Fire Department calling back.

"Only one body was recovered, and it was a charred mess.

SPD eventually identified it from DNA but I don't have the name so you'll have to use another source if that's important."

Davidson jotted down the information.

"No evidence of a second body? None at all?"

"One means one, not one and a partial."

Davidson placed two exclamation marks after the note.

"Thanks. I really appreciate this."

Davidson went online to Sterling Vineyards and ordered three bottles of a particularly nice Napa Cabernet Sauvignon Reserve to be delivered to his source's office with a thank you note. He began to pace. Arnold *was* alive.

Given that, where in hell was he?

At the window now, eyes wandering over the familiar view, he began to formulate a search strategy. But before deciding whether or not to jump down that particular rabbit hole, he needed to either accept or decline the case he'd been asked to consider. He sat down and opened the manila folder on the front sheet and dialed the phone number.

"Jose? Palmer Davidson…yeah, I know. Wait, I *am* calling…wait, let me finish…yes, I know…hey, that is your decision. The reason I am calling is I cannot do anything on the case for another week or so. If you want to retain another lawyer…no, I have not cashed the check, so no, you are not out a penny."

Call finished, he slipped his suit coat from the coat rack, paused, reconsidered, replaced it. Too nice a day for a coat.

He exited his office and said, "I will be out of the office an hour or two and will not be back until after you leave. Go ahead, lock up and I will see you in the morning."

"No problem."

She didn't bother to glance up from the monitor, much less break pace.

Chapter 4

DAVIDSON CURBED HIS Tesla across the street from the postage-stamp-sized lot where Arnold's tidy Tudor once stood. He propped his butt against the front fender and looked around. The fire had been so intense that only the concrete foundation remained. Like all houses in this neighborhood, it occupied the majority of the lot, leaving only enough room for tiny back and front yards.

Because Arnold was the property owner of record with no known heir, the city was forced to sell the condemned property at auction. The new owner—a German speculator, Davidson learned by retrieving the property record on his iPhone—was in the process of building a new home on the site, the present structure being nothing more than a skeletal frame. In contrast to the traditional architecture of the neighborhood, the construction appeared to be contemporary. Davidson wasn't interested in the house per se, but instead, hoped that viewing the lot and neighborhood again might knock lose a memory to aid his search, a strategy he routinely used when mounting a defense.

The sights seemed to be helping. Snippets of conversation began drifting back into his mind, all of which he dictated into his phone. He stepped into the middle of the street and shot a 360-degree video of the neighborhood with his phone to review back in the office. He carefully checked to make sure the recordings were satisfactory. They were. Time to head back to the office.

He jumped the 85th Avenue ramp to southbound I-5 into downtown and was immediately mired bumper-to-tailpipe in traffic, but any annoyance was smothered by newfound excitement, blue skies, and the 74-degree temperature. Yes, a break from his typical depressing routine was better than Prozac.

He took the James Street exit to Second Avenue, then south for a block before entering a multistory parking garage—a mosaic of additions and renovations, spanning more than a century of service—in the heart of historic Pioneer Square.

He exited the building and continued on foot past the Smith Tower to his favorite ratty Chinese restaurant where he ordered half of a barbecued duck and broccoli in oyster sauce to go. No rice. He'd recently excluded carbs from his diet as a way to battle the insipient weight gain of aging.

While waiting for his order, he began making a list of items to follow-up on. Ten minutes later, he whistled while walking the few blocks back to his office, delighted to once again be grappling with a seemingly insurmountable problem, a mental challenge which represented everything absent from his present skull-numbing practice—something he'd not felt for years. He looked forward to a full evening of work.

Chapter 5

DAVIDSON UNLOADED THE bag of take-out on the desk, his mouth watering from the smell. He uncapped the bottle of chilled spring water and took a long, refreshing drink.

Before sitting down to eat, he opened a mahogany wall panel, exposing a clean white-board stocked with a tray of multicolor felt-tip pens. He began transcribing his notes to the board. Another Jew seemed to be arising from the dead. He laughed at the joke.

Finished, he stepped back to study the list, but rapidly became discouraged, because none of his memories provided any clue as to where Arnold might be living. They all centered around the ill-fated trip to Las Vegas. But this raised an interesting question: did he actually move from Seattle or could he still in the city? Interesting. One thing he knew for certain was that Arnold thrived on deception. Could this work?

Probably not.

Because?

Well, for starters, Seattle was not all that big of a city. There was always the chance of bumping into someone you knew, making the risk of being discovered too high. Arnold loved deception, but he loved a sure thing more. No, the lad had moved. Okay, where?

He began to pull cities out of thin air, just to see if anything clicked: San Francisco, LA, Denver, Portland...none of them seemed more likely than the others, and this left him feeling frustrated and annoyed at himself. And made him realize just how little he actually knew about the lad.

An hour later, no further along, he noticed his untouched dinner. Ah, perfect, a distraction.

At 8:34, while nibbling a duck leg, an offhanded remark Arnold once made popped into mind: "The best vacation ever, was when my family was still alive. We stayed at a hotel in Honolulu for ten days. It was only, like, two blocks from Waikiki."

Honolulu. Hmmm...was that possible?

He dropped the duck leg on the paper plate, leaned back and thought about it. Honolulu. Arnold was clearly emotionally attached to the trip. It was, after all, a time when his family remained intact, before the cold-blooded murder of his parents destroyed his life.

At last! Here was something to work with. He stood, wiped his greasy fingers on a napkin, wrote, "Honolulu," in large red caps at the top of board, stepped back, studied it and was struck with another memory; they were standing beside Davidson's car in the Evans Pool parking lot when Arnold said, *I have limited skills. In fact, I only have computer skills. Artificial intelligence and predicting odds. Right now, I make enough good money that I'm not about to throw it away and start all over by going back to school. And I'm not about to start doing unskilled labor for a living. If I somehow make it out of this mess, I'll still have to gamble.*

By 9:30, he was no further along. His best shot, he decided—in truth, his only shot—remained Honolulu, so that was where he'd concentrate. If nothing came of it, well, at least he'd have given the search his best shot. If neither he nor the FBI could locate Arnold, chances were Naseem couldn't either. But it was definitely time for a break.

After a quick pit stop, he reorganized the white board, listing the essential details in order of potential importance.

16

What would Arnold require in a living space? That answer was easy enough. His highest priority would be to rebuild his extravagant artificial intelligence system. Which, in turn, would require state of the art security. And that would likely necessitate a single-family dwelling.

Okay, those issues were settled.

What else?

Arnold would probably want maximum security physically and digitally. The best physical barrier would be a wall around the property. If not a wall, at least a hedge. Definitely he'd need the fastest possible Internet access...the faster the better. Ideally a direct fiber-optic feed to the house, but how likely was that?

One more item to research.

Price range? He had no idea of Arnold's financial health, so estimated a net worth based on Fisher's guesstimate of his income last year; perhaps five-hundred thousand. Then again, what the hell did Fisher really know? Arnold hadn't disclosed how much he was raking in, especially in view of the income taxes he hadn't paid.

What else? His mind blanked.

Hmm...something felt wrong, a feeling...something about the Greenlake house he was forgetting. He closed his eyes and let his mind drift, trying not to concentrate on what it might be.

The thought flickered back but not clearly strong enough to get a grip on, so he began to rummage through at his notes. Ahhh, there it was; Hans Weiser, the Munster businessman who purchased the lot. Something didn't feel right about that. Why would a businessman in Germany buy a destroyed house in Seattle?

Hmmm...good question.

And now that he was on this particular subject, how the hell would Weiser know it existed? Could Weiser actually be one of Arnold's bogus identities? He laughed at the irony. Such a deception would be quintessential Gold. So much so, he was tempted to accept it as fact. Fine, but so what? This little distraction was not bringing him any closer to finding Arnold.

Back to Honolulu.

He started a search of all Oahu property transactions from the day of the fire to one week ago. By midnight, it had yielded a spreadsheet of fifty-three possible (on paper at least) properties.

Finished with that part, he began inspecting each property on Google Earth and based on those pictures, graded each one on six different criteria; security, privacy, price, etc. The grading system could now be used to order all fifty properties from the most to the least desirable.

Goddamn!

He was on a roll.

Chapter 6

"CALL ME ON the burner," Naseem said before dumping the call. She hurried into the bedroom and powered-on the cellphone purchased just yesterday in a Los Angeles strip mall. She would use the device only once and then toss it in a dumpster.

She paused to view her reflection in the mirror and turned her head from right to left and back again, admiring the attractiveness that served her well as an escort. Five foot seven inches of well-formed female anatomy. No sign of wrinkles on her smooth, flawless light-brown complexion. Silky black hair she preferred to not hide beneath a hijab, in spite of her religious beliefs. Would she live to be an old woman? She hoped so, but if not...

Two minutes later, the phone rang.

"Yes?"

"There is news. The FBI agent met with the lawyer, as we anticipated."

Ah, very good news indeed and it filled her heart with hope.

"Where?"

She wanted the call to end. Although it was extremely unlikely the phone was monitored, you never knew who could be listening...especially here in the United States.

"In the lawyer's office."

"This is good." She nodded with satisfaction. Although she didn't fully understand how Nawzer could listen to Davidson's phone calls—something about first stealing the lawyer's Amazon account and from there being able to work his way into his office computer where he'd installed a virus that quickly spread to all the man's other digital devices including his phone. "Please tell me they talked about the Jew."

"Yes. That was the point of the meeting."

"Where is he?"

"The lawyer is claiming he doesn't know and I am believing him."

The flame of excitement in her heart vanished as if wet fingers squeezed a candle wick. A year of hunting the Jew who was responsible for killing Karim and led to the capture of her husband was yet to yield one grain of actionable information.

Then, suddenly, as if from Allah himself, a message had appeared in Al Jazeera. Yes, it must have been divine guidance, a sign for her to not lose faith, for if she stayed faithful, Allah would surely reward her. She took heart, for she knew that with this news they were closer to finding the Jew than a week ago. She paused to pray for her desire to ultimately bear fruit.

"So, we have nothing?" she finally asked.

"I am being hopeful."

She waited.

"The lawyer is searching property records in Honolulu. This is new. He was not doing this before the meeting. First, he is searching for anyone with the name of Gold, but now he is looking at single properties under any name."

Her spirits soared like a desert hawk.

"Ah, excellent, this is excellent."

"But this is all I am having for you now."

"You will call me immediately if you learn anything new."

This was said as an order and not a question.

"I will."

"Excellent. Do not forget our main mission."

"Never."

She powered off the burner and removed the SIM card. She would dump them separately as soon as a flight to Honolulu was booked.

God willing, she would find Arnold Gold.

Chapter 7

DAVIDSON FINALLY HIT the sack a few minutes after 3:00 AM with the alarm set for 6:00. Luckily, he was able to snag a first-class ticket on Hawaiian Airlines—the only available seat on any US airline to Honolulu during the next week—on the 10:30 out of SeaTac.

In addition, he booked a Mustang convertible and his favorite room at the Halekulani on Waikiki. His black leather carry-on was packed with three drip-dry shirts, two pairs of cargo shorts, underwear, a laptop, comfortable walking shoes, and his favorite faded blue swim trunks. He planned to stay there for only three days. During that time, he'd either find where Arnold lived or he wouldn't, and if not, so be it. He will have given it his best shot.

"Hawaiian Airlines flight twenty from Seattle to Honolulu is now boarding travelers in need of assistance."

Standing in the boarding area, Davidson watched a woman in a wheelchair being pushed into the jetway by a man who could be her spouse. He dialed Fisher's cell. Fisher picked up on the third ring.

"Fisher, Palmer Davidson. I was thinking about our discussion yesterday. Have your people run any financials on him?"

The Bureau would be able to tap into information he couldn't, giving them an advantage. Although he suspected Fisher had already exhausted this lead, he wanted to double check. You never knew…

"No."

Now that was surprising.

"And the reason is?"

Davidson shifted his carry-on from right to left shoulder to relieve the weight.

"Thought I was very clear on that. At the moment he isn't a high enough priority to waste over-taxed resources on. Why?"

Davidson shuffled forward another step, anxious to board and stuff the bag in the footwell. It was aggravating his sore shoulder. First Class passengers would board next.

"Because if you expect me to devote billable hours to doing your work, it would be nice to know you will provide a modicum of assistance."

An aged, markedly kyphotic woman with withered veined hands wrestled a duct-taped aluminum walker as an attendant steadied her balance.

Fisher was silent several seconds.

"What exactly do you want us to do?" with a hint of annoyance.

"Well, one item would be to take a close look at the sale of the Greenlake property."

Fisher coughed a dismissive snort.

"Way ahead of you…I did that two days ago. The property was bought at auction and the title transferred to a new owner by the name…of…haven't I given that to you already?" again with a tone of annoyance.

Davidson decided he'd need to research that particular issue himself at the next opportunity and, for now, not mention his suspicion that Weiser could actually be Arnold. If Fisher elected to not share information, fine, he could play that same game. He shrug-adjusted the carry-on once more and shuffled two steps closer to the gate.

"Okay, forget the property. What about the I-R-S?"

"What about them? We checked. They don't have a tax filing

since we lowered the boom on him. It's a dead end."

Ah, so the Bureau *did* check a few things.

"Did your financial gnomes investigate the discount brokerage firms he uses? Any activity since the explosion?"

He had no idea if Arnold actually possessed such an account, but Fisher didn't know that. Maybe by dangling the possibility out there...

"No."

"In that case, would you be so kind as to look into it?"

He watched the jetway swallow the last disabled passengers.

"Yeah, yeah, yeah, okay." Fisher sighed. "On one condition."

Typical.

"And that would be?"

"You give me any information you have, or will obtain, relating to his whereabouts. We have a deal?"

"Agreed. However, as already stated, I have no idea where he might be living. I plan to explore a few thoughts and if anything pans out, I will advise you accordingly."

Davidson watched the gate attendant cast one final glance down the jetway before pulling the PA microphone from the wall holder to announce; "All passengers holding First Class seating and Gold Club Members may board at this time...", her amplified voice echoing from the overheads.

Chapter 8

DAVIDSON SETTLED INTO his seat aboard the Boeing 777 as Hawaiian music played softly in the background; steel and acoustic guitars, ukulele and two-part harmony.

It seemed to him that every Hawaiian song he ever heard sounded the same; same key, same harmony, same chord progression. Which was okay for something like preflight music...just not what he'd choose to listen to on Pandora.

As the huge plane accelerated down the runway, he checked out the films in the back of the in-flight magazine. He'd already seen the two good ones, leaving two romantic comedies, two vampire fantasies, and three kiddy flicks. He was tempted to watch George Clooney's *The Descendants* again, but had seen it three times since the 2011 release.

Instead, he spent the time on his laptop reviewing the fifty-three addresses of interest. When finished with that task, he stowed the device in his carry-on, reclined his seat, and tried to relax enough to snooze, but couldn't keep from ruminating on where the hell Arnold might be hiding.

Was this trip a wild goose chase? Did it matter?

Suddenly, he was struck by a wave of paranoia; *Am I being followed?* Was he leaving any sort of a trail?

The more he worried, the more he realized he was being sloppy. Naseem knew damn well he was Arnold's lawyer. Why did he ignore this connection until now? Hell, her people could be watching him since the Al Jazeera article hit the press.

He sat upright to scan the neighboring passengers. No one seemed to be looking at him. At least not right now, but...if they were, they'd be too crafty to be caught in the act.

Now what?

Once he's at the hotel, should he simply stay put for a three-day break and jettison the search?

Good question.

No, he decided, he must try to warn the lad. With all hope of a cat nap gone, he resumed work, spending the rest of the flight refining his search strategy. He tried to lessen his anxiety by assuring himself that the trip was so last minute and spontaneous, that none of Naseem's people could possibly be on the flight.

But he also suspected she had sympathizers in Honolulu. Not only that, but there was a computer record of his airline ticket.

How easily could that be found out?

He had no idea.

Chapter 9

HIS EARS POPPED, awakening him. He'd unintentionally dozed. Opened his eyes, he decided they were beginning their approach into Honolulu International. Seconds later the Captain came over the PA system and verified that assumption.

The moment the flight attendant popped the cabin door, Honolulu's luxuriously warm humid air bathed him, chasing away the cabin's residual chill. He'd already stuffed his leather jacket in his carry-on and was now wearing a white cotton safari shirt and lightweight slacks.

He exited the gate, passed through the terminal, jogged down the stairs to Baggage Claim and car rental booths where he initialed the requisite lines on the rental contract and signed the credit card receipt. Before handing Davidson the keys, the chubby Hawaiian forced him to listen and then repeat the directions to the rental lot despite Davidson's claim of already knowing its location.

First thing Davidson did when arriving at the car was open the doors and toss his bag on the back seat, then lowered the convertible top. Good to go. He fired up the engine and drove out of the Hertz lot onto the access road to H1, otherwise known as the Queen Liliuokalani Freeway.

Traffic was surprisingly light for this time of day, allowing him to reach the Kalukaua Avenue exit in record time. From that point on, however, it was typical blood-pressure spiking stop-and-go madness as far as Lewers Street. Two blocks later, Lewers t-boned Kalia Road. One left turn, a few feet further, and he was in the Halekulani loading zone where an attendant in a white, short-sleeved shirt and black slacks opened his door for him.

"Welcome to the Halekulani, sir."

A bellman simultaneously plucked his carry-on from the back seat.

Being in a hurry, he didn't want to waste any time going through the usual protocol, so said, "I know the drill, thank you. This is my only bag, so no point hanging on to it," while slipping the man a five. "I need the car again in...perhaps thirty minutes."

Shouldering his carry-on, he cut across the white marble floor past a huge vase of ever-present fresh tropical flowers to the front desk. He loved the rock-solid consistency this hotel offered; you knew exactly what to expect and were never disappointed.

Tanya, the receptionist, greeted him with a broad smile.

"Welcome back, Mr. Davidson. You're in luck. Your room's is ready. Mariko will show you up."

He was pleasantly surprised at the news because Seattle flights touched down by noon before many of the departing guests checked out, so typically rooms weren't ready for check-in until mid- to late-afternoon. He'd planned to use the second-floor hospitality suite to freshen up and stow his bag before spending the afternoon searching for Arnold.

Assuming, of course, the young man was actually on the island.

Mariko, an attractive Japanese hostess, led him across the marble floor to the elevator alcove.

"How long since your last visit, Mr. Davidson?"

She pressed the call button.

"Late February. I typically spend a week-to-ten-days that month as part of my mental health routine."

Although he didn't excessively suffer from Seasonal Affective Disorder, Seattle's constant, oppressive, gray winter skies were depressing.

"In that case, your room was renovated since your last visit...but the changes are so subtle you may not even notice. Most of our regulars never do. Just new paint on the walls and some of the furniture replaced."

The elevator dinged, the doors opened, and three Japanese couples—one young woman in full bridal dress—exited. The hotel made a killing catering to the Japanese wedding trade.

Davidson and Mariko entered the elevator.

Mariko opened the door to his room and stood aside so he could enter. The interior appeared unchanged from his previous visits; the bathroom to the immediate right, the bedroom straight ahead, a king-size bed, dresser, couch, writing desk, and a balcony with a dramatic view of the beach, the Orchid pool eleven floors below, and Diamondhead in the distance.

The coffee table held the hallmark Halekulani welcome basket of chocolates, bananas, apples, and papaya. It felt like a second home.

"As you see, the walls are freshly painted and the couch was replaced," Mariko explained. "Other than that, it looks exactly the same."

He reserved the same room each time he visited and considered himself especially lucky to be able to snag it on such a short notice. Mariko handed him a leather portfolio containing the registration form. He settled in at the desk to sign it while she ran his credit card through the Square attached to her iPhone. He preferred this relaxed, in-room registration to standing at the busy lobby counter.

"And here are your tickets for complimentary breakfasts."

She handed him a white envelope. The passes were a nice perk reserved for the hotel's frequent guests.

As soon as Mariko left, he showered and then ran the electric razor over his face. Sleep deprivation on top of the fatigue of travel was making him tired, so the shower was a welcome pick-me-up. He changed into a short-sleeve shirt, cargo shorts, and sandals, stuffed his laptop, iPhone, and wallet into his bro-bag, took a moment to verify he'd not forgotten anything he might need this afternoon.

After deciding he was good to go, he dialed the valet.

"Yes, Mr. Davidson?"

"I will be down straightaway for my car."

"We'll have it ready for you."

Chapter 10

NAWZER TEXTED: HE IS IN HOTEL.

A quick check of the hacked hotel registration database confirmed this. He also knew the lawyer picked up the Mustang rental from Hertz. His current problem was finding out the lawyer's purpose for the last-minute trip to Honolulu.

If he had to guess, he'd say it was to meet the Jew.

Especially with the trip occurring immediately on the heels of meeting the FBI agent. It'd taken a great deal of effort to penetrate the lawyer's electronic devices, but he was convinced it would soon lead him to the Jew's location.

Davidson curbed the Mustang at the far end of the hotel driveway, out of the flow of cabs and other vehicles, opened his iPhone to Google Maps, plugged its power cord into the USB port and suction-cupped it to the dash. He opened the laptop to the spreadsheet of properties, then studied the map for a few minutes to familiarize himself with the residential areas he planned to visit this afternoon.

Although he was extremely familiar with downtown Honolulu, he'd not driven the outlying neighborhoods, especially the ones in the foothills. With it now almost 2:00 PM, the traffic along Queen Liliuokalani freeway—the main route spanning the length of the island—would be maddening, so if possible, he'd spend the remainder of the day on the foothill side of that freeway.

Satisfied with his plan, he nosed the car onto Kali Road, drove slowly along the street, while paying particular attention to surrounding vehicles, on alert for anything that appeared suspicious, especially if Fisher had someone tailing him.

The last thing he wanted was to lead the FBI to Arnold. Assuming, of course, he was able to locate the lad. It was, admittedly, a stretch, but weirder things had happened.

He was convinced that Fisher would definitely stoop to such trickery.

Chapter 11

DAVIDSON CURBED THE Mustang along Ala Noe Place—a two-lane stretch of asphalt—directly in front of the first property on the list. The house was a single-story, 1,240 square foot, two bed, two-bath rambler, dominated by a yawning carport spanning most of the front.

The place sold for $750,000 ten days after Arnold disappeared from Seattle, thus corresponding nicely into Davidson's five-point ranking system. At least on paper.

Seeing it in person rather than on-line proved an entirely different matter because the lot and house lacked one very essential feature: security. The back of the house was supported on pylons embedded into terrain that rolled steeply into a ravine with a second, higher ridge directly across from it and covered with thick foliage.

A person with a pair of half-way decent binoculars could easily survey the house unnoticed. More than that, without a barrier between the property and the gully, property access was readily available to anyone willing to scramble up the terrain. That was, of course, if they didn't simply walk straight into the garage from the street.

All of these points chalked off this property as a serious contender. He revised the spreadsheet scores to a 0 for security but 5 for location, then revised the remaining three criteria scores accordingly.

On to the next property on the list.

The afternoon strategy was simple: screen as many homes possible in the remaining daylight and then, after a relaxing dinner at the hotel, devote the rest of the evening to more on-line research. Tomorrow he'd continue the search. Given an early start and at the rate things he was progressing, he stood an excellent chance of finishing the entire list by late afternoon.

Off he drove to the next location.

And so it went...

...until, he arrived at a residence on Ala Mahamoe Street. Outwardly, it appeared similar to the first property: a single-story rambler perched on the lip of a ravine, except for one important point; a high, Asian style, wood fence hid the property from view.

Definitely a huge plus.

At first it seemed that the property was only one floor, but on closer inspection, he realized the second floor was actually a half basement sunk into the hillside. An iron gate separated the street from a short drive to an enclosed carport.

A stainless speaker grill/keyboard recessed in the wall just a foot or so from to the right of the gate gave the place a 5 on the most critical criterion—security—elevating it to the top of the homes viewed thus far. An added plus was the three parallel arrays of angled solar panels installed on the flat roof.

Perfect.

He had no clue how much power they generated but suspected it might exceed the homeowner's needs. He realized that this green addition would fit Arnold's persona, and wondered why he didn't think of it earlier. He added this new variable to the spreadsheet and populated the field for the homes previously viewed.

The property record indicated it was purchased for $869,000 three weeks after Arnold disappeared. Could Arnold afford so much? Intriguing question. Perhaps his gambling was more lucrative than either he or Fisher suspected.

By now, afternoon was morphing into early evening with fatigue weighing more heavily.

Return to the hotel and call it a day or check this one out?

Hell, long as I'm here...

He rang the intercom. No response. Thirty seconds ticked by. He pressed the button again and, in so doing, noticed a small lens in the stainless-steel faceplate above the speaker grill; it undoubtedly was a wide-angle lens for the security system. The intercom speaker finally clicked.

"Yes?" a female voice asked.

"Hello. Is this Arnold Gold's residence?" he asked in his best friendly lawyer tone.

"Who you wan?"

"Arnold Gold. Is he in?"

Silence.

Uh-oh.

"I am the lawyer for the family estate. I need to inform him that a family member died and that an inheritance is involved."

Oh Christ, are you kidding me? Would anyone on earth believe such a hackneyed line?

"You have wrong house. No one that name live here. This Nakumira house."

Back in the Mustang, Davidson checked the property records. Sure enough, the place was owned by Mr. and Mrs. Keji Nakumira. Regardless of how clever Arnold was, he surely couldn't possibly pass for Japanes...no way. Because of these doubts—the property was just too damn perfect to completely write-off—he made a note on the spreadsheet to dive into those records more deeply after dinner.

More and more exhausted by the minute, he scanned the remaining locations on the list for the nearest one, and discovered it was only a half-block up the same street. Perfect. This would make one less property to visit tomorrow. Then, the minute he excluded this one from the list, he'd head back to the hotel for a leisurely dinner and much-needed rest.

This property looked as good as, if not better, than Nakumira's. It also featured an impressive array of rooftop solar collectors. One especially notable feature—a huge plus—was the serious concrete wall surrounding the property that included an embedded intercom/mailbox combo to the right of a retractable stainless-steel vehicle gates and smaller pedestrian entrance.

A short driveway fed an enclosed garage. The wall was tastefully constructed, giving the appearance of an expensive resort rather than a maximum-security prison. In fact, this place looked better than Nakumira's. Davidson figured he just hit the mother lode of likely candidates.

He pulled up a quick look at the Google Earth satellite view. Like most of the houses perched on these steep lava foothills, the rear of the property rolled into a deeply eroded gully that would hinder, but not prevent, an approach to the rear wall, but not the house. From the property records he learned that it was purchased four weeks after the Greenlake fire by single male, Toby Taylor.

Toby Taylor?

Why the hell did that name sound so familiar?

In a flash, he realized the answer.

Chapter 12

"THIRD AND FOUR on the twenty-one-yard line with thirteen seconds on the clock. Seahawks down by one."

Arnold perched on the edge of the black leather couch, eyes riveted to the seventy-inch Sony while his dog, Chance, lay curled up next to him, eyeing the screen too. He had ten grand riding on the Hawks winning by two.

"With only thirteen seconds left," the second announcer said. "They have time for maybe two quick plays, then it's game over. What do you think...a quick pass to the sidelines for better field position, or just go for the field goal from there?"

"Boy, that's a tough one, Mike. With their starting kicker out with a sprained ankle it's a difficult call. Plus, considering the pass defense we've seen tonight, a short-out is going to be even tougher. And don't forget...there's always the risk of an interception. Right now, I'm not sure I like the Seahawks' chances. But, like you said a moment ago, this is the kind of pressure play Pete Carroll's teams excel at. Okay, here we go...Hawks coming to the line."

Chance suddenly jumped from the couch, ran to the front door and stood at attention with eyes glued to the doorknob. He whined. Arnold's iPhone rang the distinctive tone from the front-gate intercom button. He glanced at the phone.

Answer it?

Why? He wasn't expecting anyone. Besides, the person out

there was probably just another Mormon passing out religious shit.

Really? At this time of day?

Alright, already. But not until this play. He stood, eyes glued on the TV.

"...fades back to pass, throws...oh, look at that! Wilson's pass is knocked down at the line of scrimmage. What a defensive play!"

Shit-shit-shit!

"Wow! That was some show of athleticism on the part of Morgan, the middle linebacker. He started to play an inside blitz but saw a chance to make an all-pro defensive play so hung back and took the gamble...he must have been reading Wilson's eyes."

"The Hawks are in their hurry-up offense now with no time outs left and the clock running. They're going to attempt a field goal but do they have enough time to get it off? They're sure cutting it very, very close."

Chance barked sharply. His don't-fuck-with-the-pack bark.

Ah shit.

Chance was too good to give that bark for no reason.

He barked again.

Arnold held up his phone again but couldn't take his eyes off the TV. The phone chimed once more. Alright, already. He glanced at the phone, did a double-take, brought it closer for a better look, but that didn't change what he saw.

"...is good. Seahawks win with no time left on the clock!"

No fucking way. Can't be...can it?

Sure as hell looked like him.

How the hell...?

Answer it?

Why? Nothing good could possibly come of it.

The final score of the game didn't even register. Instead, Arnold was trying to think of one reason—just one goddamn good reason, no matter how strange—for Palmer Davidson to be outside his house ringing the bell. Mistaken identity? Hardly! Coincidence?

You're joking, right? Try another one.

More importantly: How the hell did he find him?

A sudden intense gut-freeze crystallized. If Davidson is out there, who else....

Or...is this some kind of weird-as-hell freaky accident?

Oh please! An accident?

Those odds were less than winning the Powerball.

No fucking way!

The first thing he did after moving into the house was develop a "parachute" for an extreme emergency. Like this one right now. It'd allow him to vanish—to shed the house and the Toby Taylor identity—within minutes of any threat. And, just like a school fire-drill, he and Chance practiced the plan each month to keep it oiled and ready to execute flawlessly at the first whiff of trouble. The plan was similar to—albeit vastly more sophisticated and less destructive, than—his escape from Seattle.

By pulling a virtual ripcord, his finances would instantly transfer to new accounts under a well-groomed new identity. Once the money was completely transferred, his hard drives would reformat so fully—we're talking digital scorched earth clean—that not even an NSA forensic nerd could reconstruct a single byte. With his artificial intelligence system backed-up across multiple cloud sites every six hours, rebuilding it would be a snap compared to the pain he'd endured when moving in here. In other words, one simple command and Toby Taylor would vanish from the earth.

Such was Arnold Gold's whack-a-mole life.

He hated it.

But what other option did he have?

Sure, he might lose a few bucks on the house, but figured that was the cost of doing business. Truth be told, he loved this little haven in paradise...which was all the more reason to keep his present life secure and non-discoverable.

Okay, decision time. Pull the plug? Just walk out the back door with Chance and disappear? Easy enough. The plan was locked and loaded. Or...was there even one atom of hope that such a drastic action wasn't necessary? With his initial shock now beginning to ebb, he figured it might be prudent to learn a few things before making such a drastic move; most importantly, how the hell did Davidson find him? Yes, a "lessons learned" analysis might be the most prudent course of action.

And now that he thought about it, the more convinced he was that Davidson wouldn't be outside the gate unless there was a damn good reason. Davidson wasn't a threat to him. Besides, why jettison the place if there was any possibly of staying put? He loved this house. Loved the location. Practical size, killer view, Fort Knox security. To say nothing of SAM's special room. He'd hired an electrician to run a dedicated 80-amp feed to that room along with separate air conditioning to maintain it in a stable 65 degrees in spite of all the silicon generated heat.

He said, "Good evening, SAM."

A disembodied voice replied, "Good evening, Arnold."

SAM; his play on Apple's famous Siri, the AI program first introduced in Beta form on the 4s iPhone. The insider joke being that the name, Siri, was a spin-off from a Department of Defense project at SRI, the Stanford Research Institute, that was the basis for it.

"Who's at the front gate?"

A high-def close-up of Davidson immediately popped up on his phone.

"Facial identification in progress," SAM answered. Three seconds later; "Face is a ninety-five percent match for Palmer Davidson."

There it was: SAM agreed—confirming beyond any reasonable doubt this wasn't some totally weird otherworldly visual hallucination he was experiencing. Palmer fucking Davidson, for whatever reason, was standing outside the front gate with his finger on the doorbell.

He told SAM, "Intercom," which would pipe him to through to the front gate speaker.

"Yes?" he said.

"Arnold, that you?"

How the hell do I answer that?

Chapter 13

DAVIDSON WAITED AT the intercom for thirty seconds after pressing the button for the third time. He sighed. No one seemed to be home—or at least answering the call button—in spite of the muffled barks from inside. And, from the sound of if, this wasn't a dog he was in any great hurry to meet in person. Then, for no reason other than having invested a ton of effort in the hunt, he pressed the intercom button one final time, with desire for the comfort of the Halekulani growing stronger with each passing second.

"Yes?" came a voice from the speaker.

Momentarily startled, Davidson quickly ran the voice through memory, searching for a match. In spite of speaker distortion, it did carry a familiar ring. Could it be? It'd been a year since they last spoke.

"Arnold? Is that you?"

"Sorry, you have the wrong house."

This time Davidson's ears were primed and there was no question about it—speaker distortion aside—Arnold Gold was on the other end of the intercom. A surge of self-satisfaction hit.

Goddamn, I did it!

"Arnold, this is Palmer Davidson out here. I know that is you."

Careful. Do not upset or threaten him.

Silence.

Good news, the intercom light didn't go out.

"Arnold, listen...I would not be here unless it was crucially important. Believe me, we need to talk."

A pleasant breeze lightly scented with the fragrance of tropical flowers rustled overhead palms while a dog barked nearby. Evening was upon him now and lights were turning on in the neighboring homes. He wondered if the lad was already out the back door, starting his next escape.

A wave of disappointment suddenly swept away the satisfaction of a moment ago. He simply assumed that their close relationship was sufficient reason for Arnold to hear him out.

Perhaps not.

Perhaps Arnold didn't share the bond he'd felt. Davidson continued to face the lens, waiting. His peripheral vision caught movement, and he turned in time to catch a camera under the garage eve rotate in his direction.

The barking stopped, followed by a metallic click of a lock release, then the disembodied voice instructed, "Be sure the gate's secured after you."

Davidson let out a deep breath and stepped into a courtyard of cement pavers, trellised bougainvillea, and palms, the sight provoking a laugh. The Arnold he knew in Seattle was oblivious to landscaping.

After confirming the gate was secure, he paused for a closer look at the courtyard and house. Both carried a strong contemporary Zen vibe of Japanese minimalist style; tasteful, contemporary, clean. He loved the dramatic departure from the Greenlake Tudor.

The barking resumed the moment the front door swung open.

Chapter 14

OF ALL THE questions zinging through Arnold's mind, the most important was how the hell did Davidson manage to find him?

Exactly where did I fuck up?

There were people out there—Naseem being the most important one—who might *suspect* he didn't die in the fire, especially after the Al Jazeera article hit the stands. But Davidson? He'd lay down a hundred-to-one odds the lawyer never set eyes on that news source unless prompted by something.

Besides, the article had not yet triggered so much as one measly Google Alert. And he would've known, because he, with SAM's help, began to scour the Internet for fallout as soon as it appeared.

Was Davidson turning psychic on him?

In addition to wanting to know exactly how Davidson found him was a deep-rooted sense of obligation and fondness toward the man who saved his life last year.

"Heel." Chance obediently took up the correct position on his left and stopped barking. Arnold opened the door. "Mr. Davidson, come in."

Davidson stepped onto the polished gray concrete floor, his eyes sweeping the interior decorated in sleek minimalist contemporary furniture. Directly ahead, down three shallow steps, was a spacious great room/kitchen area. Glass sliders opened the entire back wall onto a large deck with a million-dollar view of twinkling lights in the distance. The hall to his left would logically flow to bedrooms and bathrooms—all of it a dramatic contrast to the Greenlake house. This one was drop dead gorgeous. Then again, he was partial to contemporary design.

"Wow. Nice place. Very nice."

"Thanks. Coming from you that means a lot." A slight blush ascended Arnold's face. "I probably shouldn't say this, but your place made a lasting impression on me. I'd never paid any attention to my own space until I saw yours and...well, it changed all that." Arnold waved him into the great room. "Come in, sit down."

Davidson paused to appraise Arnold's appearance; almost unchanged from a year ago. The only exception being a closely trimmed beard that hid some old acne scars. Still as thin as ever. Not skinny, mind you, just no excess weight. He turned his attention warily to the stout shepherd standing obediently at Arnold's side, eyeing Davidson's leg, leaving little doubt he'd lay down his life for his master if necessary. A German Shepherd? Similar general shape, but different coloring; the typical black nose-dip but with a short, glossy tan coat.

"Do I need to worry about him?"

"Chance? Naw...he's good. As long as I am." Arnold dropped to his haunches, began scratching the soft fur at the base of the pooch's ears. "Aren't you, boy," and continued the behind-the-ear massage for several moments. "He loves choobers."

"What?"

Flashing a self-conscious smile, Arnold repeated, "Choobers...those are what I call this thing I'm doing right now." Then to the dog, "Don't you, boy."

Chance threw himself onto his back, tummy fully exposed.

"And these," Arnold said, vigorously rubbing the pooch's belly, "are what we call rabber-de-jabbers."

Davidson laughed. The baby talk was wildly out of character from the young man of last year.

"I will take your word for it. Still, he *is* intimidating."

Arnold stood, brushed his hands on his shorts.

"That's supposed to be the point. He's pretty good at that intimidation when he needs to be...not that I've had any problems. Still...he's good security." Arnold nodded toward a couch and two chairs to either side of a low, black-lacquer, Japanese-style coffee table. "Have a seat."

Chance remained at Arnold's side.

Arnold watched Davidson saunter down the stairs with his signature too-cool-for-school stride. Not arrogant, forced, or jive-ass, just the confident fluidity of a man with his shit tight and the world by the tail. Davidson's self-confidence was just one other thing he deeply admired about the man. To the point of envy.

If I could only be that cool....

Davidson paused beside the couch, did a slow three-sixty, checking out the place from the new perspective.

"Yes, sir, certainly a drastic contrast. Not that I had anything against your other house. This one is just more...contemporary. And I must say, it suits you."

Chance trotted over to Davidson and started sniffing his crotch. Davidson froze, allowing him a few moments of olfactory exploration before bending down to give him choobers. Chance immediately responded with a wet doggy kiss smack in the middle of the lawyer's face. Davidson wiped away the kiss with the back of his hand and stood up.

"Did I hear his name correctly? Chance?"

Arnold nodded. "Yup."

Davidson laughed. "As in, game of?"

Arnold spread his hands in what-can-I-say gesture?

Laughing, Davidson shook his head.

"Actually, I am more surprised at my lack of surprise." Canine introductions complete, Davison continued onto the expansive deck to admire the spectacular view, leaning forward with his palms holding onto the glass balustrade, and again nodded approval. "My-my-my, moving on up."

Arnold stood next to him.

"It's too dark to see Diamondhead now, but it's right over there," Arnold pointed to their left and caught the sweet fragrance of bougainvillea again.

Just another reason to keep the sliders open during all but the hottest hours. Although the house was equipped with A/C, he only used it during the afternoons when the sun baked the house more intensely.

Davidson asked, "That picture there," with a nod toward the mantle. "Is that Rachael Weinstein?"

Arnold felt his face redden again.

"Yup."

Had he told Davidson about his deep attraction last year?

Couldn't remember. Probably. Not that it made any difference, now that it was impossible to contact her.

Davidson shot him a quizzical look.

"Are you in contact with her?"

Arnold glanced away, to hide both his embarrassment and disappointment.

"No. Why?"

"Just curious is all...I was under the impression you did not want a soul to know you are even alive. Had I thought she knew how to contact you, I would have called her and saved myself a modest amount of work. She never crossed my mind."

During their last meeting, just prior to the explosion, he'd asked Davidson to pass her a written message, the memory still so vivid it could've happened this morning.

"Did you give her the message?"

Hearing her name made him miss her even more.

"I did."

Davidson reached down to scratch Chance's head again.

"Appreciate it." Arnold motioned to the twin chaises. "Have a seat and tell me why you're here."

The gentle breeze felt pleasantly refreshing in the lingering warmth of the day.

Davidson settled in, cleared his throat.

"First, clarify a point for me."

Arnold leaned back, still upset at having been located.

"If I can. What?"

"Did you intentionally trigger the explosion?"

Arnold opened his mouth to answer, but didn't say a word...what was the up-side to admitting it? Even to Davidson. No. There was only downside. Justified or not. Killing Karim had been part self-defense and, in part, a blow (*oh, please!*) against terrorism. After all, we're at war with terrorists, right? He didn't think of himself as a murderer...but, he supposed, by the letter of the law he qualified. Technically. To make matters worse, there wasn't any question of premeditation...although, that particular point might be tough to prove in court. Regardless, there wasn't a statute of limitation in Washington State for first-degree murder. He'd made sure to check that point out.

"Why do you ask?"

"Just curious is all."

Davidson continued eyeing the view, not even glancing in his direction.

Arnold turned to the city lights too.

"What will you do if I answer?"

Davidson waved away the question.

"Not a damn thing. Your hesitation just answered for you. We can leave it at that."

Sitting here next to a touchstone of his past only increased his yearning to regain his old life, to be Arnold Gold again, to live freely without constant fear of discovery, to be able to see Rachael, to return to Seattle to resume life there. But that would be impossible unless....

Tell him? Lay it all out? Explain what actually went down—

that Karim was about to kill him? Maybe Davidson could see options he couldn't? After all, the man was a lawyer. Part of him wanted to lay it all out, if for no any other reason than to stop the deep guilt gnawing away at his soul. Do Catholics experience that kind of relief from confession?

You're off in the weeds again, dude. Get back on point. How the hell did Davidson find you and why is he here?

Okay, sure, he suspected he knew the answer, but suspecting and knowing were entirely different animals.

"Can this be one of those privileged conversations? The kind you can't divulge to anyone?"

Davidson flashed a bemused smile.

"That only applies to conversations between lawyer and client."

Arnold thought about that a moment.

"So, you're saying I need to hire you?"

"We just went full circle. I asked about the explosion simply out of curiosity. Trust me, I have no other agenda."

Anxiety began eroding Arnold's gut again. Until a few minutes ago, his Toby Taylor Honolulu life seemed bullet proof. After successfully extricating himself from the impossible double-bind of those final days in Seattle, he and Chance were living well. He flashed on a particularly poignant scene in the film, *Platoon*, Oliver Stone's iconic depiction of one man's Vietnam tour. Keith David, the squad's machine gunner, explained to Charlie Sheen that if he survived his deployment, the rest of his life would be "pure gravy." Until Davidson rang the doorbell, pure gravy was exactly how he valued every single day.

"Sorry if this might offend you, Mr. Davidson, but does anyone else know you're here or where I live?"

Davidson hesitated.

"Not as far as I could tell. I tried to check if I was being followed, but am not a professional at that sort of thing, so I cannot say for certain."

Aw shit!

His gut turned to ice again, his heart racing.

"Calm down, Arnold." Davidson raised a placating palm. "Believe me, I am here with your best interests in mind. Trust me on this, please."

Davidson seemed to be dead serious. I do trust him, Arnold realized. More than anyone I know. Well, except for Rachael. And that would be about equal. He licked his dry lips, nodded, "Sorry...go ahead and tell me why you're here."

But he damn well knew the answer...so the more important question now was how did he get involved? Had he read Al Jazeera after all? More importantly, *how* the hell did he find him?

Davidson walked him through Fisher's surprise visit, but, by then most of the words were overridden by painful memories of Seattle...the sound of the gunshot that killed Howie...the terror in the alley as Karim hunted him like an animal...the awful explosion...awakening to find himself trapped in the burning house with no way out....

Davidson was staring at him. Arnold blinked and shook his head.

"Sorry, I missed the last part. What'd you just say?"

"Nothing. I finished explaining why I am here, is all. You seem...off somewhere in your own mind."

Arnold shook his head again and tried again to focus on the conversation.

"It's these damn flashbacks...Karim and...."

He stopped shy of admitting that he triggered the explosion.

Davidson waited.

Then, he remembered the most important question.

"How the hell did you figure out where I am?"

When Davidson finished, Arnold nodded approval.

"Gotta hand it to you...pretty slick. So, what now? What'll you do with the information? Tell Fisher?"

"No," he said with a shrug. "My purpose in coming was

simple; to warn you, nothing else. I have no intention of ratting you out, if that is your worry. Unless, of course, you want Fisher to know. Do you?"

"Good question. Let's think about that a moment," Arnold said, more to himself than his lawyer. "Knowing Fisher, I wouldn't put it past him to have a TSA alert on you, so…there's a good chance he already knows you're here. But what are the odds he knows you're with me? No way of knowing that, right?"

Davidson grimaced. "Unfortunately, you may be correct. A TSA alert did not occur to me…but keep in mind…he was emphatic that you are not a high enough priority to bother with."

"And you believe him?"

Davidson shrugged. "I have no reason not to."

Neither man spoke for a moment until Davidson added, "He agreed to have their financial gnomes run a screen on you. I assume there is nothing to discover, especially with you living under a new identity."

"No, I'm clean."

Davidson nodded.

"You still have not settled the issue of what, if anything, you want him to know."

Arnold figured that once the Al Jazeera piece hit, it would only be a matter of time until Breeze showed up in Honolulu searching for him. But he was counting on the CIA, FBI, or other federal law enforcement agencies to nail her ass before she could actually touch him. The moment Davidson appeared out front, all those best-case scenarios flushed straight down the toilet.

"Aww, man—" Arnold ran his hand through his hair and shook his head. "Thought I knew, but…it might be nice to have the feds watching my back, but…and you know this too; Fisher will want to use me as bait. I'm not sure I can do that again."

Davidson nodded in agreement.

"What'd you do if you were me?"

"I am not you." Pause. "Why not look at it from this angle; if

Fisher knows where you are, the FBI *can* help protect you. Yes, you may be used to a certain extent, but—and this is crucial—if they were able to eliminate her as a threat, would that be enough of a reward outweigh the risk? That is the decision."

Arnold didn't answer.

"And as far as your exposure," Davidson continued, "you may not have to actively play the bait game in the same sense as last year."

"Why not?"

"If someone in the Bureau leaked your file to Al Jazeera you can assume that once Fisher knows your location it will find its way to Naseem." He shrugged. "If Fisher knows she's coming *here*, it makes the job of finding the leaker much simpler."

Ah, yes, the leak.

He was tempted to tell Davidson not to factor the leak into the decision, but worried that might raise some suspicions. Arnold reached down to massage Chance's neck.

"What do you think we should do, boy?"

Chance rolled onto his side, glanced up. *Thump-thump-thump.*

"I thought I was prepared for this," Arnold said. "I even have all the details set up to disappear again...even a quick way to sell the house. And if things became too urgent and I didn't have time to unload it, I'd simply walk away, like I did last year, but he's with me now," with a nod to Chance, "and he's a game changer. We're family. It makes everything more complicated. And then there's Rachael..."

Davidson held his silence.

"You know anything about her? How she's doing...anything at all?"

"No, nothing. Why?"

Davidson watched the distant shimmering city lights.

"Curious is all..."

Oh, bullshit!

For months, he'd been wrestling with how to contact her

without exposing himself, but couldn't think of a way to pull it off. Of everything in his Seattle life, he missed her the most. Problem was, he couldn't risk letting anyone—not even her—know he was alive. A secret is a secret only if no one else knows it. So...as long as Naseem was hunting him, he was toxic to anyone close to him. He refused to expose Rachael to any risk.

Shit!

"Time for his walk. Want to join us?"

"If it is no bother."

"Not at all. I'm enjoying talking to you...you're the only person from my...other life I've been able to do that with."

Plus, it was comforting to know that Davidson knew what was going on. It increased his longing to regain his real identity.

He made a show of checking out the house perimeter and street with his high-tech security system before leaving the home. Not out of any concern, but to assure Davidson that the property contained some serious, no-shit, radically sick technology.

Not only was it a necessary fire-wall against Naseem, but it was also protection against some dumb-shit meth-head burglar who wanted to steal his computers just for the street price.

Dumb shits were dumb shits, always had been and always would be. That's exactly why they're called dumb shits.

"Looks clear. If someone followed you, they're not outside now."

Chapter 15

NAWZER SAW THE lawyer's iPhone remain in one location for forty-five minutes and determined its GPS coordinates, found it corresponded to a residential area in the outskirts of the city. This was the only stop that lasted longer than three to five minutes since leaving the hotel, so had to be significant.

He pulled up the approximate location on Google Maps and made a list of all addresses within a one block radius. Then he logged into the Honolulu City property records website to begin researching the owners.

After herding Chance into the back seat of his metallic-silver Mini Cooper, Arnold and Davidson piled into the front. Arnold lowered the side windows—all of which were smeared with dog-nose-graffiti—backed out of the short driveway, waited for the steel security gate to slide shut.

He expected Davidson to make a wisecrack about his over-kill security, but remembered Davidson's own elaborate system. The lawyer probably approved.

"Where are we headed?" Davidson asked.

"A park nearby...our default walk. Sure, I could just run him around the neighborhood and be done with it, but I hate to keep him leashed when we walk, so I drive the extra distance. Yeah, it's a bit of a pain I suppose, but if you're a dog, which would you want? You'd want a shot at getting in a good squirrel chase, right?" He turned toward the back seat. "Nothing better than a good chasing a squirrel, is there!"

Chance wagged his tail but kept his nose poked out through the window.

"Good point. I get the impression you take excellent care of him."

"Spoil him rotten's more like it." Arnold laughed. "Hey, why not? He's my life now, my best friend."

Well, except for Howie Weinstein, but Howie was his best human friend.

The bond with Chance was totally different; they were pack.

They were moving up the hill now, past the last of the houses, the roadside terrain dense with jungle vegetation. A few more blocks and Arnold pulled into a parking lot and curbed the Mini under the solitary street lamp, then they were out of the car, Chance bounding ahead across a grassy field.

"Is he a German Shepherd?" Davidson asked.

Chance seemed to be enjoying himself, running, sniffing, and, after sufficient olfactory research, peeing on specific sites.

"Nope, he's a Belgian Malinois. Some people call them Belgian Shepherds on account of them looking so similar to their German cousins, and, like all shepherds they're considered working dogs. But Belgian's are exceptional. At least they are my opinion. They're the best doggie anyone could have."

"Because?" Davidson asked.

Arnold slowed.

"Well, for a couple reasons. They're exceptionally bright. Probably as smart, or smarter, than poodles, which some dog experts claim is the most intelligent breed, but don't believe it. Plus, they're loyal, hardworking, and extremely obedient. That's one of the reasons the military uses them in their K-9 corps. Remember the raid on Bin Laden's compound?"

"Who can forget that?"

"The pooch that choppered in with SEAL Team Six? She was a Malinois and did her job beautifully...in a very potentially hazardous situation, too."

"I do not remember you having a dog in Seattle. What changed your mind here?"

Arnold stopped walking, stuffed both hand into the front pockets of his cargos, and stared in Chance's general direction.

"Two reasons, I guess; protection and companionship. If he'd been there in Seattle, Howie'd still be alive and I wouldn't be in this awful mess."

"You know that's not true. Anything could have happened. First of all, that would not change the reason for that unfortunate chain of events. Naseem wanted your system. Period. The things that happened...may have been different, but in the final analysis...it is the reason we are here now, in this situation."

Davidson began to massage his right shoulder, as if working out a kink.

Arnold swallowed and bowed his head. How often did he wish he could reverse time and do things differently...if he just hadn't shot off his mouth....

"I can't accept that...Chance never would've let Karim kill Howie."

"Think about that a moment. I have only spent a couple minutes watching the two of you and I seriously do not believe you would have gone for pizza without him. You would have taken him for a walk. Look, all I am saying is, there are a hundred ways things might have played out."

Arnold shook his head.

No way was he going to accept Davidson's excuse.

"And the other reason I got him is, he's better security than all the printed circuits and silicon chips in the world. No one can get within ten feet of the house without him knowing." He was struck by just how integral Chance was to him now. Life without him was no longer imaginable. "More than anything, I love him...he's my world." He was embarrassed to hear the waver in his voice, but this was Davidson and Davidson would understand. "His love is unconditional."

Oh, how fucking trite! Gag me.

Maybe...but what he said was true.

"No argument from me on that," Davidson said with a smile.

Chapter 16

AS THEY MEANDERED along the cinder path, Arnold's car came back into view and Davidson realized they actually walked a large circle. He understood why Arnold made the extra effort to drive Chance here. For an urban doggie, this was probably as good as it gets.

He decided that the trip here to hunt for Arnold had been the right thing to do. At least now the lad was warned. What he chose to do with the information was up to him and only him. Which left him wondering what information, if any, did he owe Fisher? He thought about this a moment and finally decided that, as Arnold's lawyer, he could not break his trust, that the decision was Arnold's. What he could do, however, was tell Fisher he confirmed that Arnold was alive, in hopes this news would elevate the FBI's level of concern over Naseem. He was relieved and pleased with this decision. However, he still believed that it was in the lad's best interests to ally with the FBI.

His job here in Honolulu was now finished. Soon as they returned to Arnold's place, he'd bid him goodnight and return to the Halekulani, call the airlines and, if possible, bump up his return flight.

He asked, "Do you enjoy living here?"

Arnold appeared puzzled by the question.

"What do you mean?"

"For you personally. Is there a girlfriend in the picture?" Uh-oh! That sounded wrong, so he quickly amended it. "It strikes me that Chance is your only roommate."

Arnold laughed.

"I'll never find another friend as close as Howie. And that, Mr. Davidson is just another reason Chance is my world."

"That is a non-answer if have I ever heard one."

Arnold glanced away.

"Yeah, I'm dating someone, but nothing serious."

Considering Arnold's historical difficulty interacting with the opposite sex, seeing a woman represented a quantum leap in social integration.

"Tell me about her. What is she like? How did you meet?"

Davidson watched Chance slip between two bushes on the edge of the park, arch his back, assuming the classic doggie poo-position. Thoughtful dog, not doing his business in the middle of the field where it'd have to be doggie bagged and disposed of.

Arnold stopped walking to wait for Chance.

"Not much to tell, really. Her name is Loni. She's a realtor…" He laughed. "The one who sold me the house."

Arnold's tone suggested this was a touchy subject, and this piqued his curiosity.

"Nothing wrong with that. It is probably better than other ways of meeting a woman. Tell me more."

"Well…let's see…" Arnold kicked at a fallen palm-frond. "She's about my height…slender…black hair…she's a good realtor," with a shrug in his voice.

"But?"

"Christ, Mr. Davidson, I hate questions like that. What exactly do you want to know?"

"For starters, do you like her?"

Arnold began walking again, slow and casual.

"She's easy. Whoa, that doesn't right. What I mean is, she's easy to hang with. Like…when we go out for dinner? I don't have to struggle to make conversation."

"Good. I take that as a sign of progress. Does she know how you, ah," at a temporary loss for words, "earn money?"

Arnold let out a soft dismissive snort and glanced away.

"Are you kidding? I learned that lesson the hard way."

Davidson found the conversation interesting. Arnold Gold, aka Toby Taylor, dating a woman.

Yes, definitely a sign of progress.

"What are some of the things to you have in common? So far, your description is purely physical."

Arnold stared back.

"What's with all the questions? Am I under interrogation?"

Davidson raised his hands in supplication.

"Sorry. No malice intended...just interested, is all. Not many people have an opportunity to start life anew like you. But if the topic makes you uncomfortable, feel free to change it."

"I dunno..." Arnold said, slowly shaking his head. "She talks about work a lot. She's never asked what I do because she's convinced I'm independently wealthy and, truth is, I've never said a word to the make her think otherwise." He glanced at Chance before returning to Davidson. "She likes to talk about business. That's interesting...I guess," with a shrug.

"Do I sense some reservations?"

Davidson immediately regretted probing. Answering such personal questions was undoubtedly difficult for the lad.

"Ah, man..." Arnold kicked at another palm frond. "It's a problem. The best way to describe it is she always wants to *close the deal.*"

Did he mean what that sounded like?

"Sorry, can you be more specific?"

"You're kidding, right?"

Arnold's face showed genuine surprise.

"Not at all. Explain what you meant by that."

"She's always making hints about marriage. She's never really gone nuclear and dropped the M bomb, but that's pretty much what she's not-so-subtly hinting at."

"I take this to mean you have different ideas."

Arnold nodded. "Waaaayyyy different."

After a deep breath, Davidson pushed further. "Because?"

Arnold glanced away. "Aw, man...this is embarrassing."

"Sorry. Feel free to change the subject. What would you prefer to talk about?"

"No...it's weird...I'm totally comfortable talking to you about it. I've never discussed this with anyone, and I guess it's the kind of thing I'd toss around with Howie, no problem. Oh, man, do I totally miss having a friend like that!" He held up his index finger. "Give me a second...while I search for the right words..." and stared at the bright twinkling stars overhead. "Okay, see if this makes sense; she thinks I'm a little rich kid. Probably on account of me buying the house with my own money. She's totally convinced I'm a trust fund brat."

Davidson laughed.

"We both know that is far from the truth. The trust fund part, that is. I have no idea of your net worth." Davidson began to massage his right shoulder again, working on easing the dull deep ache that began a month or two ago and never let up. "Are you are saying she is more interested in your money than you? A gold digger, if you will forgive the pun."

"Exactly!" Arnold nodded. "I'm surprised I didn't think of that word."

Davidson gave him a good-natured shoulder punch.

"That, my friend, is the reason I am your lawyer." He cleared his throat. "Back to Rachael. Is she the one you want to marry?"

Wow, another subject not discussed with anyone.

Especially Howie. He glanced at Davidson, who kept eyeing him with this curious-as-shit expression.

Just admit it?

Davidson seemed to know anyway. Why hide it?

"Yes. But right now, with the Naseem thing going on, I'm super toxic, so there's no way to risk contacting her."

Davidson nodded. "Well then, we will just have to see if we can remedy that."

"How? I can't do a damn thing until Naseem is..." He cut himself off. And substituted, "out of the picture" for *dead*.

Chance was next to him, looking up.

"There you go...that, Mr. Gold, is a good reason to partner with Fisher. But that is your decision. In the meantime, what about Loni?"

Arnold realized Davidson was hinting he should break off thing with Loni if they wanted different things from the relationship, but...at the moment, his life was too off the rails to even think about dealing with it.

Besides, how the hell would he even broach the subject with her?

Davidson was giving him a fatherly look.

"Whether you want my advice or not, here it is: settle things with Loni before anything...happens."

Yeah, this sounded more and more fatherly.

"Like?"

Oh, please! You know exactly what he means.

"Use your imagination. You are a vulnerable young man with hormones and, apparently, wealth for your age. You have every right to have concern over her motivation, and I, for one, do not want to see someone take advantage of you. That is all I wish to say on the matter."

Arnold nodded, eye averting, now feeling a pang of guilt for continuing their relationship for all the wrong reasons.

"Let's get back to the Fisher thing."

They were almost back to the car now, but he wasn't in a hurry to head home just yet. He motioned Davidson to a picnic table, plunked down on one side with Davidson settling in on the other. Chance flopped on the ground next to Arnold's foot and rolled onto his side.

"You said you did not want him to know where you are," Davidson said.

Arnold, stalling, took a moment to study the scarred wood picnic table, running a fingertip back and forth over initials carved into the weathered grain.

"I don't know...it's...complicated. I mean, having the FBI's help would be nice."

Davidson nodded. "I agree."

Arnold sighed.

"You never said what you'd do if you were me?"

Davidson fished a roll of breath mints out of his pocket, offered it to Arnold, who waved it off. Davidson popped a mint into his mouth.

"Well, I am not you. However...the pivotal issue is; can Naseem find you?" Pause. "That all hinges on whether or not you ever mentioned Honolulu to her. After all, that is the only reason I found you."

"Yeah, that *is* a problem; I can't remember. Maybe. Maybe not. Oh, man, we talked about so many things..."

Why did I ever make that fucking trip?

"Okay, say I did mention it. The question is, would she remember? Yeah, maybe...maybe she took notes. Hey, grubbing around for intelligence was what she did."

What a mistake!

He continued, "Okay, the odds are small, but playing small odds is exactly how I earn a living. Somehow that bitch will figure it out. Sooner or later." He shook his head in disgust. "Why the hell did I have to use this name!"

"And if you disappear again? Does that really solve anything? Naseem will continue to hunt you until the day she dies."

"I know, I know." Arnold sighed. "Oh, man! Working with Fisher last year...Christ, I hated it. And I really don't see any of that changing."

"There *is* a bright side, however. If the FBI does neutralize her, you will can be Arnold Gold again and stop worrying about all this."

Arnold palm-wiped his face. Last week, when this situation was purely hypothetical, he was rocking along not giving too much thought to the reality of Naseem showing up. Yeah, he knew damn well she was out there someplace...but now...now, this was real, and a pain stabbed his gut.

"I'll do just about anything to have my old life back. This constant worry...the whole Rachael thing." He swallowed hard, blurted, "I want to be with her *so* much." He glanced at the twinkling stars again. "When I was in that house with Karim...oh, man, I was scared so shitless every damn minute of every damn day. I knew he was going to kill me...I just didn't know when. Now it feels like the same shit's starting all over again..."

Arnold grabbed a chunk of coconut shell from the table, threw it angrily into the night.

Chapter 17

"YOU *DO* NEED to make a decision fairly soon," Davidson said. "You have been warned. You know full well she is coming after you."

"I know, I know," Arnold said sharply. He turned around to lean against the picnic table and slowly shook his head, "...it's just...I'm having trouble with this. I can't make this decision right now...I need time to think."

"I understand, but with the leak..."

Davidson let it hang.

That damn leak again! Tell him? No...wait.

"Here's the deal; right now—unless you're being followed—Fisher and Naseem don't know anything for sure. Okay, Fisher *suspects* I'm alive or he wouldn't't've conned you into trying to find me. Naseem *probably* suspects it, on account of Al Jazeera...so if you don't tell anyone anything, I'm safe just staying put...and who know, maybe the FBI will nail Naseem before anything happens."

Arnold looked around for Chance, realized he was sitting at his feet, staring up, so reached down to give him choobers.

"That sounds as if your mind is made up."

"Probably..." Arnold nodded. "It's that I can't stand the thought of being bait again. The stress...ah, man, that was too much. Besides, it's Fisher's job to hunt terrorists, not mine."

"Sorry to have wasted your time, then," Davidson said with a note of regret. "I realize this trip is causing you nothing but grief."

Arnold waved off the remark.

"That's not true at all. You did what you thought was best...I'm just telling you what I think. Hey, who knows, things can always change. I can always change my mind, right?"

Davidson nodded; happy the darkness would hide his disappointment. He firmly believed Arnold would be better served under FBI protection, but he did have a point; being used as bait again carried some huge risks.

Arnold slapped his knees, stood.

"Probably best we put as much distance as possible between us now." He brushed off his shorts and waved Chance over to the car.

"C'mon, I'll take you back."

Chapter 18

"THANKS, MR. DAVIDSON...." Arnold offered his hand. "You put in a ton of work on this for nothing. I sincerely thank you."

He wished he could find more eloquent words to describe how deeply his gratitude ran. He also believed in the old saw; actions speak louder than words, so would start looking for an appropriate thank you gift (in spite of having no idea what that might be). Material tokens could never express one's true appreciation.

"At the time," Davidson said, "it seemed to be the appropriate thing to do. Now, I am not sure I did the right thing by showing up at your doorstep. I sincerely hope I have not inadvertently placed you in harm's way. My guess is only time will answer that."

They stood beside to the driver's door of the rented Mustang.

"Hey, no worry...I'm okay. Odds are nothing's going to come of this."

"Notify me straightaway if that changes?"

Arnold felt like shit.

Why not tell him the truth?

Not now. Not at this point. Someday, for sure, once the situation is stable.

"Don't worry, I will. After all, you're my lawyer."

"Okay, *Toby*, take care. I mean that. Stay vigilant."

Arnold backed away from the car, holding Chance protectively by the collar.

"Safe flight."

Davidson slid into the bucket seat, fired up the engine as Arnold saluted. With a laugh, Davidson returned the salute, pulled a U-turn and drove away. Arnold he stood on the sidewalk and watched the tail-lights disappear before he and Chance entered the courtyard, locked the gate and secured the front door. The interior of the house felt safe and secure, like a good home should, and this sense of security reaffirmed his decision to simply wait and see how things played out. If Davidson was followed, it'd only be a matter of days before things came to a head. In a way, he preferred knowing this instead of the way it was before...when there was no way of predicting when or if Naseem would arrive.

He pulled a longneck pale ale from the fridge, flipped the cap into the recycle bin, wandered out onto the deck and dropped into his favorite chaise. Chance plopped down beside him on the deck, yawned and nestled his snout between his forepaws. Together they watched the twinkling lights of downtown Honolulu. Out of habit, Arnold began running his fingers back and forth through the shepherd's tan fur.

"What do you think, boy? Are we in trouble?"

Thump-thump-thump.

He absent-mindedly kneaded Chance's neck while mulling over the situation. If Fisher told Davidson the truth, that Naseem wasn't a high FBI priority before now, then the Al Jazeera story and subsequent terrorist chatter certainly had to bump that priority higher.

After all, she was the reason Fisher reached out to Davidson, right?

Wasn't this was good news?

Well, not entirely; because now a day-glow red and white bulls-eye was painted smack dab in the middle of his chest...soooo, it was time to ratchet up his security. Twenty-four hours a day, hundreds of SAM's bots would continuously explore the vast reaches of the World Wide Web and Darknet looking for any information on Naseem, Nawzer, and others in her terrorist group.

He'd encountered a picture of Breeze, AKA Naseem, for the first time last year while browsing a website of Las Vegas escorts. One glimpse at her thumbnail image and he was immediately attracted.

A mouse-click on the image hyperlinked him to her homepage which featured pictures of her in various provocative poses, complete with a detailed description of the various services she provided. He'd booked five days and nights with her, and boy, was a horrendously bad decision—and the basis for his present clusterfuck of a life.

Now, one year later, his best friend Howie was dead and *Arnold Gold* no longer existed. At least not on paper. Worse yet, he didn't dare contact Rachael.

He knew this intolerable situation would reach a climax soon; just how soon was the question. The Al Jazeera article had tipped the first domino in line, so, how would this skirmish end? Naseem knew he was alive, so he guessed it'd take her maybe three or four weeks to figure where the hell he was. Nawzer would be—if he wasn't already—digging around in files on Davidson's computers.

He hated the stress, but welcomed knowing they were in the end game.

Davidson...since Howie's death, Arnold had never felt as close to another person as him. Felt almost as if the older man was an adopted father. He pushed aside his practice to fly half-way across the Pacific for what, two nights?

Probably.

But hopefully, he'd be able to enjoy a few vacation days before returning home. Then again, knowing him, probably not. He'll be on the next flight home. His solo practice wasn't set up to accommodate impromptu vacations.

How to show his appreciation?

Send a check? No, that was a non-starter. Davidson would

never cash it.

Well, shit, at least reimburse his expenses.

Perfect! For now. But there just had to be a better thank-you than that.

Arnold ran inside, grabbed his Surface computer and settled back in the chaise. After a gulp of beer, he started in. First, hacking into the Halekulani main server and into Davidson's account where he replaced the credit card number with his own. From there he found the airline and paid that charge.

What else?

Ah, yes, the car rental. Which agency was it? He remembered a rental sticker on the back bumper. Before polishing off the beer, he settled those costs too. At least now Davidson wouldn't be out any cash, but unfortunately there was no way to reimburse him for time and hassle. One day...he'd make sure to do that.

Another beer?

Hell, why not.

Another trip to the fridge.

Back on the chaise again, he thought through his next steps, the situation being eerily similar to last year. Naseem was hunting him while he was hunting her.

Who would end up on top?

Last year, before the shit hit the fan, Arnold occasionally logged into his Facebook account, but, for obvious reasons, hadn't touched it since disappearing from Seattle. He'd give twenty-to-one odds that Nawzer's bots monitored the account, constantly on the look for a hint of activity, just as he had SAM continuously monitoring Naseem's old account.

Now that Naseem was clearly back on the FBI's radar, it was time to bait the trap. Using Tor to access the Darknet, he resurfaced and logged into Facebook to post a smiling selfie on Waikiki with Diamondhead in the background. Attached to the posting was a virus similar to the famous Stuxnet launched years ago specifically to disable certain centrifuges in one of Iran's nuclear facilities. The totally cool thing about Stuxnet was that it ignored everything but the target computer, so when it did unleash its magic, the damage would appear to be nothing more than a programming error instead of a virus.

Task finished, he signed out of Facebook while making sure his digital footprints were completely erased.

Chapter 19

THE NEXT MORNING, before taking Chance for his walk, Arnold stood at the kitchen window and called Loni, enjoying the view with a mug of freshly brewed coffee in hand.

"Hi, it's me. Have a question for you. A guy knocked on my door yesterday, said he's here on vacation and loves Honolulu. So much so, that he wants to buy a vacation home here. He was driving around a few neighborhoods at random when he came across this place…and fell in love with it. In particular, he loves the privacy. And asked if I'd be interested in selling…you know, for the right price."

He took a sip of coffee.

"You're not actually considering it, are you?" her words dripping incredulity.

Which was pretty much exactly the response he expected.

"I have no idea…maybe…it all depends on how much he's willing to pay. I could always throw out a ridiculously high number and see if he bites," with a shrug in his voice.

"Of course, but the problem with that is, anytime you do that, there's always the chance they'll write you an offer."

"I know, but that doesn't mean I have to accept it."

"Yes…but…where would you go?"

"I don't know. I don't know anything at this point. I haven't had a chance to think that far ahead and I certainly didn't give him an answer...so, for now, everything's hypothetical. And who knows what he'll want to do tomorrow."

"I'm not sure I like the sound of this," now sounding petulant.

"Okay, so here's my question. He's a busy guy. He plans on leaving town in the morning. *If* I did decide to sell—which I haven't—he wouldn't be able to be here in person to sign the papers, so all of that would need to be handled through his lawyer. Is something like that possible?"

He was pretty sure it was, but wanted to run it past a real estate agent to make sure, if for no other reason than discussing the topic now would grease the skids if he was forced to liquidate the house in the near future.

"I've not personally dealt with that specific situation before, but have a couple people in the office who have, so I will ask around and find out. Off the top of my head, I can't see why that wouldn't work." Pause. "Just how firm is this deal? Hypothetically, that is."

"Like I said, I haven't even thrown out a price. That could be a deal breaker."

The coffee was cooler now, so he took a bigger sip.

"I can't believe you'd actually consider selling," now sounding eerily like his mother. (Bless her soul.) "I thought you love it there."

"I do." He polished off the remainder of the cup in a gulp. "Look, nothing's concrete. Change of subject. Are we still on for dinner tonight?"

"Yes, it's locked on my schedule. Why do you ask?"

"Just checking if you had another appointment pop up. See you there."

Chapter 20

DAVIDSON'S LUCK HELD. Having substantial Hawaiian Airline mileage in addition to possessing a full-price, first-class ticket bumped up his priority, allowing him to score a seat on the 1:00 PM Honolulu-Seattle flight.

After hanging up the phone, he headed to the bathroom for a shower. He'd pack—a trifling job, considering how little there was—after enjoying a leisurely breakfast.

His frequent guest status allowed him complementary breakfasts from their elaborate buffet. Dressed in cargo shorts and a white safari shirt, he rode the elevator to the lobby and walked through to Orchids where a hostess ushered him to an outside table in the shade of a palm tree. He ordered grapefruit juice, black coffee, and two pieces of whole wheat toast before visiting the parallel buffet serving tables that featured both Japanese and American fare. He piled his plate with Japanese-style pickled veggies, three pieces of very crisp bacon, a modest heap of scrambled eggs (with catsup and Tabasco sauce), and a healthy dollop of orange marmalade.

His juice, coffee, and toast were waiting upon his return to the table. He popped the linen napkin draped it over his lap, opened his laptop to the *New York Times* website.

Ahhh, grease, salt, and caffeine. What more could a person want to start the day?

Especially a travel day.

But his mind was too consumed with gnawing worry to concentrate fully on the news.

Had he unwittingly exposed the lad?

If so, could he do anything to correct the mistake? Talk to him again? And say what, exactly? That he firmly believed he would be safer if he were allied with Fisher? Arnie was brilliant, but was he sufficiently canny to remain hidden from Naseem? What exactly did he disclose to her in Las Vegas?

Appetite now gone, he shoved aside the plate of eggs and tried unsuccessfully to convince himself that Arnold was no longer his responsibility, that he'd been warned, and as an adult, was perfectly capable of choosing his destiny. But the rationalization did not assuage his anxiety. Nervously, he glanced around, searching for anyone watching, then realized how ridiculous he was behaving and tried to return to reading the news.

He checked out of the hotel at 10:03 AM, tossed his bag in the passenger seat and drove away—already eagerly anticipating his scheduled return mid-February when he'd be relaxed and far removed from this current mess.

Squeeze in a bonus week in late September or early October?

Hell, he could afford the time off. Why not? He loved his mini-vacations here. Loved the sun, the warm tropical air, spending days in shorts and t-shirts and being spoiled by luxurious hotel amenities. Yet Honolulu wasn't a city in which he'd choose to live year-round. He suspected the relative confinement of being on an island in addition to endless sun and balmy temperatures might grow monotonous. He should've asked Arnold about this.

Naseem and Akmal handed the TSA agent fake passports. After a cursory glance to compare their faces to the pictures and a quick barcode scan, the agent waved them through to the waiting line for the body scanner.

So far, things were going flawlessly.

Her brothers and sisters in Hawaii were awaiting their arrival.

"You are planning something, Naseem. I can see it in your eyes."

They moved closer to the scanner.

"Do not say another word until we are completely away from TSA."

Akmal nodded and Naseem returned to her thoughts.

She was certain that the Toby Taylor who owned the house in the Honolulu suburbs was the Jew. She was also certain that if the lawyer visited him, it was to warn 'Toby' about her.

Which undoubtedly indicated that the FBI was now watching him closely, lying in wait. She smiled at her good fortune: it'd be sweet to use this opportunity to not only kill the Jew, but in the process, kill as many federal agents as possible before slipping away once again.

A plan began solidifying in her mind.

She'd use the six-hour flight to forge the details into a strong, effective attack, one worthy of Allah.

Chapter 21

ARNOLD AND LONI Lee sat at a window table for two in Taormina, a small Italian restaurant off Lewers, his all-time favorite place for Italian food in all of Honolulu.

In his mind, pizza really didn't count pizza as Italian food *per se* because he delegated it to a category all by itself (Big Kahuna's was his favorite). They lucked out and were seated immediately at their favorite spot, one of the two tables next to the window which allowed Arnold to watch the tourists pass by.

They were enjoying a glass of overpriced Chianti before ordering dinner, the same wine the waiter recommended on his first visit here. Loni seldom drank more than one or two sips of alcohol of any kind. On their third date, he finally summoned enough nerve to ask why, but she artfully deflected any answer and he never pressed the issue. Whether or not she drank wine made no difference to him. He was simply interested in learning a person's reasons for self-imposed dietary restrictions.

Especially alcohol.

He suspected it wasn't because of any deeply guarded secret—such as a dark family history of raging alcoholism—but instead it was in character with her obvious aversion to calories in any form. She proudly maintained a reed-thin body of well-toned aerobically-trained muscles. True, her hectic schedule often resulted in missing lunch, but even when time permitted a leisurely meal—tonight, for example—she pushed her food around the plate without nibbling more than a few bites. Arnold found this practice head-scratchingly weird, especially because he was a card-carrying eater. Rachael, on the other hand, loved food, but unlike Loni, maintained her weight by being very active.

"What's wrong?" Loni asked.

The question jarred him from the street scene and he realized his thoughts were elsewhere. He returned his attention to her mildly annoying habit of rubbing an index finger around the lip of her wine glass, creating soft screeching sounds, but doubted she realized how it might bother anyone within earshot.

He was struck again by her stunning beauty. Luxurious long black hair and exotic facial features expressed through a mix of Asian and Caucasian genes, all packaged in a sleeveless silk dress of tropical blues. Her beauty was just one more reason to seriously suspect her motive for dating him. He believed most people paired-off with mates of approximately equal physical attractiveness.

There was, of course, a major modifier to the rule: money. Money seemed to allow ugly guys to attract beautiful women. He was a case in point. Yeah, sure, he was the first to admit this prejudice was extremely cynical, but...

Rachael's hair was also black, but in a short practical cut of a busy nursing student.

"Huh? Oh, nothing," he answered.

She made a dramatic show of folding her hands and leaning forward, narrowing the gap between them.

"Really? You could've fooled me. Your body is the only thing here all evening. Your mind's in a galaxy far, far away. You're not sharing and you know how much I hate that."

True.

Hard as he tried to focus on their conversation, it was impossible, due to his continuously ruminating over the increasing danger Naseem presented. What once had been a purely hypothetical situation had suddenly turned intimidatingly tangible and dangerous and was scaring the shit out of him. Since Davidson's visit, the stress and tension were unrelenting. He felt like a nervous wildebeest at a watering hole. He didn't want to die. Especially at the hands of that fucking terrorist Naseem. Only a few minutes ago it dawned on him; even if he allied with Fisher, he was now officially and totally hosed. So, given that, why not improve the odds of survival by tossing in with the FBI? More and more that seemed to be the right move.

"Come on, Toby, tell me what's bothering you."

He slumped into the chair, opting for a sip of Chianti rather than concocting some lame-ass story. Besides, what the hell could he say? He'd never uttered a single word about his life before Honolulu, a historical vacuum that created a void stupefyingly easy to maintain by never filling in the blanks.

She, on the other hand, eagerly concocted an elaborate backstory fabricated on total fiction built entirely from...he wasn't quite sure where. In hindsight, was a major-league slip-up to not have ginned up a reasonable line of bullshit to account for having the funds to purchase the house.

Hell, winning the Lotto would've been a better story than handing her a blank slate. *But*, he reminded himself, he'd been a victim of circumstance; having fled Seattle on the spur of the moment and arriving in Honolulu with nothing more than the false ID from Vegas. Realistically, in his own defense, he never imagined he'd end up sleeping with his realtor.

Hey, it wasn't like he'd planned on that, right?

When the Bagley Street house blew up, he escaped with nothing more than the clothes on his back and the contents in his pockets. Which, luckily, included a driver's license and a Visa card with the fucking Toby Taylor alias. Oh yeah, there was a cellphone too; which he promptly tossed. His plan, the night of the explosion, was to convince Karim he was just running over to the nearby pizza joint, and then, when safely out of the house, trigger the explosion with the phone. Didn't work that way. Not even remotely close.

Yes, the explosion detonated...but there were a few minor wrinkles, like ending up trapped inside. Shit, if he hadn't been able to bust out that window...

But he did escape.

You work with what you have, right?

After running out of the alley and putting as much distance between him and the inferno, he'd cut across Greenlake Park to Aurora Avenue and jumped the first bus downtown, transferred to the SeaTac Tram at Westlake, then spent the night tossing and turning in a flea-bag motel off US 99.

The next morning, he scored a one-way ticket to Honolulu. His first order of business upon deplaning was to find an affordable hotel room. Easy enough. For the next three days he searched every Seattle news source in existence for word of the fire. Interestingly, the only mention was a two-paragraph filler the *Seattle Time* the following day.

Nothing appeared in any other media.

Why not?

Was the death of an international terrorist that unremarkable? *Or*, was Karim's body too damaged to identify? *Or*, were Karim's remains mistaken as his? *Or*, did no one give a shit? He pondered these questions time to time since then. Something just didn't feel right about the radio silence. After all, the FBI knew full well Karim was in his house. On the other hand, so many things were happening in his life that these questions faded from consciousness.

Until now.

His first days in Honolulu had been hellishly hectic. With nothing but the clothes on his back, he devoted his first efforts to procuring the myriad basic essentials; clothes (not a huge problem in the tropics), a laptop and unraveling the mysteries of a city visited only once before.

As his immediate situation began to stabilize, he turned his attention to rebuilding SAM. And that was no trivial task. The first step required procuring a suitable location, and because of secrecy of his work, precluded a roommate or landlord. Translation: he needed to own a single-family house which had to meet special criteria. Reflecting back on what those were, he applauded Davidson for having nailed them all. Well...except for the Toby Taylor fuck up. He owned that one.

"What's so funny?" Loni asked.

Uh-oh.

"Nothing. Just thinking about our house search."

Well, sorta.

Finding the right place took more time than anticipated. Then, after signing the papers, came a thirty day wait for the deal to close before he could to move in, which, on account of having no furniture, amounted to nothing more than schlepping in a rucksack and Hefty bag stuffed with his entire new wardrobe.

Next came the formidable task of acquiring all those little items he'd previously just taken for granted: furniture; housewares, a high-speed Internet connection, a car, on and fucking on...leaving him with new respect for those poor people who lose everything in a natural disaster. He realized how little we relate to other people's tragedies until we have been hit with one.

After dumping the sack of clothes in his new bedroom, he drove to Best Buy to acquire all the hardware required to rebuild his Artificial Intelligence system. Tons of it. Servers, routers, cables, the whole enchilada.

By then, he and Loni were dating.

That began innoxiously enough. Aware that he was new to the city, she offered—as a full-service realtor, of course—to help him become established and delighted in advising him on what furniture to buy. She loved having carte blanche in selecting his furniture, wardrobe, and choice of vehicle.

One thing naturally led to another until...well, shit, here they were.

"What about it?" she asked.

"Huh?"

"Toby!"

By then, she'd concocted an elaborate backstory for him. Her various iterations followed one basic theme: he was a trust-fund brat without job skills, a privileged young man who need not rely on employment for financial survival, whose career was singularly devoted to enjoying the life of a Ralph Lauren advertisement.

Which, in reality, was light-years from reality.

But, he never saw an up-side to correcting her fiction. And, truth be told, the story served him exceeding well because he never risked becoming entangled in a lie. She quickly came to believe—again without a word from him—that his parents were wiped out in a tragic freeway pileup (or was it a plane crash?), leaving him a sizable chunk of wealth, perhaps in a trust he couldn't fuck up until he hit thirty-five, at which point he'd have hopefully matured sufficient to carry on his parents' fiscal duty of clipping coupons from tax-free bonds. That particular melodrama held an irresistibly appealing flair for her.

"You're thinking about the sale of your house again, aren't you!" she said, leaving no room for debate.

Deny it? For the love of God, why?

She just handed him the perfect excuse for tonight's distracted behavior.

"Toby?"

"Huh?"

"You're not listening to a word I'm saying. Where are you?"

"You're absolutely right," he admitted with a nod. "It's the house...sorry, what did you just say?"

A broad smile flashed across her face, clearly pleased at being correct. Yet again. Early in their relationship she'd bragged that her meteoric real estate success was directly attributable to her uncanny ability to read people.

"So...do you plan to leave the island or are you just looking to make money?"

He produced his best innocent shrug.

"Dunno…haven't made up my mind whether to sell or not."

She frowned.

"Well, that raises an important question, doesn't it? What about *us*?"

He peered into piercing, dark-brown eyes.

"What do you mean?"

"Stop it." Her frown deepened. "You know exactly what I'm talking about. What about our relationship? Doesn't that influence anything?"

Well, maybe a few days ago, but now? No. Not with Naseem back on the FBI's radar. The Al Jazeera story dramatically altered the equation. If Fisher could capture Naseem, he could be Arnold Gold again, which would allow him to safely contact Rachael, which would mean…

This brought him right back to Davidson's advice about Loni.

"I guess that says it all," she said, throwing her napkin on the table and ending an awkward silence.

He scrambled for a diplomatic way to weasel out of the topic.

"I didn't say a word."

C'mon, you pussy, here's the perfect opportunity—

"That's the *point*. I wanted you to say *some*thing. Anything." Swallowing obvious anger. "We've been seeing each other for, what, a year now? This whole time you've never said one word, not *one*, about how you feel about me…about us!" She stopped abruptly, staring hard. "And now that you've brought it up, how *do* you feel about me?"

He turned toward a group of tourists on the sidewalk, embarrassed by the other customers eyeing him. A moment later, he turned to her and took a breath.

"I like you."

True, but…

She recoiled.

"You *like* me? That's *it?*" shaking her head sadly and a tad too dramatically.

He wanted to tell her to calm down but knew that'd only fan

the flames.

"Yes. I like you."

Repeating the words, it felt wonderful to finally respond to her probing.

I should've had the balls to say this months ago, when she first started making noise about where the relationship was heading. Again, Davidson was right.

Eyes now down to slits, she continued staring.

"You're seeing someone else! Aren't you! Yes, that *is* it, isn't it!"

"No." he shot back too emphatically.

He immediately realized the lie. He *was* in love with someone; Rachael. And unless he could resolve the possibility of being with her, he shouldn't be in any other relationship.

She cocked her head to the right, as if selecting her next words carefully.

"Where do you see us in, say, six months?"

Aw man...

"You folks decided yet?"

The waiter was collecting their untouched menus, and, in the process, mercifully threw him a life raft.

Arnold thought; matter for fact, I just did decide.

Instead, "We need a few more minutes, please."

Loni sat back with her anorexic arms folded defiantly across small breasts.

"I'm waiting."

He shrugged.

"I have no idea."

Well, at least that was the unblemished truth. He knew for fact their relationship just took an unrecoverable nosedive...and realized it was for the best.

Jesus, stop acting like a pussy, dude!

Her eyes crystallized into tiny granite pebbles.

"Know what? I don't believe you."

What's not to believe?

"Okay, so what do you want me to say?"

The evening became a total disaster. There was no way to avoid it.

Why even try?

"I just don't believe *anything* about you anymore. I don't believe you're a day trader."

Day-trader?

Oh right, just another of her out-of-thin-air conclusions based solely on his elaborate computer setup.

She was convinced he spent hours playing the markets, gambling the monthly trust fund stipend.

He decided to minimize further damage by responding in only monosyllables.

"Why?"

She nodded as if accepting this to be a capitulation, although he wasn't sure what exactly what he could be capitulating to.

"I'm beginning to think that everything you've told me about yourself is nothing but fake news. All that extravagant security of yours? If you're simply a day-trader, why do you need that?"

And off she goes again...he'd never said a word to justify his computer lab.

"See! This is *exactly* what I'm talking about!" stabbing an index finger at his chest, leaning forward, narrowing the distance between their faces. "I find it very interesting—no, make that highly unusual—that you never discuss your family. Why not? What's the big secret?" now speaking in a harsh whisper barely perceptible above the restaurant din.

Seeing no up-side to any answer he could possibly come up with, he decided it best to just let things play out. He knew—or hoped he knew—where this was headed.

But why he didn't have the guts to do it himself?

"Know what? I searched the Internet for you again today. Guess what I came up with? Nothing! Not a damn thing. You're not on Snapchat, Twitter, LinkedIn, or any place any normal person should be."

She paused, as if loading the bazooka for one final blast.

"You know I don't do social media." he was growing irritated at the harangue. "So what?"

"That's the point! You're not *normal*."

She was whipping herself into a lather. The patrons at the next tables began staring instead of sneaking the furtive glances of moments earlier.

"To be truthful, I think all this...this *crap* about an anonymous buyer is nothing by a cover for something else going on. Know what I think? I think you're into something illegal and the authorities, or maybe the Russian mafia, or whatever, are getting close and you know it and that's why you're talking about selling the house."

Wow. Close on that one.

But there she went again, engineering another elaborate answer to an unanswered question. She sat back, arms crossed defiantly, waiting for his defense. Instead, he sat back too and waited. Her tirade would either blow over or she'd storm out. Whichever of those she chose, this was the first step in ending the relationship. Still...he felt like shit for taking the coward's way out.

"This conversation we're having? Wait," she paused for a dramatic sigh. "Correction: this *monolog I'm* having, is going nowhere. Let me ask you this—and if you don't answer me, I'm walking out of here. Why are you seeing me?"

"Because I like you."

Truthful enough. Just not what she wanted to hear.

Another exasperated sigh.

"What does that *mean*, you like me?"

Alright, already.

"Look, Loni, I'm not sure what I can say...I like you, okay? I enjoy our hanging out together. I like listening to you talk about your work...I don't know what more to say."

She cut him off with, "Where are *we* going?"

And there it was.

"I don't know."

Oh, for christsake, you pussy, cowboy up and tell her it's over.

She shook her head.

"From the very beginning of this relationship you've been hesitant about something...and don't dare deny it, we both know it's true. What bothers you about us? Well, maybe bother isn't the right word, but I think you know what I'm saying...something's off-kilter and I want to know what. I'm being totally honest and I want you to be totally honest with me."

He had no doubt about that last part, but that was beside the point. Explain? She genuinely seemed to want an answer, but he couldn't say a word about his past or about SAM or the gambling...and he certainly wasn't wild about any mention of being in love with Rachael...so...what the hell could he say?

And now that the subject of their feelings was out on the table, she'd never volunteered—nor had he asked—about how she felt about him. Perhaps because he always assumed any answer would be manipulative. Yeah, he was a first-rate asshole to hold that belief, but at least he was honest with himself about it.

He thought back to the first time they walked his house and she had immediately zeroed in on his finances.

"Sorry if this is too personal—and if so, no need to answer—but I can't help ask...what's with you being so young to afford a house in this price range, I mean...oh, and may I call you Toby instead of Mr. Taylor?"

He smiled at her. "And your question?"

"May I ask what you do for a living? You're not a trust fund brat are you?"

Those words quickly became the crux of the issue of her nonstop interest in his finances rather than him. That, and her incessant need to Close The Deal. Tonight was a prime example. Okay, sure, if he were shopping for a house, she'd logically want a handle on his financial qualifications, but that part of their relationship was so far in the rear-view mirror that...

"Okay, I admit it. I'm strange," he finally offered. "I don't tweet or promote myself on social media. I didn't realize that's a felony in Hawaii."

"That's not the point."

"No, Loni, that *is* the point. I'm not going to be forced to defend how I choose to live. So, if that's unacceptable, let's just call it a night and I'll pick up a pizza on the way home."

There! It was out.

He felt a flood of relief! He locked eyes with her, figured if she walked out, to hell with it. At least it would save him the pain of ending things two or three days from now.

After a shocked moment, she dropped her gaze. Her angry pout dissolved into a thin, weak smile.

"Let me tell you about the showing today..."

Chapter 22

THE BOEING 777 touched the SeaTac runway at 10:30 PM. Because of being in Seat 1B, Davidson was first out the door the moment the flight attendant cleared them to exit.

He streaked to the down escalator for the North Terminal tram station. As he reached bottom, the subway train hissed to a stop, so he jogged the platform and jumped onboard seconds before the doors whooshed shut, then was out again, bee-lining for the up escalator to baggage claim, cresting the moving stairs and immediately spotting a black suited man holding up a white plastic sign with, "Davidson," printed in thick black Sharpie letters.

He waved.

"That's me"

He continued toward the sky bridge to the garage beyond. The driver caught up.

"No baggage to claim?"

"No baggage."

The cool, humid Seattle air jolted his skin, completely deleting residual any warm Honolulu glow.

"This way," the driver quickly took the lead.

They rode the escalator to the third floor of the parking garage and a waiting black Mercedes. Davidson tossed his carry-on on the seat beside him for an easy exit when they pulled up to the Smith Tower. As the darkened sedan sped along I-5 toward downtown,

Davidson debated whether to phone Fisher now or wait until morning. He decided to call tonight, but to do so in the office.

The limo braked at the curb in front of the building at 11:10 PM. Davidson slipped the driver a five-dollar bill in addition to the tip built into the charge and stepped out to wait at the lobby doors until the car vanished. As a defense attorney, he fostered a healthy paranoia of allowing anyone to know his home address.

Anyone meant anyone, including limo drivers.

When traveling to and from to the airport, he always arrived and departed from work. But tonight, instead of crossing Second Avenue to the garage, he used his access card to open the door the ornate marble lobby.

"Evening, Mr. Davidson."

"Evening, Sampson."

He was on a first name basis with the graveyard security guard for years now as a result of the long nights spent in the office during the days of trial preparation. He continued into the elevator alcove where, at this time of evening, one brightly lit cage always waited with open doors.

When he flipped on the office lights he was immediately struck by how dark and dreary the interior was in contrast to the brilliant light he'd left at Honolulu airport. Stranger yet was how distorted the short absence from the office seemed; felt like he was gone a week.

"Agent Fisher, Palmer Davidson. Oh, sorry, did I wake you?"

"Hell yes." Fisher voice was thick with the rasp of sleep. "The more important question is, why? What just couldn't wait until morning?"

"You said to call you if I learned anything."

Davidson leaned back, stretching stiffness from in his legs.

"And this gem of information just had to be told to me now

instead of in the morning?" with a distinct note of irritation.

"I was able to locate Arnold Gold and warn him of the threat."

Once again, he savored pride for having solved a difficult puzzle.

"Wow, that was fast. Especially for someone who didn't know he's alive."

The words per se didn't irritate—Fisher did have a point—the irritation came from Fisher's arrogance and sarcasm in his tone. It served as another example for why Arnold might be hesitant to work with him.

"I remind you—you are not the only person missing sleep over this."

"It that it? Or is there something else? Will he assist us?"

"I only call to confirm that he is indeed alive and well hidden. In addition, it would be difficult, but not impossible, for Naseem to find him."

Arnold's safety depended on her missing the Toby Taylor angle.

"Are you going to tell me where he is or are you just jerking me around?"

Davidson wiped his face but it did not lessen the grimy fatigue that irritated his eyes.

"We discussed it...he is considering his options. I explained it would be to his advantage to help the Bureau, but he is understandably concerned about the obvious risks."

"In other words, you called to fuck with me."

Not even thinly masking his hostility.

"No. I called to confirm what you previously only suspected. I hope that this confirmation increases the case's priority. Again, sorry to have awakened you."

"Wait! Before you go...any chance you were followed?"

Bingo. His greatest worry.

"I really do not think so, but have no way to know. The trip was spur of the moment, which makes tailing me problematic," and caught himself before mentioning he flew. "Unless, of course, I was under Bureau surveillance."

After a sarcastic snort, "I didn't need to. I know you flew to Honolulu."

Goddamn it!

"How—"

"Put out a TSA alert on you ten minutes after leaving your office."

Davidson was sitting bolt upright now, blood pressure pounding his temples.

"You did that knowing you have a leak in your office? Why not buy an ad in Al Jazeera? This is a prime an example for why Arnold is hesitant to work with you."

"Get off your fucking soapbox, Davidson. If you'd been truthful with me from the start, I wouldn't have to do shit like that."

Davidson slammed down the phone and turned to the window, hands of white knuckles, unsure who he was angrier with; Fisher or himself? Not an easy answer. Hanging up like that was an embarrassingly juvenile response and did not square with the character he tried to be.

He took a long, slow breath while studying the familiar view to the north, and told himself to relax and try to think through his options.

What could be the repercussions of Fisher knowing Arnold was somewhere on Oahu?

The best case scenario would be for Homeland Security to focus attention on flights in and out of the islands as part of the government's hunt for Naseem. But what about the FBI leak? Would that only facilitate Naseem's search? Because the moment she knew Arnold's approximate location, it'd be relatively easy for Nawzer to do the rest. At that point, there would be little possibility of effectively protecting the lad. Every action carries the risk of unintended consequences.

Goddamnit! What have I done?

He slapped the top of the desk hard enough to sting like hell. He massaged his hand.

Come on, think.

What to do now? Warn Arnold? A glance at the phone sent a chill slithered along his spine. Did Fisher have his phones monitored too?

Don't be ridiculous! He wouldn't have enough to claim just cause. Or did he?

No.

You sure about that?

That would all depend on how Fisher might spin a request, especially if he was able to couch it in terms of national security. He decided that at this point it was probably best to do nothing, that Arnold had been warned. Yet...to do nothing felt wrong.

A glance at his watch.

It was now past midnight and he could feel fatigue and anger muddying his objectivity, so he decided this was not the optimal time to make a decision, that instead, it was time for some much-needed rest in his own bed. Thank God, tomorrow—correction, today—was Saturday, with nothing scheduled. Nevertheless, he'd be back later to catch up on all the work he neglected these past couple days.

Wearily, he grabbed his carry-on bag, locked the office and went home.

Chapter 23

ARNOLD AWOKE TO barking. Not Chance's playful bark, not even his warning bark. No, this was his dead-serious, don't-fuck-with-the-pack bark warning that something was radically wrong.

He slipped out of bed knuckling sleep from his eyes, headed through the darkened house straight to the computer room and security monitors. He scanned all the images from the six strategically-placed HD Sony cameras mounted under the eaves of the roof, each capable of panning a one-hundred sixty-degree arc and switching from color to infrared. Every element in the system was state of the art.

He immediately homed in on a person on the sidewalk peering through the driveway gate, scoping out the house and courtyard. He switched to infrared and adjusted his glasses, but the face was obscured by the angle and a hoodie. He switched to a feed from another camera and looked again.

A woman?

Yeah, a woman, but not just any woman; he was looking at Naseem Fucking Farhad.

Really?

How can you be so sure with that hoodie on?

Well, the image sure as hell gave him that impression. What was that she was holding in her hand? A gun?

"Launch RAID."

RAID was his radio-controlled drone docked on the roof which could be deployed with just this simple verbal command. He'd built the aircraft two months ago with no particular use in mind other than a radically sick robotics project using a new computer chip and printed circuit. RAID was way more technologically sophisticated anything available on the hobby market, although its shape appeared typical of most; basically, a pentagonal star with propellers. The kicker, though, was RAID's payload, which included a multi-lens, normal and infrared, HD video camera with 50X digital zoom, a directional microphone, and 2.5 gigahertz 5-watt transmitter. As such, it was the epitome of operational reconnaissance stealth and provided a cool complement to his overall security system.

"No bark."

Chance gave a soft protest whine but obeyed.

Arnold switched the primary video feed from perimeter cameras to RAID, inserted a Bluetooth ear-bud to listen to the drone's directional microphones and donned his modified Oculus Go goggles so he could watch and control the camera while moving around the house. RAID flew to the south corner of the lot where palm fronds would partially hide it from being seen by Naseem.

"Move left...more...more. Descend ten."

He zoomed in the video.

The hoodie still prevented seeing a full facial image, so to compensate, he snapped several pictures from various angles and instructed SAM to digitally merge them into one composite image. With RAID now hovering at a higher altitude he scanned the rest of the property with the infrared lens, searching for any other human heat signatures.

"Attention," SAM said. "External probe in progress."

Okay, rather than a gun in her hand, she was sampling his Wi-Fi network and his security system. No problem. Not yet, at least. His encryption algorithm would be impossible for her to crack. But the fact she was even bothering to scope out his Wi-Fi indicated her crew was likely searching out a way to penetrate it. Which also told him they were technologically more sophisticated than expected. Undoubtedly Nawzer was still with them. Boy, *that* sonofabitch was a real piece of work, a huge pain in the ass.

Okay, so now what?

Send out a decoy to see how they deal with it? No, it was probably best to reserve that strategy. Although it'd potentially confuse them, it would do so only temporarily and, in the end, accomplish nothing other than providing them with additional security information. He was sweating now.

Fuck! Think! Do something!

He sucked down a deep breath, closed his eyes.

Okay, okay...odds are she's not out there alone. Right? Christ...check out the rest of the property.

If it hadn't been for the infrared lens, he would've flat-out missed the second one. This one, built like a male, was crouching at the up-hill corner of the property, approximately fifteen feet from the street, right hand against the wall to help him work his way down the steep side of the property. Arnold watched him flick on a small red LED for a few seconds, explore the ground at his feet, then turn it off again.

Fucker!

Call 911? And then what? How before the cops get here? Assuming they did. No, he'd watch a little longer, then, depending on what happened, decide.

Oh, Christ! How the hell did she zero in on him so quickly? Did it matter? Not really. He knew she'd end up here. Sooner or later. Just didn't expect it to be this soon. Now what? What would happen when that fucker reached to the back of the house? Try a break in?

Maybe.

But Naseem surely knew he'd be equipped with some crazy-sick security. Most definitely, but she had little to lose by finding out exactly what they were dealing with, and then use that information for refining their next attempt. After all, Naseem's biggest agenda was to get her hands on SAM. And then, kill him.

In that order?

Why not just kill him and disable the security? If they were a smart as he suspected, they'd count on a police response taking ten to fifteen minutes, so why not burn a few seconds to gather as much information as possible, split, then come back another time? Made sense, but what if they *did* try to physically break in? He wasn't armed and he hadn't called the cops. Shit, time to get the hell out of Dodge.

"Dock RAID. Initiate cellphone scan."

SAM's sophisticated programs included an automatic protocol to land RAID on the battery charger.

SAM's synthesized voice replied, "Docking protocol initiated. Two cellphones detected."

"Infect cellphones," Arnold said, pulling off the VR headset while jogging into the bedroom.

He again signaled Chance to not bark, threw on shorts, a MSFT Forum t-shirt, shoes and socks, stuffed a change of clothes and the Surface Pro in the black rucksack that was always stocked with spare cables for just this sort of emergency.

With the combination of dark-adapted eyes and the glow from various electronic devices, he had no difficulty moving quickly through the familiar space. He led Chance silently downstairs into the basement.

Had that asshole made it down the side of the house by now?

He peeked out a basement window but saw no one at the back gate. Light from the moon and stars was enough to navigate his escape path in the ravine. With his left hand masking the glow from his iPhone screen, he dialed 911.

"911. What is your emergency?"

"Someone's breaking into the house," Arnold whispered.

"What's your address, sir?"

He quickly recited it.

"A car has been dispatched. Stay on the line, do not hang up."

To hell with that.

Naseem must have a lookout to warn if a cop car got within two blocks of the place. Besides, for their next visit they'd be armed with jamming devices. Like it or not, his fate just solidified; the time had come to put all his chips on Fisher.

Arnold removed Chance's collar and wrapped it securely in a shirt to keep the tags from clinking while scrambling down the rocky terrain, stuffed the wad in his rucksack, unlocked the deadbolt, cracked back door, listened…heard the soft crunch of a footstep on volcanic debris. Close. Probably to the corner of the wall now. Time to make his break.

They slipped out, silently closed and locked the door, listened again.

Yeah, the asshole was getting too goddamn close.

Again, shielding the glow of the iPhone screen as much as possible, he opened the app to remotely control the exterior floodlights. With his other hand shielding Chance's eyes, he closed his own eyes, thumbed the app. The property exploded in blinding, high-intensity LEDs. He counted off three seconds before cutting off the lights, then opened his eyes, quickly cracked the back gate, slipped through, and started scrambling down the steep rocky path, Chance scurrying silently along with him.

Chapter 24

CLEAR SKIES, STARS, plus the bright moon provided enough light to hurry down the path memorized during their numerous routine drills. A shout came from the back of the house. It was immediately followed by the sound of someone crashing through brush.

Dumb shits were actually trying to follow him.

Advantage, Arnold.

With such a good head start and knowledge of the terrain, he and Chance could move steadily but no faster than he felt was safe. A broken leg would be a disaster for him now. After another fifty feet he paused to listen, heard more clamoring from the trail above. A few rocks skittered past, bouncing down the ravine. Chance remained at his side, nose raised toward their pursuers, tracking their scent but still obeying the no bark command.

The steep path cut a snaking course through dense foliage to the mouth of the ravine where it eventually leveled out at two concrete Jersey barriers before continuing on as a residential street. The closer he got to the road the more streetlight helped him move quickly. Five feet from the barriers he stopped, a sixth-sense warning him to not walk straight into the open street. Just in case...

In a crouch, he scanned the immediate surroundings.

And noticed the car.

Cars held little interest for him other than their utility, so he didn't know the make or model but took note of the stickers in the upper right corner of the windshield. A rental. Which, by itself, was no big deal in a city perpetually overrun with tourists. But a rental in this neighborhood? At this hour of morning? What were the odds? Slim, but not insanely impossible.

He slowly worked through the foliage toward the property to his right, where a bougainvillea-covered trellis could shield him. Assuming, of course, the house wasn't armed with motion-activated floods, or worse yet, a burglar alarm. If that happened, he could kiss his sorry ass goodbye. Chance moved silently beside him, alert for problems, obviously aware of the seriousness of the situation.

Twenty feet of low groundcover now separated him from the trellis, making it impossible to cross that stretch without being exposed. The footsteps from the trail were growing louder now, leaving him little choice but to continue moving and pray no one noticed. He duck-walked the perimeter of the property, sticking as close as possible to higher foliage, keeping one eye on the car, ready to drop to the ground at the slightest hint of being seen.

As soon as he reached the trellis, he dropped onto his haunches to listen, Chance on his left, panting. Slowly he pushed the vines aside, for a clear view of the car across the street, but the interior was too dark to see inside.

Seconds later, two hooded figures emerged from the trail into the street, halted to scan their surroundings. After a few whispered exchanges, they casually approached the rental. The driver and passenger doors opened but the interior lights remained off and two people stepped out.

The four huddled, whispering harshly, pointing, shaking their heads. A minute later, they piled into the car, pulled a K turn, and proceeded slowly down the street.

Arnold waited five minutes before he dared leave the protection of the shadows. Satisfied they were now gone, he cautiously stepped from behind the trellis to the sidewalk. Nothing happened, so he started walking slowly along the street toward the intersection where the neighborhood would enlarge with parallel streets. If Naseem and company were still searching for him, a larger area lowered the odds of being spotted, but, he figured, they were probably long gone anyway.

He continued toward the freeway, to more populated streets where the risk of being spotted would drop even more. Vehicular traffic was sparse with no pedestrians in sight, making him feel excruciatingly exposed and obvious. Now within two blocks of the freeway, he pinged Uber, and then, while waiting for the ride, phoned Chance's vet. The clinic would be closed but he knew someone always answered.

"Sorry to wake you. This is Toby Taylor...Chance Taylor's father. Hey, listen, an emergency just came up and I have to fly out this morning. Is it possible to board Chance a few days?"

"No problem. You know he's welcome anytime. When do you want to drop him off?"

"Soon as I can get there. Thanks!"

Chapter 25

ARNOLD KNELT ON cool concrete, Chance's head held gently between his hands, peering into those large, clear doggy eyes, the air smelling of fur and disinfectant.

An occasional random bark came from kennels in the rear of the clinic. Leaving his best friend for even a few days tore at his heart. Animal behaviorists claim dogs understand only about fifty words, but Chance knew many more than that. Plus, he understood a ton of non-verbal communication that non-dog people never appreciate. The pooch apparently knew something bad was about to happen because his flaps were down and his usual smile was gone.

"Daddy has to go. Chance stays. Daddy will be back."

He used the same phrases each time he left Chance at home in the belief that simple consistency was crucial to clear canine communication.

Leaning in, Chance delivered three quick doggy kisses. Arnold returned the love with choobers.

Goodbyes finished, he stood.

"He understands. He'll be good."

The vet nodded.

"We know he will. He's a great dog. Any idea how long you'll be gone? Not that we don't have room for him."

"No. But, I'll pick him up soon as I get back."

She smiled at that.

"He'll miss you but we'll take good care of him."

"I know." Arnold nodded, cast a final glance at his best friend. "That's why you're the only one I trust him with. Thanks again for taking him on such short notice."

Chapter 26

ARNOLD TOOK AN Uber to an all-night café. He'd never set foot in the place before, but had always noticed the garish red neon "open 24 hours" sign when he drove past in the last year. The long, narrow interior was surprisingly humid with the thick air smelling of grease, coffee, and Clorox. A scarred laminate counter ran most of the left side of the room and a parallel row of booths ran the right wall. Luckily, he was able to grab an empty booth in the back, as far as possible from the front window. He was amazed at the number of customers sitting around eating and chatting.

What the hell are all these people doing up at this hour of night?

He decided they probably worked in various segments of the service industry that supported the city's huge tourism trade.

A walking tattoo in a white t-shirt, shorts, and catsup smeared apron lumbered over.

"Know what you want or you need a menu?"

He had no clue what her body art cost, but this honey had obviously sunk a sizable chunk of coin into ink and piercings, and, in the process, undoubtedly immunized herself against an impressive number of diseases.

Arnold figured the minimum price of admission for killing an hour or so would be a cup of coffee and slice of their triple coconut cream pie. With a nod of approval, she lumbered away. He opened his Surface and signed onto the café's complimentary Wi-Fi.

Email Davidson?

Tempting, but decided that wouldn't be too smart. Naseem had zeroed in on him waaaaaay too quickly. The most logical conclusion was that Nawzer had somehow gained access to Davidson's email. And the more he considered this, the more it seemed there was no other way to explain all the totally weird shit that had just happened over the past few days.

And...as long as he was on this subject, where *was* Davidson? Still at the Halekulani? Oh, man, that'd solve a few problems in a damn wicked hurry. He Googled the hotel's number and dialed.

"Palmer Davidson's room, please. That's spelled—"

"Sorry sir, but he's not registered here."

Well, that settled that.

Davidson probably checked out yesterday for the return to Seattle. Another pang of regret tapped his heart for so inadequately thanking him. No one else would drop work to fly over to warn him. *Well, Howie would've*, but...no one else. There had to be a kick-ass way to show his gratitude, but nothing came to mind. Besides, he had other, more pressing matters to deal with at the moment.

This brought him straight back to the most important question: Naseem. The only way she could've possibly known where he lived was by following Davidson either physically or digitally. Most likely the latter. Meaning Nawzer's fucking fingerprints had to be all over Davidson's electronics. Probably every goddamn device he owned.

"Here you go."

He glanced at the generous slice of phenomenally enticing pie sitting next to a white ceramic mug of steaming black coffee. For some strange reason, this sight triggered a weird out-of-body image of him alone at the counter just like the famous Edward Hopper painting.

It took only the first bite to understand why this ratty little diner was so busy at such an ungodly hour. Smooth, rich coconut cream. Pure ecstasy, orders of magnitude more than anything he could've anticipated with a silky texture of absolute, drop-dead sensuality. He sat back, replaced the fork on the plate, and savored the nutty flavor...which made him want to run up and down the aisle screaming.

He hadn't been hungry when he walked through the front door, but now...holy shit!

Pie finished, he checked the time: 3:30. A login to the Alaska Airlines website showed all mainland flights—regardless of destination—waitlisted. Same thing for Hawaiian and American Airlines, although their standby lists were shorter. His only chance of getting off the island in the next twenty-four hours would be to pester airport ticket agents in person. Then, with a little bit of luck, he might be able to snag a last-minute opening.

Bill paid, he moved outside, stood for a moment on the sidewalk, and decided to kill more time by walking over to the Royal Hawaiian before catching an Uber to the airport.

Chapter 27

THE AIRPORT WAS more deserted than expected, but what the hell did he know? He was never here this time of day. With the ticket counters unmanned, he opted to kill time by strolling the lobby on the off chance he'd stumble across an airline he hadn't considered. This was exactly the how he happened on Allegiant Air. He'd never flown the carrier, but remembered reading about their inaugural flight from Honolulu to LA. Unlike the bigger airlines such as Delta or Alaska, they only had two automated ticket kiosks.

What the hell, he had nothing better to do at the moment, so why not check? He swiped the screen, activating it. To his surprise and good fortune, he was able to snatch the one remaining seat on the early LA flight. Using his Robert Kay identity, he purchased the ticket; an aisle seat directly across from the rear toilet.

Okay, whatever. It'd get him to the mainland.

Five minutes later, with his boarding pass stored safely in his rucksack, he found an empty row of molded plastic chairs and stretched out as best he could over the scalloped surface using his rucksack as a pillow. He figured that falling asleep would be impossible, so just closed his eyes to concentrate on planning his next move. Later, once the departure gate was assigned, he'd to wait there. How Chance was doing? Did he feel abandoned?

Man, I miss that pooch!

By 6:00 AM, the lobby was rapidly beginning to congest with passengers for the crush of outbound flights to Asia. He stood, stretched, knuckled his eyes, decided to hunt for breakfast.

Thankfully the TSA lines were short, allowing him to zip through in record time. Unfortunately, Starbucks had yet to take delivery on his beloved classic breakfast sandwich, so he was forced to wander the seemingly endless string of fast food concessions in search of an alternative...hmmm...a Cinnabon or a McDonalds breakfast sandwich?

Tough choice.

With the memory of coconut cream pie still fresh in mind, he opted to stick with something outrageously sweet. Minutes later, armed with a gooey Cinnabon Classic and Starbucks triple-shot grande latte, he headed for the waiting area at the assigned gate. His luck held; he nailed a seat next to the only 110-volt power outlet in sight. He plugged in both his Surface and iPhone to top off their charges while surfing the web. You never knew when the next opportunity to charge might present itself....

As preboarding began, he queued up with the other passengers. Call Loni? And say what, exactly? He didn't have a good answer to that. Still...her tirade of the other night left him feeling strangely...what? Guilty? Perhaps. About? No good answer for that either. Who was he kidding? Truth be told, he was feeling very guilty. From their first date he knew they had no future...not as long as Rachael was foremost in his mind.

He'd asked Loni out for the simple selfish reason that he felt completely alone and desperately in need a friend. He knew no one in Honolulu. She was single and obviously interested in the young man who could afford to buy the house. So, in a way, he'd used her. Yeah, he was definitely feeling guilty. He boarded the flight, settled into his seat, and dialed.

"Hey, it's me. Just called to say I'm sorry about the other night."

He watched a burly man repeatedly try to hammer an oversized suitcase into the overhead rack, ignoring all the obvious laws of physics and dimensions. The guy seemed dead set on not checking the bag.

Loni sighed.

"I am too, but I needed to say those things. Your life seems a little...strange to me."

He watched as a flight attendant tried to reason with the man, but he continued to ignore her while ramming the suitcase this way and that as the aisle jammed up with passengers unable to pass.

"This probably isn't a great time to tell you I'm at the airport. An emergency came up suddenly and I have to fly to the mainland. In fact, I'm on the plane now and need to shut down any second."

"You're leaving?" she said with a strong note of disapproval. "Now?"

The flight attendant finally prevailed and the passenger grudgingly relinquished the suitcase, but continued to block the aisle and glare as she snaked her way through the other passengers toward the front door.

"I'll probably be gone a couple days, maybe more. You up for dinner when I get back?"

"What's the emergency?" this time with a distinctly leery edge.

Uh-oh, here we go again.

"It's complicated and I don't want to get into it right now."

Perhaps calling wasn't such a hot idea. Hang up before she gets argumentative?

"Hold on...uh-oh, they're closing the cabin door now, have to hang up."

"Don't bother calling again."

She disconnected.

Chapter 28

NASEEM RESTED HER elbows on her knees to stabilize the binoculars while studying the Jew's house across the ravine, Akmal sitting silently to her left, watching, searching their surroundings for any sign of a dog or another human approaching. Not that this was likely, given their location. They'd been surveilling the house for an hour now without any sign of activity inside.

"He is gone," Akmal muttered.

"Yes. This appears to be so."

"We are waiting how much longer?"

"We go now."

She lifted the lanyard from her neck, wound it around the middle of the binoculars before replacing them in the case. Akmal disassembled the rifle and packed it and the high-powered scope carefully into the black duffle bag, making sure to protect the scope.

Finished packing, they inspected the ground, making certain to leave nothing to give away their presence. Satisfied, Naseem started making her way the edge of the ravine to easier terrain back to the street where their car waited.

"I am thinking," Akmal said. "There may be another way to find him."

Chapter 29

SIX HOURS LATER, Arnold exited the gate into LAX and melded into a swarm of passengers pushing to the main terminal. At baggage claim, he rode an escalator up to the departures area, located the Alaska Airlines ticket area and secured a seat on the next shuttle to SeaTac. He'd need to hurry because the flight would begin boarding in fifteen minutes.

In route to the gate, he ducked into a gift shop where he purchased a UCLA hoodie, ball cap, and an I Love LA t-shirt, thinking they'd be warmer than what he was wearing in addition to providing a simple disguise if Naseem had sympathizers in the airport watching for him. Once seated aboard the 737, waiting the flight to push back from the gate, he used his iPhone to reserve a Hertz Mini Cooper similar to his own because the controls would already be second nature to him.

At 6:04, Arnold pulled to the curb across the street from Rachael's parents' house. At least, this was their place before Howie was murdered.

Was she still living there?

Or, as she planned last year, was she now graduated nursing school and working? Did she have her own place now? Was she still living in Seattle? More importantly, was she involved with someone? He had no right to worry about these things, especially considering that she, like the everyone else, assumed he was dead. Still…

Well, that last point wasn't exactly true anymore. As of a week ago, several people, including the one he feared most, knew damn well he was alive. An idea hit: now that the whole fucking world knew he wasn't dead, what was the risk in contacting her? Well, it was still risky, just not *as* risky.

He picked up his phone, reconsidered, stopped.

Okay, she answers the phone. What the hell do I say?

"Hi, it's Arnold, I'm not really dead."

How would that fly? Would she be angry at him? Would she even give a rat's ass?

No, wait for a better time, after you've thought this through.

He'd only get one chance at this, so needed to plan the call very carefully and script his opening words. Perhaps when his life stabilized…

Focus! There are more important things to do, and quickly.

He fired up the engine and headed for Queen Anne Hill.

He drove slowly past a short, downward-sloping driveway to a large stucco rectangle of wide windows and a garage door painted the same color as the walls. The first impression was a driveway dead-ending into the wall. Davidson's home. A minimalist contemporary statement. And a hell of a nice one at that. Every window was dark. Apparently, Davidson wasn't home.

Arnold glanced along the street for a place to park.

Fat chance!

Par for the course in this neighborhood. Same problem on the next block. The third block finally yielded an opening perhaps big enough to squeeze in a Mini Cooper or Smartcar, but only if the driver possessed extremely canny parking skill. Miraculously, he shoehorned it in without dinging paint. He trotted back to Davidson's house and rang the doorbell. No answer. Waited, rang again.

Hmmm...out for the evening? Or merely at the office catching up on work? Did he even intend to come home tonight? Now that he thought about it, maybe Davidson was out on a date. Was there a girlfriend in Davidson's life?

A date? A *girlfriend*? Wow, that sounded so freaking...weird, for a man Davidson's age. Partner? No, that sounded too gay. Thinking back on it, had he ever mentioned a wife? For some nebulous reason, he'd assumed Davidson was divorced. How the hell did he come to that conclusion? Davidson hadn't a word either way.

Whatever. The point was, he could be any number of places.

Just because Arnold spent all his time holed up at behind a computer, didn't mean other people didn't have a life.

The easiest way to find out would be call his cell. Really? How stupid was that considering his suspicion his devices were bugged? No, the best course of action would be to wait for him to show.

That settled that, so now what?

He looked at the neighboring houses, decided he was too suspicious to not be noticed by some gung-ho Neighborhood Watch nut.

Drive up to Starbucks and kill an hour or so?

Seemed like a reasonable option.

Back in the car, he asked himself if he really wanted to give up the parking spot. Might not find another when he returned. How about walking to the coffee shop? With the Cinnabon gut-bomb still weighing down his gut, he certainly could use the exercise, but...that slog up such a steep hill would be a total bitch. Besides, he'd had enough exercise since fleeing the house. *Home.* This was his first time away from Honolulu since arriving there last year. He realized just how much he missed Chance and the house. *I'll return soon enough,* he told himself. First things first.

He retrieved his rucksack from the car, walked back to Davidson's street, crossed West Highland Drive to Kerry Park where he found an empty bench with an insanely sick panorama of the glowing business district, Harbor Island, and West Seattle. The sight made him aware of just how much he missed this quirky city too!

The lingering warmth of an Indian Summer day felt lovely, in stark contrast to the relentless rain routinely depicted for Seattle in movies. He watched kids roughhouse on the well-groomed lawn as sightseers stood at the guardrail admiring the view while taking selfies. A smattering of dog walkers passed by, which made him long for Chance. He'd never been separated from him so many hours.

Go ahead, contact Rachael. Why wait for the perfect wording? Just bite the fucking bullet and do it. And, as far as the risks, wasn't that minimized on account of Naseem being on the FBI's radar now? Perhaps...but why expose her to any risk at all? Tough decision.

How to do it? Message her? Yeah, a short text might be the best way to test the water.

He crafted a short message, double checked it, triple checked it, decided what the hell...so pulled the trigger and sent it.

To distract himself while waiting for a response, he fired up his Surface and searched for a neighbor's unsecured Wi-Fi network. He found one with two bar strength. Perfect. He was good to go.

He wanted to see if anyone—other than Davidson—had searched for his Honolulu property records. After buying the house, he routinely monitored the site to see if anyone was searching for his name. After several months of coming up empty he was lulled into complacency and his diligence tapered off. He found Davidson's query, but, in addition, another one occurred two hours afterward.

Arnold checked the name used to log into the records but figured anyone with an IQ in excess of 20 would use an alias, so instead searched for any residual digital footprints. Surprisingly, he found one. Hmmm...puzzling. Why would someone of Nawzer's caliber leave evidence?

Could this be an oversight or a trap?

Were they waiting to see if he'd take the bait and, in the process, pick up a cleverly hidden Trojan horse or virus? Tough questions. To be safe, he simply copied the information to a separate file. Now, if they suddenly realized their mistake and came back to erase it, it'd appear untouched.

His phone pinged. His heart accelerated as he switched to the messaging app.

Rachael; WHOEVER U R, STOP IT. HES DEAD.

He stared at the hunk of printed circuits and Gorilla glass in his hand, feeling as though the living, breathing woman he loved so much was right there. He raised the phone to his lips and kissed it. He realized must look like a fool and glanced around. No one seemed to be paying attention to him.

Oh, Christ, what do I do now?

What could he type to convince her he really was Arnold? His mind began flying at warp speed, grasping for the words...something only the two of them would know, a shared personal experience...

Ahhh, yes...

He tried thumbing the letters but his hands were shaking too badly. He took a deep breath, closed his eyes, counted to ten slowly, tried again. Better, but still a mess. Finally, he sent:

REMMBR THE CHAMPAGN AT HOWIE'S BAR MITZVA?

And waited, staring down at the screen...

Ding. WHAT SONG DO I H8?

Oh, man, easy one.

TOTAL ECLIPSE OF THE HEART

OMG!! THAT REALLY U?

YES!

No response.

He was convinced that every sightseer within a radius of ten feet away could hear his heart and breathing. He typed, GO FACETIME.

Seconds later the screen opened to a fish-eye view of Rachael's tear-streaked face. She stared back at him. A fist-sized lump filled his throat and his eyes misted over.

A second later, grinning like a village idiot, he croaked, "I'm so sorry, Rach...I wanted so badly to contact you but...I just couldn't. Not until now."

"I thought—"

"I know, I know. I'll explain *every*thing the first chance I get."

"Why? What's going on?" her face now etched with concern.

"Trust me, I'll explain...just know that I really want to see you and will do everything I can to do that."

"I want to see you too, now that—"

"How about you tonight or tomorrow?" he blurted impulsively without the slightest idea how he would pull off such a miracle. "For only a minute of two, okay?"

"Tonight? When?"

Good question. One he didn't have an answer for, but..."I don't know...yet, but...I'll find a way. Remember Palmer Davidson...the lawyer?" his words tumbling out.

She smiled. "Yes."

"I have to meet him first. Tonight, if possible. I'll contact you soon as I have that out of the way, okay?" He swallowed hard. "I...I really missed you," which wasn't all he wanted to say, but, hey, it was a start. By now, he was getting totally paranoid-antsy that somehow Nawzer or Fisher might have an alert on his phone.

Cut it short, dude!

"I miss you too, Arnold."

He blew her a kiss, "Bye," before disconnecting.

For several minutes—he lost track of exactly long—he savored the precious memory of the conversation. Finally, as he began to get his shit together, he realized his bladder was about to explode.

He glanced around.

No Sani-Can in sight. Did he actually expect to see one in this neighborhood? There was, however, a thick clump of high rhododendrons anchoring the west corner of the park. He shouldered on the rucksack, casually strolled to the large bush, glanced around to make sure no one was paying attention before slipping behind it.

Later, at the view spot's concrete balustrade, Arnold gazed at the twinkly lights of his beloved city with his heart still galloping from the brief chat with Rachael. Now, more than ever, he needed to get his life and true identity back. But this couldn't happen until he and Fisher neutralized Naseem—which had been his plan from the start of this gambit. It was a long shot, he knew, but a gamble well worth the risk.

Another glance at his watch.

Time to see if Davidson was home.

Chapter 30

ARNOLD KNOCKED ON the front door and pushed the intercom button twice. No answer.

Come back tomorrow?

He could do that, but he had to settle things with Davidson before seeing Rachael, soooo...he believed, no, it was more like a hunch, really, that the lawyer would return sometime this evening, so why not wait until 9:30, 10:00, 10:30 at the latest? If he was a no show by then...

Yeah? Then what?

He wasn't quite sure, but would decide when the 10:30 PM deadline rolled by.

He glanced at the house across the street and decided it was probably not a good idea to be seen standing at the front door for what could potentially be a few hours, so he looked around for a better spot, a place that'd partially hide him from nosey neighbors and occasional dog walker.

The property was on the south of Queen Anne hill, where the land rolled steeply downward, allowing the back the house the same drop-dead city views as the park a half-block to the west. Large, mature rhododendrons grew in heavily mulched beds to either side of the driveway, a foot or so from the stucco exterior. Arnold walked over to the driveway in search of a suitable spot to wait, a spot out of sight of prying eyes. He wedged himself between a rhodie and the house, settled in, leaned his back against the rough stucco and closed his eyes to fantasize about seeing Rachael again.

He was awakened by strong light in his eyes and the groan of a heavy garage door raising. He stood, brushed beauty bark from his butt, stepped into the driveway and waved both hands overhead so Davidson wouldn't mistake him for a burglar or disgruntled client.

Davidson drove the Tesla into the garage. Instead of a typical interior of exposed sheetrock and bare, dusty concrete, this one was immaculate. Painted walls, tidy built-in storage cabinets and a shiny, epoxy-sealed floor clean enough to walk barefoot on. Davidson stepped out of the drivers-side door carrying two brown paper sacks. Arnold slipped inside the garage a second before the heavy door started groaning its way back down.

Davidson looked him up and down.

"My, my, the prodigal son returneth. Pray tell, why? A change of mind perhaps?"

This said with a hint of a smile.

Arnold came around the right side of the car to the kitchen door.

"We need to talk."

Davidson raised the bags in case Arnold hadn't noticed them.

"And eat, I hope. I am famished. I picked up a couple things at Uptown China if you are interested. There is enough for both of us. Crispy walnut prawns, lemon chicken, Szechwan beans. Hungry?"

Arnold realized he was starving, especially for just about any dish from Uptown, one of his favorite restaurants.

"Aw, man, sounds great!"

"Fine. Now, if you will excuse me so I can open the door…"

Recessed into the wall adjacent the doorjamb was a gleaming stainless-steel intercom grill and keypad. Davidson placed his right index finger on a circle one inch below the grill. A synthesized voice said, "Name?"

Davidson spoke toward the speaker.

"Palmer Davidson."

Last year, Davidson had introduced Arnold to his extensive home security system that included fingerprint identification, a retinal scanner, and voice recognition. Overkill? Perhaps. But effective nonetheless.

A satisfying metallic *clack* followed. Davidson opened the door, automatically turning on the interior house lights. For Arnold, the sight of the kitchen triggered bad memories of the days in the immediate aftermath of Howie's murder, when he stayed here.

A moment later Davidson called, "Are you coming inside or are you into playing statue hacker?"

Arnold sucked a deep breath and stepped into the stunningly contemporary kitchen of stainless steel, polished concrete floor, high-gloss white European cabinets, and a wall of floor-to-ceiling doors that could be accordioned open to a deck running the length of the house—a deck with an eye-popping downtown panorama. Seeing it again underscored just how strongly his present home was influenced by this one.

The lawyer set the paper bags on the counter.

"What would you prefer to drink? I have chilled Tsingtao or a not-too-buttery Chardonnay. There are, of course, red wines in the cooler, but obviously they are not a drinkable temperature."

To the right of the refrigerator stood Davidson's prized six-foot high wine cooler.

"Oh, least I forget, I also offer Seattle tap water."

"A Tsingtao would be perfect."

For whatever reason, although he loved that beer, he never brought it. And now, thinking about it, he never looked for it at when grocery shopping.

"Excellent choice, considering our dinner menu." Davidson took two green bottles from the fridge, uncapped both, handed one to Arnold. They clinked, said, "Cheers." Davidson took a long pull and nodded approval. "Have a seat while I fix dinner," pointing toward the counter stools.

Arnold sat while Davidson busied himself collecting paper plates, napkins, and wooden chopsticks from a drawer.

"Hope you do not mind paper. I prefer not to load the dishwasher on days like this." He arranged the plates and chopsticks on the counter. "Chopsticks work for you?"

Arnold laughed.

"Can't believe anyone doesn't know how use them."

"Not in this city."

Davidson arranged the open containers just so, before taking the stool to Arnold's right.

Without another word, Davidson opened a container and passed it to Arnold.

"Dig in. There is more here than I can eat, hungry as I am." He dished three prawns from another container onto his plate. "And while you are at it, explain your sudden visit. Did you change your mind about Fisher?"

Arnold recounted a summary of Naseem's visit, his escape and subsequent chase. The lawyer ate slowly while listening.

After a sip of beer, Davidson said, "It seems like you just endured a great deal of effort to talk to me. Why not simply call or email? You have all my contact information, do you not?"

"This is where things get complicated. I'm convinced that the only way Naseem could've found me so quickly is if they're into your computer and maybe even your phone."

Davidson slowly set his chopsticks on the plate and stared at him.

"I'm dead serious," Arnold added.

Davidson's face morphed into a mixture of anger and fear as he glanced toward his home office.

"Whoa, easy...I don't know it for sure, so let's not get ahead of ourselves. I don't want to have to call Medic One for you."

Davidson's eyes drilled him.

"There *is* no other explanation," Davidson said. "It is Occam's razor." He sucked a deep breath, ran his hand over the top of his head. "Can you find out? Now?"

Arnold raised both hands.

"Absolutely, but you need to chill first, Mr. Davidson, okay? Seriously."

"Chill? How?"

"No, really...take a deep breath. You need it. Let's think about this a minute and see if we can turn our situation into some sort of advantage."

Davidson was off the stool now, pacing, not saying a word as Arnold watched. He finally calmed down and took his seat again, kneading the muscles in the back of his neck and right shoulder.

A moment later; "Are you absolutely certain it was Naseem outside your gate?"

Arnold replayed the memory.

"It was the middle of the night...so the best images were infrared. You've seen that kind of picture before...details aren't the same as normal light. Wait, let me show you." Arnold retrieved the Surface from the rucksack. "Your password still the same?" referring to Davidson's Wi-Fi.

Davidson nodded.

Arnold connected to SAM through the Internet, found the best images and handed the tablet to Davidson.

"Take a look. What do you think?"

Davidson studied the images from that night.

"I see what you mean...the hoodie makes a positive ID impossible, but under the circumstances, Fisher needs to be made aware of this. Tonight. I will call him now. If she is still on the island, he might be able to catch her."

"Exactly why I'm here. I want that bitch either dead or locked up for good."

Davidson drew his phone from his pocket.

"Why go through the delay of flying here? Why not go straight to the Honolulu field office?"

"Believe me, the thought crossed my mind, but there's still the arson thing hanging over my head."

"True, but Fisher assured me there is no evidence against you."

"So you said, but I need more than that. I need immunity or something on paper you think will protect me."

"I agree." He patted Arnold's shoulder. "Ever considered of law school?"

"Not a chance," without hesitating a second.

With a nod, Davidson returned to his cooling food.

"Before I call, I have another question for you; you have an escape plan...why opt for this route?"

Arnold paused to dislodge a piece of chicken from between his molars.

"Two reasons. The bitch has to be stopped. I mean for good. Not just because of who she is, but because I can't keep living like this...in constant fear of being discovered. Plus," he paused, embarrassed at what he was about to disclose, "I want to see Rachael. And that means I need to get my real life back."

Davidson nodded.

"Makes sense. Are we ready to proceed?'

"Go ahead, call. But there's no meeting until the legal issue's settled. I don't look good in orange."

Chapter 31

FEARING HIS PHONE was compromised, Davidson used one of the three Tracfones he'd purchased for calls to several of his less respectable clients. He set it on speakerphone so Arnold could hear Fisher's words.

"Sorry to call so late, but I was just contacted by Mr. Gold. He agrees to assist in tracking down Naseem Farhad."

"Yeah? What's the catch?"

Restaurant clatter could be heard in the background.

"We require written resolution of the legal liability issue before any negotiation can proceed. This must be agreed and signed within the next twenty-four hours or the offer is off the table."

"What legal issue we talking about?"

"He is given complete immunity from prosecution for any alleged activities concerning the unfortunate events that occurred on his property last year."

"I hear you, but you know damn well I can't make that decision. I'll need to run it past several people, including the DA. But if I were to obtain it, how soon would he be available?"

"Upon receipt of a signed agreement and I expect an answer within forty-five minutes."

Arnold could almost hear Fisher's mind grinding away, running the possibilities.

"He there with you?"

"No," Davidson shot back, too quickly.

"Bullshit! You're on speakerphone. I can tell. There's no other reason—"

"Notify me within forty-five minutes at this number. In the meantime, I plan on finishing dinner."

Grinning, he disconnected.

Davidson's burner phone rang exactly forty-five minutes later.

"We have a deal. On one condition."

Davidson raised his eyebrows at Arnold.

"And that is?"

"He explains exactly what went down the night of the fire. I'm talking specifics, not generalities."

Arnold nodded agreement.

"I suspected you might ask that. He agrees."

"Good, it's settled then. Where are you?"

"Do you mean where is Arnold? He left me minutes ago. The lad is exhausted, in need of rest. After you hear what has happened in the past twenty-four hours, you will understand why. We can meet first thing in the morning."

"Doesn't work that way, Davidson. Have him in my office in thirty minutes or no deal."

Again, Davidson raised questioning eyebrows. Arnold shook his head.

"No deal. He is my client and I want him well rested before any meeting takes place. Believe me, it is in everyone's best interest for all involved parties to be well rested."

A long pause ensued before Fisher said, "Have him in my office. Seven sharp."

Davidson set down the phone and picked up his chopsticks.

"He sounded relieved to have a night off. You too, from the looks of it."

"A few extra hours aren't going to make a difference, but I appreciate it. Now I need another favor."

Davidson paused, his chopsticks hovering over a string bean.
"What?"

"I need to see Rachael. It's important. I'll only take a few minutes."

"Can it wait until tomorrow, after we meet? After all——"

"No, it can't."

He knew that in the greater scheme of things, it could, but he couldn't. The sooner he saw her, the sooner he could start sorting out things.

Davidson shrugged.

"You can do whatever you wish, I suppose. But I *am* completely serious about rest. We need to be as fresh as possible when entering the lion's den. How long do you have in mind?"

"I don't know. I need to ask her first."

Davidson checked his watch.

"Okay, son, but make it brief."

Son?

Arnold paused, momentarily stunned, iPhone in hand.

"Sorry, it is just an expression," Davidson muttered with obvious embarrassment. "Go ahead, make your call."

Arnold returned to thumbing a text.

"I'll be quick. It's just that I need to settle something."

Davidson busied himself with finishing off the crispy walnut shrimp.

Arnold arranged for a quick visit to Rachael's apartment in the Belltown neighborhood, ironically only about a two-mile straight line from Davidson's home. Davidson insisted on driving, which Arnold figured would guarantee a short visit. The high-rise was under construction when Arnold fled the city, making this the first time he would see the completed project. Davidson braked the Tesla at a bus zone outside the Third Avenue entrance to the lobby.

"I will park around the corner, space permitting. If not, I will circle the block. Either way, count on being back here ten minutes from now."

"Yes, Mom," Arnold said, slipping out the passenger door.

Jesus, he felt like a twelve-year-old being driven to a movie by his parents. Through the large window he could see Rachael on a couch in the lobby. He studied her a moment, searching for any hint of her mood. She sat nervously clasping and unclasping her hands. Uh-oh, must be a bad sign. Was she planning on how to break bad news? An engagement? To a doctor maybe. Wasn't that what nurses did, marry doctors? He decided to simply suck it up, to just do it. He needed clarification. The doors were locked, so he knocked on the glass. She flinched, startled, turned to the window and stared a moment before jumping up and running to the door.

"Oh my god, it *is* you," she blurted, her hand to her throat.

He ducked into the lobby, letting the door swing shut behind him. She appeared as beautiful as his memories. Not the Loni-type stunning beauty, rather an easy, familiar, comfortable one that only heightened his need to be with her. Black hair cut practically short, no makeup, smooth complexion in no need of enhancement. They stood still, silently staring into one another's eyes.

Rachael finally broke the spell with, "Why don't we sit over there," with a nod toward the couch just vacated.

The lobby was a muted neutral with clean contemporary lines. An unmanned concierge desk displayed a will-return-at such and such time sign. Rachael settled into the center of the couch. Arnold opted for one of two chairs directly opposite her.

"Where have you been?"

Oh, man! Things were too damn complex, too complicated for a pithy answer. Another time when, and if, he ever had the opportunity.

Finally, he said, "Honolulu. I live there now."

He realized how evasive that must sound.

She stared down at her interlaced fingers for several beats before slowly shaking her head.

"All this time...I thought you were dead."

He wanted to wrap his arms around her and hold tightly for as long as possible. Instead, he simply leaned forward and reached for her hand.

"Oh, Rachael..."

She stared at his proffered hand, then up at his face, making no effort to accept his gesture.

"I mourned for you, Arnold. I *really* mourned. It broke my heart to think you died...especially in such an awful way."

Until this moment, he'd never thought what, if any, repercussions his sham death might have on others. Perhaps because he had no family or friends after Howie died. He never thought for one moment that Rachael might have...panic gripped his gut.

"Oh, Rach, I'm *so* sorry. Believe me, I didn't intend to upset you. It's just..."

What? A quick explanation? Impossible.

But, would he ever have another chance to explain?

"Someday I hope to tell you...but I just don't have time right now...please believe me, I never meant to cause you any..."

She shook her head.

"I *don't* understand...why contact me now? After a year? Can you at least explain that to me?"

"No, not tonight. There's not enough time. Another time...I promise." The seconds were flying away, his ten minutes evaporating. He needed to quickly salvage whatever link they might have. "Rach, have you known me to lie? Ever?"

"No."

"And I never will. Especially to you. Believe me when I say that one day—and I hope that's very soon—you'll know everything, but not tonight. I'm trying to get my life back."

Shit! How totally insanely weirdo did that sound? Could mean anything from drug rehab to electroshock therapy.

He grimaced, sucked in a deep breath, blurted, "I'm working undercover for the FBI."

Well...sort of. Starting tomorrow.

Had he just lied?

She recoiled.

Before she could say a word, "That's why I couldn't contact you until now. That's all gonna change soon...and I can be Arnold Gold again. Very soon."

There! It was out.

She appeared even more confused.

"You're not Arnold Gold now?"

Uh-oh, here we go.

"No. My undercover name's Toby Taylor."

Stop it, you're just creating more questions. And you're not even close to the reason for this visit.

She slumped back in the couch, arms limp at her sides.

He swallowed.

"Rach, listen...I have your picture in my living room so I can see you every day. I want to..." he swallowed again. "I want to know if there's any chance...any way at all...you and I might be able to see if we can..."

He shrugged, embarrassed at his bumbling.

"See if we can what?" she said, eying him differently now.

He sighed.

"Get to know each other better."

She frowned.

"We've known each since we were in diapers."

What was that? A twinkle in her eyes. Was she messing with him now? Just like she used to?

"Are you seeing anyone?"

"Arnold!"

He raised both hands in self-defense. "Okay, okay, sorry...it's just...I have to go. Would it be okay if I call occasionally?"

He stood, not wanting to push her. Besides, Davidson was probably already out there waiting, but he didn't dare take his eyes off her to look. He'd explain as much as possible in texts or on Skype. But wow...what an awesome step toward regaining normalcy. He was totally, totally amped.

She also stood.

"I work crazy hours. I'm at Swedish now." Referring to a large medical center in the heart of the city. "Probably best if you message me first to see if I'm free. If I am, I'd love to talk to you, Arnold Gold."

She punched him good-naturedly on the shoulder.

His heart started racing. This was turning out better than he could've hoped for. They walked to the glass doors, looked deeply into each other's eyes. He pulled her to him and wrapped his arms around her, buried his face in her black hair to inhale her familiar scent, and wanted to burn this memory into his brain forever.

He fought to keep from blurting, "I love you."

Don't mess up a tenuous situation, dude.

Surprise! She hugged back.

Chapter 32

"UP FOR ANOTHER beer?" Davidson asked, reentering the kitchen from the garage.

"I'll get it," Arnold said, nerves still tingling from the memory of Rachael in his arms. A beer might just be calming.

Davidson waved him toward the living room.

"No, go on over and sit down."

A moment later, Davidson set two Tsingtaos on the coffee table before settling into the opposite chair. Neither man spoke for several beats, which was fine with Arnold, still savoring the sweet memory.

"Let me ask you something; do you enjoy living in Honolulu full time?"

"Didn't you already ask about this?"

Davidson swiped a streak of condensation from the side of his bottle.

"Yes, so let me explain what I want to know. I love my visits there. Enough that I flirt with the idea of owning a condo. Nothing fancy or terribly large, mind you...a *pied de terre,* so to speak. A place to visit when time permits. For years I have had the itch, but, for some reason, I hesitate to actually act on it." Davidson paused for a sip of beer.

"Wow, you're serious. Cool! What about work? Aren't you busy as hell?"

"That is part of the problem. I suffer from a mild case of burn-out. Especially in view of the type client I represent. I chose to study law for the intellectual challenge. And chose to defend criminals because I believed—and still do—that too many people are victimized by the system. However, over the years, my view has evolved. Too many of my clients are maddening repeat offenders who make the same bad choices time and time again and I see no way to help them change. Hell, most of them are not even the least inclined to change. Consequently, shepherding their cases again and again through the system has become...unfulfilling." Davidson's eyes grew sad. "Sorry, I did not intend to complain."

"Are we talking early retirement?"

Arnold had no idea of Davidson's age, but suspected he was too young to begin kicking it on Waikiki.

Did he have hobbies or interests outside of work?

Truth be told, he knew nothing of the man's personal life.

"No, not retire. However, I could easily scale back my caseload and be perfectly happy. In fact, the extra time would allow me the flexibility to fly there whenever I chose." Davidson gave wistful chuckle. "Funny, just discussing the concept gives it more allure."

"Then why not just do it?"

Buying a small get-away seemed like a perfect remedy for his burnout. He suspected there was more to Davidson's conflict than simple burn-out.

Davidson tipped his bottle toward Arnold, then took another sip.

"What are *your* long-term plans? How long do you plan to gamble for a living?"

"Ah, man...haven't thought that far ahead. My system is my work. It'll never be perfected, so I gamble to support myself as well as test its performance."

"Yes, but life is change. People change. Circumstances provoke change. You are in this present unsavory situation precisely because of your gambling. Do you seriously think you will support yourself this way forever?"

Davidson's point was dead on, of course. He'd been acutely made aware of this very pitfall since Vegas. He set his beer on the table and leaned back in the chair. He'd made a point of not discussing personal finances with Loni, but this was Davidson, and Davidson was, well, family.

"You're absolutely right. There are other ways to test the system, and I do plan to stop the gambling, but only when I'm convinced my portfolio is strong enough to support me."

"What age will that be?"

A shrug, "All depends. Late thirties or early forties...somewhere around there."

Davidson whistled.

"Late thirties? I *am* impressed, I had no idea you were doing so well. But I suppose your house should have given me a hint."

Arnold's face reddened with embarrassment.

Did he detect admiration in Davidson's tone?

"I don't mean retire-retire. Not in the sense of stopping work entirely. There're a couple jobs I'd be interested in working on if given the opportunity."

Davidson raised his eyebrows in surprise.

"What would that be?"

Arnold began rubbing his forehead, working out the first twinges of a fatigue headache.

"Building more artificial intelligence into cybersecurity fascinates me."

"What does that mean for a person who knows nothing about either subject?"

"You know what artificial intelligence is, right?"

"Not exactly."

"AI is intelligence," Arnold said, using finger quotes, "exhibited by software...devising software that can problem-solve on its own. The idea's been around since computers were invented.

Remember HAL in the movie 2001?"

"Of course. That is a classic."

"There's a good example of a computer that could think on its own. It's what SAM is doing 24-7. Got it?"

"Okay."

"And you know what cybersecurity is, right?"

"I have a general idea."

"Okay, so I want to work on using AI to solve security problems. To make software that can identify problem more complex than spam filters or antivirus software. My dream job would be to work for a cybersecurity company, like FireEye to guard against cyberterrorism."

"What keeps you from applying for a job?"

"One very basic thing; no degree. I never went further than two quarters at the U-W. Unless I have that degree..." letting it hang. "Enough about me. You never finished your answer about a Honolulu condo. Why not just buy one?"

Davidson sat back, fingers interlaced behind his head.

"When the urge hits, I check Zillow to see what is available." He chuckled. "Inevitably I find a place; right price, layout, perfect location. But I always get cold feet."

Such indecision from Davidson shocked Arnold, especially knowing how much he loved his Honolulu vacations.

"Why?"

"I worry that if I do buy something, I would feel *compelled* to use it. And once that happens, I would end up hating it. I have seen this happen too many times, mostly with friends who buy a boat. Initially, they are thrilled, but after a couple years feel trapped by *having* to use it to justify the cost. They end up hating it. Does that make sense?"

Arnold laughed at the irony.

"Absolutely." Then became dead serious. "Think that happens with couples?"

"To couples?"

"You know...two people who want to be with each other...then, once they are, they lose interest in each other? Like, I've wanted to be with Rachael for so long..." A blush warmed his face. "She likes me too...I think. But we've never had a chance to..."

He let the words hang.

"There is only one way to find out," Davidson said with a smile.

They chatted about Davidson's law practice and Arnold's fascination with artificial intelligence a while longer, Arnold finding the ease of conversation—considering their generational divide—both amazing and refreshing. Instead of a professional lawyer/client relationship, their conversation became eerily intimate...more like discussions with Howie or dad, and underscored (once again) how little he knew about the man.

Did he have close friends?

Did he read?

If so, what?

Davidson stood and began cleaning up the dinner mess. Arnold jumped up.

"No, let me do that. After all, you supplied dinner."

Davidson shrugged.

"Fine. I will prepare the guest room for you."

The guest bedroom—which also served as a small home office—was directly off the kitchen with the combined space spanning the entire back of the house.

And, like the kitchen, it had floor-to-ceiling, openable glass doors with the same killer view. The remaining walls were paneled in dark wood and, like the rest of the first floor, furnished with sleek, contemporary, minimalistic furniture.

A sturdy tubular chrome and glass desk held an Apple

computer and a Bang & Olufson BeoCom phone. Arnold had fell in love with that phone last year and purchased a used one on eBay.

With the press of a wall switch, Davidson lowered a built-in Murphy bed cleverly disguised as wall paneling.

"The sheets and bathroom towels are fresh and the alarm is set for six. Breakfast will be courtesy of Starbucks en-route to our meeting."

"Thanks so much, Mr. Davidson." Arnold held out his hand. "For dinner and everything else you've done for me."

Chapter 33

AS ARNOLD AND Davidson walked into the Federal Building, lattes in hand, Fisher was already in the lobby to escort them upstairs. They passed through a metal detector, signed in, and were handed lanyard visitor badges with instruction they should be worn in clear view at all times and to surrendered before leaving the building.

Fisher herded them into the elevator that would take them to his floor, but instead of stopping at his office they were led to a conference room three doors further along the hall. Being Sunday morning, most of the offices and cubicles were deserted and many of the overhead lights were off. A vente-size Starbucks cup sat at the far end of the oval conference table. Arnold figured that if nothing else, he and the FBI agent shared that particular preference.

"Have a seat," Fisher said, shutting the door.

The room was windowless. For security reasons, Arnold assumed, to prevent a spy with binoculars from lip-reading conversations. Which made him wonder if the walls were constructed with special sound-attenuating materials? And the air-vents? He knew similar precautions were elementary counterintelligence measures often used by intelligence agencies. No notepad or computer in sight, which, to Arnold, indicated that their audio conversation—and perhaps the video—would be recorded in spite of no obvious cameras.

Fisher folded himself into a chair, leaned on the table, got straight to the point.

"Why the sudden change of heart, Gold? Davidson said you wanted to play lone wolf on this."

"Well, so much for foreplay," Arnold said with a glance at Davidson.

His lawyer nodded for him to continue. Arnold detailed the events of the night Naseem visited the house.

Fisher mulled that over a moment.

"You absolutely sure it was her?"

Arnold smiled, having anticipated the question.

"Here, you decide." Arnold opened his tablet to the pictures he'd shown Davidson the previous night and slid the tablet across the table to Fisher. "What do *you* think?"

Fisher agreed it was likely her, but emphasized the hoodie prevented absolute identification. He nodded in approval.

"Man, that was a really quick thinking to take these. Damn shame more people aren't as resourceful. Sure as hell would make our jobs easier." Apparently satisfied, Fisher slid the tablet back across the table. "I assume you don't have a problem sending me a copy?"

"Not at all." He suspected the FBI wouldn't allow him access to their Wi-Fi, so removed a thumb drive from his pocket. "Here."

Fisher inspected the drive before setting it on the table next to his coffee.

"Thanks. Just to make sure we're all on the same page, you intend to help us take down Naseem. This correct?"

Again, Davidson nodded for him to answer.

"Hell, yes, I want her captured."

"Good. Then here's what I want you to do. Fly home today. We already have your flight booked. Once back, you go about business as normal...just keep on like nothing's changed. We'll do all the rest."

Arnold considered the implications. This time, it'd be far less risky than last year when he was tethered to Karim. Still….

"That's it? I just keep on keeping on? Like nothing's happened? Won't that seem…a bit suspicious?"

"Not unless you act like it is."

"But—" Davidson started to say.

"—we're coordinating with the Honolulu police to increase patrols in your neighborhood. They'll put the word on the street there's been a spike in burglaries in your area. If Naseem's intel is as good as we think, we believe that word will work its way back to her and keep her from becoming too paranoid."

Hmmm…did and didn't make sense.

His nervousness increased.

"We in agreement, gentlemen?"

Fisher glanced from Arnold to Davidson.

"Not entirely," Arnold said before Davidson could respond. "I have a stipulation."

"Stipulation?" Fisher asked. "We don't—"

"—remember Rachael Weinstein, Howard's sister? Until now, I haven't felt comfortable contacting her. But now with everyone aware I'm alive, I want to…so here's the deal: you, meaning the Bureau, come up with a way for us to spend a few days together some place other than Seattle or Honolulu."

Fisher laughed.

"That's a ridiculous. We're law enforcement, not eHarmony."

Davidson opened his mouth to speak, but Arnold cut him off.

"No, it's not. Think about it. You guys spend a shitload of bucks on informants every day, right? Well, consider me an informant. Besides, you guys make an art of moving people all over the place without anyone knowing."

Fisher shook his head.

"Will never happen."

"With all due respect," Davidson countered. "Do you want my client's help in apprehending a dangerous terrorist or not?"

Fisher appeared to bite off his first reply and paused for a deep breath.

"Don't start with me, Palmer."

"Agent Fisher," Davidson continued evenly. "You are asking Mr. Gold to put his life on the line to aid in capturing a dangerous terrorist. Considering the magnitude of your need, his request not unreasonable. His point is valid; the cost can be accounted for as a confidential informant."

Fisher a paused a beat.

"I'd buy that argument if he had nothing to gain from this. *But* we both know that's not the case. By neutralizing Naseem, he benefits greatly. And that includes being able to see the Weinstein woman."

"True. But only *if* you capture her. Until then, he assumes one hundred percent of the risk. We just provided evidence that she is probing his security systems, so we are certain she will return. It takes only one bullet to the head for him to lose everything." Davidson paused. "Do not forget, he has other options."

Fisher seemed to be growing more annoyed.

"Such as?"

"He can just as easily disappear again."

Fisher didn't respond.

Davidson added, "In the greater scheme of things, his request is trivial compared to the potential payoff."

Fisher tipped his chair back, studied the ceiling a moment.

"I'll need to kick it up the chain of command before we can negotiate anything solid."

"But you'll do that?" Arnold asked.

Fisher nodded. "Sure...after we've clarified a few things."

"Such as?" Davidson interjected.

"The information I asked for last night *on the speakerphone*," Fisher said. Arnold started to open his mouth, but Fisher wagged a finger at him. "No, no, no. Don't even think of denying it. Did you trigger that explosion?"

Arnold looked at Davidson for guidance.

"For the record: are we being recorded?" Davidson asked.

"No."

Davidson recoiled in mock shock.

"You expect us to believe that?"

"Did you expect me to believe you last night?" Fisher replied.

"In that case, my client respectfully declines to answer all questions relating to the fire."

"Then this conversation is over." Fisher glared at Arnold. "You're free to go."

Davidson motioned Arnold to remain seated.

"I will, however, describe a hypothetical scenario that may or may not bear resemblance to the actual events of the night in question."

He described the detonating mechanism, the explosion, and the terrifying escape through a smashed-out bathroom window, carefully omitting any mention that Arnold was aware Karim was trapped inside the house. Fisher then asked several pointed questions, all of which were clearly stipulated as being hypothetical. Although Davidson's approach seemed overly cautious to Arnold, he admitted his lawyer was doing a great job protecting him.

With the questioning over, Fisher pushed back from the conference table and stood.

"Any agreement will be performance-based. Meaning you need to meet several milestones before we are under any obligation to fulfill our end of the agreement. Until my superiors sign-off, I can't speculate what those milestones might be, but *if* I can arrange a week for you and Ms. Weinstein, where would that be?"

Arnold warned himself to not be hopeful, that this seemed too good to possibly come true.

"Maui."

Fisher nodded approvingly.

"I'll be back when I have a decision."

Chapter 34

FISHER RETURNED FORTY minutes later with a smug grin, a manila folder, and pad of legal paper in hand.

"This is our agreement," he said, handing Davidson the folder. "We fly Weinstein and Gold to Maui under assumed names for two weeks and put them up in a reasonably priced hotel. Gold will be responsible for any miscellaneous expenses. That's it, take it or leave it."

Arnold was surprised the FBI agreed to anything, and suspected Fisher went bat for him with the main office.

Astounding.

But, he reminded himself, the deal wouldn't have happened if Davidson hadn't pushed.

"Perfect. Assuming she agrees."

"She doesn't know?" Fisher asked with a bemused smile.

"Nope. Didn't want to mention it until I actually had something. I mean, what's the point, right?"

Arnold grinned.

Fisher jotted a note on his legal pad.

"Before we get ahead of ourselves, you need to agree to a few of our stipulations," encasing the last word in finger quotes.

"Absolutely."

He was willing to agree to just about anything if it meant seeing Rachael.

Fisher consulted the yellow legal pad.

"The Bureau is allowed to conduct a complete security assessment of your property within twenty-four hours of your return. You must agree to any security changes we deem necessary for your protection."

He looked at Arnold.

"No problem."

It was a relief, actually. Although he had faith in his system, it wouldn't hurt to hear the FBI's take on things.

"We assume," Fisher went on, "that Naseem traveled there by air, so we now have a team working up a list of all passengers that arrived from the time of Davidson's arrival to the evening she appeared outside your place. We assume she traveled under false documents, so don't we expect her name to show up with any of the airlines, but we're checking anyway. We'll also put in a huge effort into reviewing airport security videos. We first run them past our facial recognition software, but as I'm sure you're aware, it still requires a human to examine all potential hits. That's where you come in."

Arnold was ecstatic. At long last, Naseem was firmly in the crosshairs of an FBI manhunt.

"Expect the work to be tedious. And unless we're incredibly lucky, extremely time consuming. Any problem with what I just said?"

"Believe me, I'm happy to do whatever it takes to get the job done."

He meant every word.

"Special Agent Jose Rios—from the Honolulu field office— will meet you at the airport. He's our go-to guy on this." Fisher pulled an eight by ten color headshot of a Hispanic male from the manila folder. "Memorize this. I want you able to recognize him at the gate. From now on, he's your guardian angel until this issue is resolved. Where's your luggage?"

"That's it," he said, motioning to his rucksack. "But I have a rental car at Mr. Davidson's. I need to return it."

"We don't have time for that. Your flight pushes back from the gate in less than three hours." He held out his hand. "Give me the keys, I'll have someone take care of it. Any questions before you're out of here?"

There had to be something he was forgetting, but couldn't think of it.

Game on.

Chapter 35

ARNOLD SPOTTED RIOS standing beside a row of handicap seats the moment he exited Gate 21 at Honolulu airport. Rios apparently recognized him too, because they headed straight toward each other and identified themselves. Rios looked to be six-feet tall, stocky and buff—the type of guy who could bench-press two-hundred fifty without breaking a sweat—black hair and beard trimmed short and precisely. He had on a green floral aloha shirt, white slacks, expensive looking sneaks, with black wrap-around Ray-Bans that screamed law enforcement. Arnold assumed his fancy designer athletic shoes was some sort of fashion statement.

"What name you want to be called, Toby or Arnold?"

Arnold thought about it. Much as he longed to be Arnold again, he preferred staying in character. For now. A slip-up might end in disaster.

"Toby."

"Done."

Rios appeared to be constantly scanning the area around them, although that was difficult to tell on account of the Ray-Bans.

"Have a ride?" he said.

"No. Ubered out when I came here."

A nod, more scanning.

"Anyone picking you up?"

"Nope."

A friend picking him up? Didn't have any friends in this city except Loni.

"Good, I'll take you home."

"If it isn't too much trouble, I need to make a stop along the way."

Arnold slipped the rucksack over his left shoulder and headed for the breezeway that would take them to the main terminal and parking area beyond.

"Where and for what?" Rios answered, scanning the crowd as they walked.

"My dog's at the vet. I need to pick him up soon as possible. If that's a problem, I'll run over after you drop me," not wanting Rios to feel like a chauffeur.

"No problem. I got work to do at your place anyway, so we might as well take care of things now. Any luggage?"

By now they were almost to baggage claim.

"No, I left in a hurry. Everything's right here."

They blew past the baggage carousels, out the door, straight across the street to the parking lot where Rios led him across a patch of sweltering cement to an aging gray Crown Vic sporting government plates and a small roof-mounted whip antenna. Arnold laughed at the cliché. Anyone who didn't make it for exactly what it was would have to be brain-dead. Then again, maybe being blatant was exactly the point. Rios popped the locks.

"Hold on...let me crank up the A/C before we get in. Has to be close to a hundred and twenty in there."

With the doors open and the engine running, they stood on opposite sides of the vehicle chatting over the roof, letting the interior temp blow down a few degrees.

Three minutes later, Rios leaned, held his hand in front of a dash vent and nodded. He slid into the driver's seat.

"Okay, we're good to go. Where we headed?"

Rios caught the on-ramp to the main highway and merged into

traffic. Once in the appropriate lane, he settled in and relaxed.

"I know what Fisher told you, but this office doesn't have the manpower to devote to twenty-four-hour coverage, so here's the deal...got a phone?"

"Thanks for reminding me."

Arnold fished his cell from his pocket and turned it off airplane mode. With everything zipping around in his brain, he forgot to do it when the plane was rolling to the gate.

"Here's my number. Ready?"

Arnold opened the Rios contact.

"Shoot."

Rios recited the number.

"Call me at the slightest whiff if something's not right, no matter how minor it seems. I'll be the one to decide priorities. In addition, I want you checking-in with me each morning and evening between seven and eight until this business is finished. If I don't hear from you, I'll assume we have a problem and believe me, you don't want me assuming that. As of now, we have a constant ping on your cell. We clear?"

"We're clear." Arnold glanced from the phone back to the road. "You need to move over to the right lane and take the next exit."

Rios glanced in the side mirrors, "Homeland Security upped the terrorist threat level for the island a couple hours ago, so every law enforcement agency around here is on alert for your friend. They've all been sent copies of her picture, so we have eyes on the street in addition to HPD running increased patrols through your hood."

Arnold wasn't overjoyed at the prospect of uniformed cops hanging around his house, but if that's what it took to lessen his risk, hey, he was all for it. He called the vet's office to tell them he was on the way.

When Arnold pushed through the front door, Chance was stretched out on the cement to the right of the reception desk. The moment he saw Arnold, he was up and skittering across the floor, tail wagging, whining. Arnold dropped to his haunches in time for Chance to plant three wet doggy kisses on his face. Arnold responded with a barrage of two-handed choobers. Reunion finished, Arnold settled the account and thanked the staff. This was the only place he'd ever consider boarding Chance.

When he walked out the clinic door, Rios had his butt propped up against the front fender of the Crown Vic, facing to the sun, Ray-Bans reflecting sunlight. The FBI agent nodded.

"Man, that's one very handsome dog you got."

Arnold thumped Chance's chest.

"I couldn't agree more. And if he could talk, he would too."

Tail wagging, Chance trotted to Rios but Arnold immediately called him back. Some people were intimidated by Shepherds and he didn't want them to start off on the wrong foot.

"Hey, no problem, we need to get to know each other."

Rios dropped down, held out his hand and made the universal no-fail kissing dog-call sound. Chance trotted straight over and began sniffing his hand.

"Thanks," Arnold said as Rios drove out of the parking lot. "I know this was out of our way, but I needed him back soon as possible."

"Don't blame you. I'd do the same. How long were you gone?"

Arnold thought about that.

"Three days? Yeah…guess it's three."

Felt like a week…maybe longer. A very intense week, at that.

Rios curbed the Crown Vic in front of Arnold's driveway and they all piled out. As Arnold opened the security gate Rios clasped him on shoulder.

"Hang on…Fisher said you had a few visitors the other night.

Tell me about that."

Arnold pointed to the location where he first saw Naseem and then the spot where he saw her partner working his way down the side of the wall toward the rear of the property.

"That squares with Fisher's report. Before going out to pick you up, I swung by here for a look, but with so much security," jerking a thumb in the direction of a video camera, "I didn't do more than a quick look-see through the gate. Before we go inside the house, we need to inspect the perimeter and you can point out anything that might be out of place. C'mon, let's go."

Makes sense.

Slowly, carefully, they worked down the right side of the house, the steep grade and jungle grass making their footing slippery. They eventually made it to the back of the lot and the small lava path under the deck. Even in the shade, the sweat-popping humid air was pushing eighty-five degrees.

The basement door and windows appeared untouched. No surprise there. SAM would've alerted him if there had been an attempt to breech the house and he doubted they came armed with technology capable of defeating the sensors and alarms. But you never knew...Naseem had surprised him in the past.

For the sake of completeness, they worked up the opposite side of the house and around the garage and driveway. Arnold showed Rios his iPhone screen.

"I just checked the inside. It's clear."

"Okay then, we can go in now, but I still need to personally clear the house. Electronics are wonderful, but actual eyes are better."

Arnold appreciated Rios' thoroughness but believed that if SAM said the intruders didn't make it inside, there weren't inside.

Period.

He opened the door for Rios.

Chapter 36

SOON AS RIOS drove away, Arnold tossed his rucksack in the back of the Mini and turned to Chance.

"Want to go for a walk?"

Tail wagging, Chance bounded across the driver's seat to passenger seat to press his nose to the side window. Arnold lowered the glass, the simple task making him feel that he was really home again.

After parking at their usual spot, he let Chance jump from the car without a leash. A real plus for this particular area was how infrequently others used it, which allowed him to give Chance complete freedom to roam.

What's the point of going for a walk if you can't sniff out all the new scents?

Chance exploded into a circuitous sprint of pure doggie joy.

Lost in thought, Arnold plodded the familiar path as Chance ran ahead, occasionally disappearing but never for very long. Perhaps a deep-rooted hunting instinct from his wolf ancestry made him always keep tabs on the pack. During times like these, Arnold was struck by how profoundly Chance was an integral part of his world. If anything ever happened to him...he shuddered at the thought.

Does Rachael love dogs?

Strange, after so many years—admittedly, knowing her only as Howard's sister—he didn't have the vaguest clue. And thinking about it now, Howie and Rachael never owned a pet, not even the usual childhood classics like hamsters or goldfish. Certainly, no cat or dog. Well, neither did his family. Dogs required too much attention—what with his parents working such long hours—so he wasn't allowed to even float the idea past them. He gave them credit for having enough good sense to know their limits and not abuse a pooch with neglect.

Forty-five minutes later Arnold loaded Chance into the car for the trip home.

We he turned into his street he was surprised to see Rios's car at the curb in front of his house.

Something must be up.

Arnold opened the driveway gate with the remote and parked in the garage. Rios was walking into the driveway before he was out of the car. Man looked dead serious, too.

This can't be good.

"Just gave Fisher a download on your security," Rios said. "We see no deficiencies in need of shoring up. He said you had things under excellent control last year in Seattle, so he wasn't all that surprised with what I described here. Having said that, he wants me here in the house until things resolve. That means 24/7. You cool with that?"

Seemed like overkill to Arnold, but he wasn't about to argue. After all, the whole point of this exercise was to take down Naseem. Besides…the added protection was reassuring.

"No problem. C'mon, I'll show you your room. Hope you don't mind bunking with a few computers. If so, guess you can always take the couch…I'm not giving up my bed."

Rios laughed.

"Thought that's what you were going to say. Not a problem."

Arnold was unlocking the front door when it dawned on him

that Rios wasn't carrying an overnight case.

"What about your things?"

Rios nodded toward his car.

"My go-bag's in the trunk. I keep it there for exactly this kind of situation. I'll bring it in later. Tomorrow I'll swing by my apartment for a few things."

Arnold typed a six-digit code into a security pad to the right of the jamb and peered into a small lens.

"It's scanning my retina," he explained.

Same as Davidson's system. The door opened and Chance bolted ahead to check things out.

"You know where the guest bathroom is." Arnold pointed in spite of Rios having walked the interior earlier. "Drop your things in there," referring to the computer room.

With evening rapidly approaching, Arnold became aware of hunger pangs and realized he hadn't eaten since breakfast.

"Hungry?"

"Only twenty-six hours a day. And that," with a hand to his belly, "is the problem."

Rios paused on the steps to the great room, apparently admiring the room and view again. Arnold occasionally did this in spite of seeing it every day for a year. He vowed to never become blasé and take his good fortune for granted. He flicked on some lights.

"How does pepperoni and Italian sausage pizza sound?" Arnold asked.

"Perfect. I'll make a beer run. What's your preference?"

"No need. I'm fully stocked. Just grab a one for me too while I call in our order. I'll catch up with you on the deck."

Rios nodded approval.

"Roger that. Man! Can't get over this view. You're one lucky sonofabitch," he said, pulling two long-necks from the fridge.

Arnold had the pizzeria's number in his phone's contacts.

Order placed, Arnold joined Rios on the deck. The FBI agent's legs were crossed and stretched out on a chaise, fingers laced behind his head, scoping out the ravine and distant city. The area was too dark to make out many details in the thick foliage and volcanic rock below, but the distant lights were beginning to twinkle. Arnold settled in. Chance circled three times before plopping down on the deck beside him, sighed, and curled up. Life felt comfortably back to normal.

Rios raised the bottle, the lights from the kitchen glistening off the condensation.

"Big Swell IPA. Nice."

The Maui Brewing Company bottled the beer, which, despite its name, was made on Oahu.

"I don't know a thing about beer," Arnold admitted. "I buy it simply because it's brewed here and I like to support local businesses. You a beer drinker?"

"Guiltily as charged, your honor." Rios took a pull from the bottle. "Couldn't help but notice all those computers. Pretty impressive set up you got there."

Arnold wasn't sure where Rios was headed with that, so didn't answer. Did he know about the gambling? If so, to what detail? He meticulously hid that part of his life for obvious reasons.

Rios leaned closer to Arnold, "For real, you make a living off gambling?" as if this somehow made the question more confidential.

Well, shit, that answered that. Now what? Minimize it?

"Not actually *support* myself...sure, I place a few bets now and then during football season, but what I actually do is work on statistics...as a sorta hobby."

"Uh-huh," Rios said one second before the left side of his head vaporized into a trail of red mist.

A split-second later Arnold's ears registered the whine of the bullet, although his brain didn't compute it as such. Primal self-preservation instinct kicked in, sending him rolling off the chaise for the deck a half second before a second bullet shattered the glass slider directly behind him.

Chance was up, lunging at the glass balustrade, barking. Spread eagled on the tiles, Arnold's brain scrambled to process what just took place. The only thing he knew was that he was under attack and he was scared shitless.

What do I do?

Move!

Where?

Rios way lying next to him in an expanding pool of blood.

Fuck! He's dead.

Move for christsake!

The bullet had to come from across the ravine, so his best protection—his only protection—was behind the thick concrete pillar supporting this corner of the roof. Was it massive enough to shield him? Was there any other choice?

He slithered behind pillar and frantically punched 911 into his cellphone.

Chapter 37

ARNOLD REMAINED CROUCHED behind the pillar, just like the 911 dispatcher repeatedly told him to do while also assuring him that the police were on their way...not that he planned on going anywhere, not with a fucking sniper on the other side of the ravine.

Was the bastard still there?

He ordered Chance inside, out of the line of fire.

"What's the other person's condition?" the operator asked again.

He forced himself to look.

"Sir?"

The back Rios' head was blown away and the pool of blood was turning brown and no longer expanding. He remembered hearing on Dateline that bleeding stops when the heart stops.

"He's dead."

He closed his eyes, gagged, swallowed, and tried not to vomit.

"Why do you say that?"

What fucking difference does it make? The man is dead. What didn't she understand? Or was she just trying to keep him on the phone?

"Sir?'

"The back of his head's...gone..." and flashed on the infamous Zapruder film of President Kennedy's assassination in Dallas, when the back of his head blew away exactly like—

"The officers are very close now. Can you hear the sirens?"

Arnold listened. Yes. He saw that Chance was still inside, away from the sliders, watching, panting, sniffing, waiting for a command.

"Good boy." He raised his hand and repeated, "Stay," so at least Chance was safe.

"Mr. Taylor, you there?"

His fucking ear was hurting major bad. Was he hit? He began up to reach up, realized his hand was already there, pressing the phone crazy hard against it, so eased up.

"Yes."

"Good. An officer's at the gate outside your house. Do you feel safe enough to open it or should he use force?"

How long since the second shot? Minutes? Hours? The house and deck were suddenly eerily still and silent and so damn exposed.

"No no, I'll get it."

"Please do that. I'll advise the officer. You stay on the line until you confirm contact."

With the pillar at his back, Arnold counted three, then bolted through the house and out the front door to the security gate. A uniformed officer was peering in.

"You call 911?"

"Yes. In here." Arnold opened the gate, motioned him to follow as another patrol car screeched to a stop in the middle of the street, misery lights flashing blue and red reflections off surrounding surfaces. Arnold pointed the cop through the house to the deck, decided no way was he going in there again, so simply sat numbly on a paver and waited for someone to tell him what to do.

Dazed, Arnold held Chance by the collar as if protecting him from the ebb and flow of police and the lingering specter of a sniper somewhere out on the hill, vaguely registering the sound of an overhead helicopter, terse voices, radio squawks, his mind incapable of processing anything other than; just as long as Chance is safe. Which made him feel guilty for being more concerned for Chance than Rios. But, he told himself, it was not a choice. It's fact.

Chance is alive, Rios isn't. I love Chance, not Rios.

Still...

Knowing that his Vegas trip was the root cause of everything bad that had happened in his life festered in his heart. Rios would be alive if...unintended consequences. Collateral damage. His fault.

"Hey, Taylor. You there?"

A short, thin Asian guy was crouching in front of him, rocking his shoulder. Arnold looked blankly at his face and blinked.

"Taylor, we need to talk."

No words came.

"Look, Taylor...I'm Detective Jim Tanaka, Honolulu P-D," and flashed identification.

Arnold blinked again.

Am I being arrested?

He thought back to a year ago, the female detective grilling him, her intense blue eyes boring into him.

If he hadn't gone to Vegas...

"Mr. Taylor?"

"Huh?"

Tanaka sat down facing him.

"Look, Taylor, I need to hear what happened. You willing to talk to me?"

Arnold glanced around again, realized he was sitting on pavers in his courtyard and a helicopter was up somewhere overhead.

"What?"

Tanaka eyed him.

"We need to talk. I need to understand what happened out there. We can do it in my car, if you want, but honestly, I prefer someplace with more privacy...your call, but there's a lot going on here. What do you say, you willing to take a ride with me?"

They don't know the story, so of course they want a statement.

"That man inside...he's an FBI agent...Rios. Has Special Agent

Fisher been notified?"

Tanaka smiled.

"Hey, don't worry about a thing, got it all under control. All you need do is ride with me to the office, tell me what happened."

He stood and motioned toward the gate.

"Okay, but only if I can bring my dog." He saw Tanaka's eyes and added, "Seriously. If he can't go, I can't either."

Tanaka nodded approval and took a step toward the street.

"No problem. Bring him. C'mon, let's go."

Arnold glanced at the inside of the house he loved so much.

Could I ever live there again?

"Can someone close the door when they leave?"

"No problem, but we'll be back before they're done. Don't sweat it."

Chapter 38

TANAKA LOADED THEM into the back seat of his unmarked car, made sure they were comfortable, closed the door. As they were pulling away from the curb, Arnold's mind cleared sufficiently to wonder what to hell he was going to say: That terrorists were trying to kill him?

How crazy would that sound? And why would an FBI agent be babysitting him?

He needed to call Fisher and Davidson immediately to give them a heads up. Fisher would know how best to handle the things.

Arnold tapped his Apple watch, said, "Call Davidson.

"Arnold?" Davidson answered in a voice gravely with sleep.

Which, considering the hour in Seattle, was most likely the case. The familiar sound of the lawyer's voice calmed him. Slightly. He could advise him.

"Sorry Mr. Davidson, but..." and quickly synopsized the shooting.

"I will notify Fisher straightaway," Davidson said, sounding wide-ass-awake now in his uniquely crisp manner.

"Great, but here's the thing." He turned away from the front seat and shielded his voice with his free hand. "A detective's taking me to the police station for a statement. Like, I'm in the car right now...what do I tell him?"

Allen Wyler

"Tell them everything *except* your real name and occupation. Take your time, do not attempt to lie or fabricate a story, just tell him the bare facts and nothing more."

Arnold lowered his voice further.

"So, which name do I give him? How will it look if they find out I gave them an alias?"

"Taylor is the name on your property records, so stick with that for now. We will resolve the finer points once Fisher is brought up to speed. Which, as of now, is my highest priority. Talk to you later."

Davidson hung up.

"In here," Detective Tanaka said apologetically, opening the door to a small interrogation room with a bare concrete floor, cinderblock walls, three chairs, a small desk bolted to the concrete, and recessed fluorescent ceiling lights. "Sorry. Our conference room's in use right now, so this'll have to do."

Arnold led Chance inside, selected one of three metal chairs for himself and told Chance to sit.

"Would you like something to drink? Water, Pepsi, coffee?" Tanaka offered.

"Coffee's good."

He immediately reconsidered. Caffeine might just jack his nerves way past the melt-down point. Then again, it might paradoxically focus his thoughts. Either way, getting Tanaka out of the room—if for only a minute or so—would give Davidson more time to lay the ground work with Fisher.

"Black? Milk? Sugar?"

"Huh?...oh, milk, no sugar."

He hoped the milk might settle the herd of buffalo stampeding through his gut.

"Unless I need to brew a fresh pot, I'll only be gone a minute. Door's unlocked and the men's room is straight down the hall, second door on the left, in case you need it."

160

"Thanks."

He began to pet Chance while whispering reassuring words, but the pooch was calming him more than vice versa.

And thought about Rios again...what's his story? Married? Kids? Who'd break the news to them? He only knew the man a few hours, yet immediately liked him. Personality-wise, he was tight-ass Fisher's polar opposite: friendlier, less detached, more laid back.

Tanaka and another Asian male returned minutes later. The new guy looked mid-thirties, tall, and remarkably buff in a gray polo shirt. The new guy offered his hand.

"Mr. Taylor, Special Agent Lee, Honolulu Field Office. I just spoke with Special Agent Fisher. For the moment, I'll serve as the Bureau liaison until he arrives. In the meantime, we'll be ironing out a few jurisdictional issues," with a glance at Tanaka.

Just how much did Lee—or Tanaka, for that matter—actually know? His real name, for example. Were they aware of the Naseem connection?

Then again, if the FBI was involved, everyone probably knew, and realizing this gave him a twinge of relief. Arnold shook hands without saying a word and decided to let things play out until reinforcements could arrive.

"At the moment," Tanaka said, "this is a Honolulu homicide investigation."

The detective offered Special Agent Lee his choice of the two remaining chairs before dropping into last one. Chance nudged Arnold's hand, his way of suggesting the choober session wasn't over yet, but Arnold ignored the hint.

"I know you told the other officer what happened," Tanaka said, referring to the first cop on the scene, "but you need take us step by step through everything—and I mean everything—that happened from the moment you met Rios at the airport."

When Arnold finished, Lee asked him to go through the entire story again, but by now Arnold needed a break. It was past midnight and Chance hadn't been outside for hours.

"I'm happy to that, but my dog needs to be walked."

"Mr. Taylor, this is important," Lee said, with a mildly condescending smile. "We still have questions."

"Yeah, I totally get it," Arnold said, standing. "But I'm here voluntarily, right? And I need take care of my dog, so soon as we do that, I'll be happy to go through it as many times as you want. In fact, why don't you guys join us?"

The two law enforcement officers exchanged glances.

Tanaka nodded.

The four of them walked along Beretania Street to Thomas Square where Arnold could unleash Chance. The small park was deserted except for a scruffy male curled up on his side with his head resting on a wadded-up coat. They moved along the park perimeter, Arnold taking them through another detailed description of the events, Tanaka and Lee asking questions, clarifying details point by point. By the time they returned to the police building Tanaka and Lee appeared satisfied with the information.

"Are we finished?" Arnold asked, eager to leave.

How much of the terrorist aspect surrounding him did the FBI share with the locals?

He found comfort in knowing that Fisher would be arriving in a next day or so, to take charge of things. After all, Rios' death held far greater implications than a murder case.

"We're good for the moment," Lee answered. "No question we'll have some points to clarify in the next twenty-four hours, so count on hearing back from us."

Tanaka nodded.

"Keep your cell charged and with you at all times. Never know when we'll need to reach you."

Now what?

He wanted out of the building, away from any reminder of Rios' murder, but then what? Home eventually, but how safe was that? Hell, no place seemed safe for him anymore, not with Naseem out there. Why the hell did he shoot off his mouth last year? All he ever wanted was to live a private, peaceful life, but that had been shattered the instant he first contacted the bitch. He was as frightened now as he had been with Karim last year. He needed fresh air and time to think.

"In that case, it's okay for me to go?"

"One more thing," Lee said, "before you take off. We're obviously concerned for your safety, so think it's best if we put you up in a hotel until this situation's stabilized."

Okay, that's one solution...but he wasn't going to leave SAM for an indefinite period and would not board Chance again.

"I appreciate the offer, but can't do it."

"You kidding? After someone takes a shot at you?"

Lee nudged his glasses up the bridge of his flat nose, only to have them slide down again.

Arnold scrambled for another good reason to decline.

"If I hide, Naseem will hide. And that reduces the odds you'll ever find her."

"You underestimate us," Lee said. "She's on an island. That makes it harder for her to hide and escape."

"Easy for you to say, but considering the hordes of tourists flying in and out of here every day, hiding is probably easier than you think."

He could tell that Lee didn't agree.

"Hey, look at it this way; she wants two things. My software and payback for last year. In that order. She can't get past my firewall...so that leaves her only one option; break into house and physically steal the computers. What I'm saying is, if I'm in a hotel, you'll need to guard me *and* the house. Wouldn't it be best to concentrate on just one place? Believe me, I don't want either of us," with a nod toward Chance, "in harm's way, but that's not going to get any better up until that bitch is dead or locked up."

Tanaka said to Lee, "He's making sense. Hey, if the man's willing to take the risk, why not?"

Lee studied Arnold a beat.

"Long as you acknowledge it's your decision."

"It is." Arnold turned to Tanaka, "Should I call Uber or can someone give us a ride back?"

Tanaka glanced at his watch.

"I'll take you. You need to show me where the shots came from."

Chapter 39

"DON'T MIND LEE," Tanaka said, as they sped along the freeway. "He's just doing his job. For what it's worth, I agree with you; whoever pulled the trigger is probably long gone from there and won't be coming back until the dust settles. And when they do resurface, it won't be back to that site again. As long as we're on the subject, you have an approximate idea where the shots came from? Catch a muzzle flash, anything at all?"

"No, nothing."

He'd been mulling that over since leaving the police station. He was pretty sure he knew the spot.

"The back of my property rolls off into a gully and a ravine, then climbs another slope to a narrow crest that's maybe fifteen feet lower than mine, which is the only reason I can see Diamondhead. Only way a person could have enough height to hit Rios would be further uphill fifty feet or so, which narrows it down to one place."

Tanaka glanced at the sky.

"By time we get there, it should be light enough to point it out to me," He tapped the turn signal. "You obviously know that area well. How would a sniper get there?"

Arnold knew the ravine well from his extensive explorations when developing his escape route.

"You got a couple ways...up the ravine but the terrain's really steep to reach the spot I have in mind. The easiest is to simply walk through the property on the other side of that ridge, but that has it's own problems. I'll show you that route on Google Earth."

By the time they parked, the sky had morphed from purple to magenta and was now rapidly shifting to vibrant pink hues.

"Crime scene techs are still here," Tanaka muttered, apparently referring to a blue utility van blocking the driveway. A Honolulu patrol car was at the curb and a uniformed cop was guarding the open gate to the courtyard. The helicopter was gone as were most of the looky-loos. Tanaka motioned Arnold to remain by the car. "I need to check on what they're doing before I can allow you inside."

"No problem."

He was in no hurry to look at the pool of blood again.

"Should only take me only a couple minutes."

Arnold and Chance stayed out on the sidewalk and exchanged a silent glance with the cop. He stared through the open gate and the courtyard, past the wide-open front door. The interior looked unchanged, but he knew it'd forever be different in his heart. Tanaka was at the top of the steps facing the great room talking to a tall, stout, black-haired woman in khakis and a blue polo shirt.

A minute later, Tanaka came out.

"They're about done, so we're free to go in."

The sky was light enough now to see the suspected sniper spot.

"Let me point it out and show you the easiest way to get there."

They walked inside. Chance bounding ahead, stopped and sniffed at the spot where Rios died, where only a pool of dried blood remained, the sight an eerie reminder of Howie's death. Suddenly, exhaustion and sadness were weighing him down. Once again, his home was a crime scene and the death directly attributable to the fucking Vegas trip.

He was aware of Chance licking his hand. Doggies know when

you're not right. He dropped onto his haunches and nuzzled him, and fought to not embarrass himself with baby-talk in front of strangers.

"Yo, Taylor, c'mon over."

He glanced up. Tanaka had one foot in the kitchen and one on the deck, waving him over.

Tell him?

Part of him wanted to. No, not now. Maybe later. Maybe never. When, or if he did confess, it'd be to Fisher or maybe Davidson. One day....

Taking a deep breath, he walked onto the deck, Chance running ahead to sniff blood spatter. The police would leave soon, never giving a second thought to who would have to clean up the mess. There were, undoubtedly, businesses that specialized in crime scene cleanup, but where the hell would you look for one? Google? Really? Ask Tanaka for a referral? No, he needed to do this himself, if for no other reason than to show Rios due respect. He'd start the moment they closed the gate.

Tanaka was standing at the railing, the tech on his left, pointing to a clump of dense foliage across the ravine.

Tanaka turned to him, "I see what you mean...that the spot?"

Arnold followed Tanaka's finger.

"Yep."

The detective turned a slow one-hundred-eighty, the tech doing likewise.

"This the pillar?"

"Right. I was here," tapping the spot with the toe of his shoe, "when I called 911."

Tanaka took a step back, crouched, glanced from the bullet hole in the slider to the ridge, back again.

"Get a picture from this angle?"

The technician nodded. "Several."

"One through the hole?"

"I did."

Tanaka stood and slowly turned 360 degrees.

"In that case, we should be good."

"Let me show you the easiest way to get there."

Arnold retrieved the Surface from the kitchen counter, opened it to Google Earth and zeroed in on the neighborhood directly across the ravine. Using the stylus, he drew the preferred route on the image. Tanaka thumbed a few notes into his phone.

"Got it."

"You might want to check with the homeowners first," he warned Tanaka. "A hundred-and fifty-pound Rottweiler lives there...Pork Chop. A real sweetheart but protective as hell."

Tanaka laughed. "Good to know."

Arnold walked Tanaka and the female tech to the front gate as the photographer and one other crime scene tech drove away. Tanaka watched her pack equipment into the van before turning to Arnold.

"You still believe staying here's the right move? Offer's still good, you know."

Arnold reached down, thumped Chance's chest a few times.

"No disrespect, but I feel safer here. You've seen my security. Do you really believe a hotel would be safer? Especially after what just happened."

Tanaka opened the driver-side door.

"Good point. Alright then...my number's in your cell. Call if anytime for anything."

With that, Tanaka slid into the front seat as the crime-scene van began pulling away from the curb.

Chapter 40

ARNOLD WATCHED THE detective's car disappear down the street before locking the front gate. Back inside the house, he scanned the perimeter of the property with his security cameras to make sure no one had slipped in unnoticed during the confusion. All clear. He was finally alone.

Chance settled in on the great room floor—probably intending to nap—but Arnold knelt down and rolled him onto his back, started in with tummy and chest rubs, babbling away in the high-pitched baby talk he'd been too embarrassed to use in front of the cops. Might feel comfortable enough in front of Rachael—she'd understand—but definitely not Loni.

"Chance is a good boy, yes he is...a good boy."

Eyes closed, the pooch lolled on the cool marble, neck flaccid, tongue hanging limp out the side of his mouth, happily submitting to Arnold's outpouring affection.

Tears welled up in his eyes. He hoped Rios' spirit could feel his sorrow and grief. Had he only known...if anyone should die, it should be Naseem. And if she were detained without being killed, he hoped she'd rot in a shithole like Gitmo.

Why Rios?

He buried his face in Chance's soft tan fur while the pooch lay motionless, telepathically nursing Arnold's grief.

Doggies know.

The sky was now bright blue in the full morning intensity, a time of day he would usually be working with SAM. But now, with every bit of emotional reserve exhausted, the only thing he felt capable of was curling into a ball beside Chance and sleep.

Instead, he forced himself to his feet, patted Chance's tummy one last time, schlepped to the bedroom and dropped onto the bed.

He'd deal with Rios' blood later.

Chapter 41

ARNOLD AWOKE SHORTLY after 11:00 AM with a severe case of molasses brain and cougar mouth. Three hours of dense, dreamless sleep had done nothing to dent his funk, fatigue, or guilt over Rios. Eyes closed, he kept curled up on his right side, wishing to hell he could sleep for as long as it took to feel better. But knew that wasn't going to happen.

Suddenly, he felt eyes staring at him, so slowly cracked his lids and found himself staring at a wet black nose and dark brown eyes just inches away. Doggy telepathy. Time to get on with it. A wet doggy kiss landed squarely on his nose. Arnold wiped it off with the back of his hand, reached over and scratched the soft fur at the base of Chance's ears.

Nothing's softer than doggy ears.

Stay put for a few more minutes? For what?

Stop with the self-pity, already. Get to work.

He sat up, unplugged his cell from the charger and unmuted the ring, saw that he'd missed five calls from Davidson, so immediately dialed.

"Where are you?" Davidson asked without introduction.

"At home."

"What!?"

Arnold explained his discussion with the police.

"Should I fly over?"

"Thanks for the offer, but that's not necessary. There's nothing to do here. Besides, Mr. Fisher will be here in a day or so."

Davidson said nothing for several seconds.

"Good to know, but I want you to check in daily until this matter is resolved. If you cannot reach me, leave a message. Agreed?"

Arnold ran the Norelco over his face, showered, cleaned and replenished Chance's food and water dishes, then drove them to their favorite park.

Later, during the return from the park, he swung by Starbucks for a latte and breakfast sandwich, which he ate under one of their three green umbrellaed patio tables just outside the store's front door, Chance snoozing on a shady patch of concrete next to him, the air a perfect t-shirt temperature. Breakfast finished, he stopped by Safeway to re-up on dog food and cold cuts.

As he waited in line, eying the front page of the gossip rags, his phone rang. Fisher. The customer ahead of him grabbed his bag and walked off. The cashier began ringing him up zip-zip-zip. Arnold answered the call.

"Gold? Fisher. How you holding up?"

What do you say to that? Like shit?

"Where are you?"

"These all your items?" the clerk asked, moving him along now that people were stacking up behind him. Arnold nodded.

"Just touched down at the airport."

The clerk sighed impatiently for him to pay.

"Look, I'm in the middle of something. Let me call back in, say, two minutes?"

After stowing the groceries in the back of the car, he returned Fisher's call, Chance ten feet away sniffing the trunks of nearby palm trees.

"We're making outstanding headway with the airport videos, but as you know, these things take time," Fisher explained. "How about you swing by in two hours." It didn't sound like a question. "I should be completely up to speed by then."

Arnold was planning to research several items, but figured they would likely yield little, if anything.

"Two hours. You sure?"

"Yes. We'll make this as easy as possible. You'll only need to review segments with greater than sixty percent probability of a match. Three o'clock good?"

Again, not really a question.

"Just so you know...Chance will be with me. Hope that's not a problem."

At the moment, Chance seemed very interested in one particular trunk.

"Chance? What? Your dog?"

"Uh-huh."

If there were no other option, he'd leave him home, but it felt safer if they were together. They were pack.

"No problem. Just needed to figure out what you were talking about. Look forward to meeting him."

"Where are you?" Arnold had no clue where the local FBI field office was.

Fisher told him.

Back home, groceries stored, Arnold grabbed the white plastic pail from under the sink, and, as it filled with water, searched for the large sponge he reserved for washing the car. Found it under the sink, shoved way in the back, behind a row of cleaning supplies. How the hell it got there was a mystery.

He lugged a pail of water out to the deck and started in on Rios's blood, the job taking forty minutes, three water changes, and a shit load of Scrubbing Bubbles to remove as much stain as possible from the tiles, grout, and glass. Two very pale grout stains wouldn't wash off no matter how hard he worked, but unless you knew exactly where to look...

The most difficult part was dumping the blood-tinged water down the drain. Felt as if he were callously discarding Rios' only remaining remnants of physical life. Which, he supposed, was literally true. For him. The body, of course, waited at the coroner for an autopsy. The thought of the corpse laid out on cold stainless-steel made him nauseous.

Fucking Naseem! First Howie. Now Rios. How could there be a God if people like Naseem were allowed to exist?

Finally finished with the task, he took Chance downstairs, out the door and through the back gate. They scrambled down the trail into the ravine as they had done several nights ago.

This time, instead of following the path to the end of the ravine, he began scrambling the steep slope toward the sniper spot, the terrain tough climbing, forcing him to hang onto vegetation in the steepest parts. Chance, on the other hand, had the advantage of four-paw-drive and had no problem scrambling on ahead. The mix of hard work and blazing sun was causing fat drops of sweat to roll down his face and chest. He scolded himself for not bringing the rucksack. They could really use a drink.

Finally, the terrain eased up, then abruptly leveled off onto a narrow crest that continued up a much gentler grade, the other side dropping precipitously into the next gully, making this ridge impossible to develop. He stopped at the suspect spot, hands on hips, sucking deep breaths, thigh muscles aching, Chance next to him panting rapidly. He swiped his dirty hands across his t-shirt before palm-wiping his face. First thing he'd do when he got back would be to freshen Chance's water, drink a gallon himself, and then shower.

Across the ravine the entire length of his back deck was fully exposed. His limited knowledge of rifles and sniper tactics came only from movies. Which basically boiled down to zilch. In spite of this, he suspected the shot might be pretty easy. Which raised an interesting question; why was Rios hit rather than him? Bad luck or a mistake? Or, was Rios' execution meant as some fucked-up message, perhaps softening him up enough to hand over his system? He'd probably never know.

He decided to get to work. The sooner they were out of this hellish sun and baking ground, the better.

The vegetation around him appeared trampled, but by whom? Kids? The sniper? Police? He knelt down to search the ground for anything unusual. After ten blazing minutes, he decided there wasn't anything to be gained by continuing. Had the police had found anything important? More to the point, what had he expected to learn? Was it a mistake to even come? Maybe, but he needed to do *something*—just anything—to help track down Naseem.

He called Tanaka.

"Hey, it's Toby Taylor. Have a minute?"

He watched two fluffy white clouds skitter overhead, thankful for the breeze that just came up. Chance was stretched out on his side, panting. Arnold petted him with his free hand.

"S'up?"

"You check the sniper spot across the ravine?"

"Right after I left your place. Why?"

"I'm up here now taking a look for—" For clues? Jesus, would that sound idiotic! "—did I mess anything up by coming here...like, maybe it's a crime scene or something?"

"The groundcover pretty well trampled?"

"Uh-huh."

"Okay, then. That's the spot. Nope, didn't find anything, so you're good. Thanks for asking."

"If I come across anything on the way back what should I do with it?"

"Nothing. Don't touch it. Take a picture and call me. We can discuss what to do with it after I have an idea what it is...but I seriously doubt you'll find squat. We combed that area thoroughly."

Time to head home.

Instead of climbing back down the way he'd come, he walked the narrow downward-sloping spine two-hundred yards to a spot where the terrain gave easier access to the ravine, then crossed the gully to his side, cut through a neighbor's lot to the street and continued home.

Why the hell didn't he take this route in the first place?

Chapter 42

SHOWERED AND REHYDRATED, with Chance stretched out on the cool marble, Arnold donned his Oculus Go and virtual reality glove. He'd modified the system to allow him to interact with SAM from anyplace within range of his Wi-Fi, specifically out on the deck where his voice commands wouldn't work. He settled into a chaise and started work.

Although his most recent Internet searches for Naseem had yielded nothing, he decided to give it a fresh try. Couldn't hurt, and who knew, it might just reveal something he previously overlooked.

Soon as he moved to the house, his primary task had been to rebuild SAM, his artificial intelligence system, from the ground up. And as soon as SAM was up and running, he constructed a dynamic database of every scrap of information he could dredge up about Naseem and her relatives. A dynamic database differs from a standard relational database in that it isn't made up of rigidly defined categories, like name, address, etc. SAM used bots— automated search engines—to constantly scour the Internet for scraps of information on Naseem and her group. Each new piece of information was then added to, and improved, SAM knowledge base, which in turn, better directed the search strategies.

This ability to constantly refine and improve itself is the most important feature of a dynamic database. Although SAM always alerted him to any new piece of information, Arnold periodically ran quality control checks on the system to verify it hadn't missed a lead. And confirmed that SAM hadn't missed anything.

His last personal contact with Naseem had been in Seattle two days before the fire. Then she simply vanished until appearing outside the gate, then vanished again. And her known associates? Well, Karim was dead. An extensive search for Firouz had yielded only one skimpy article in the *New York Times* five days after the fire when he was arrested on a subway to Kennedy Airport. Nothing had appeared since. Where was he now? Was he a long-term guest at Hotel Gitmo or another federal detention center?

SAM had hit a digital brick wall.

He double and triple checked every possibility he could think of, but all traces of Naseem had been meticulously scrubbed. Her defunct "escort" service website had been cleanly dismantled within twenty-four hours of the fire. Nawzer's work most likely.

There had to be a way to find her.

What was it?

He suspected she actively communicated with Firouz. The question was; how? They certainly didn't leave any trace of a digital means. Being skilled Jihadists, they surely knew enough to use only trusted third parties, quite possibly family members of sympathetic internees, but only the Feds possessed the knowledge and capability to pursue that lead.

Meanwhile, he was spinning his wheels and praying that law enforcement could find her before she could make another attempt to capture and kill him. Made him feel as if he were walking around with a bright red bullseye on his forehead. Go back over everything for a fourth time?

What had he missed? What had he overlooked?

He shook his head in an attempt to clear his brain. There just had to be a digital footprint somewhere out there. Where? It was, he knew, extremely difficult to erase every trace of something that had been posted on the Internet. Especially if it was shared on some form of social media. Even private files were not always immune from discovery. Arnold always marveled at the stupidity of people who emailed or messaged an X-rated selfie. Did they really believe it would never end up in Google News?

With a resigned sigh, he initiated a new search by opening the year-old confirmation for his "appointment" with Breeze last year. As he did previously, he focused on the message header rather than the text. Complete headers—typically hidden by an email app, such as Outlook—list important information including the address of the originating computer in addition to the various servers used in routing the message to the recipient. He worked meticulously through the complex path the message had traveled, but, as in the previous reviews, saw nothing of value.

He searched for her old escort webpage, the one he initially encountered while scanning a site of escorts serving any variety of persuasions. Breeze paid the site a monthly fee to direct customers to her personal webpage. He hacked into the site's server to find her method of payment (PayPal), but all other information had been wiped out. Ditto for the backup files. Whoever cleaned up the evidence was extremely savvy. Had to be Nawzer again.

Her domain name remained was registered with GoDaddy, so he checked those payment records. They too were scrubbed clean and the account was had expired a month ago.

Arnold sat back, convinced of was missing something...but couldn't think what that might be. He reached down and began massaging Chance's neck.

Thump-thump-thump.

He was losing concentration. Time for a break.

The next fifteen minutes were spent cleaning the kitchen counters and vacuuming the floor (yet again) to make sure he'd not missed any shards from the slider.

Now what?

Text Rachael? He checked the time. Bummer; she was at work now.

Break finished, he brewed an espresso and returned to the computer still haunted by the suspicion of missing something. What?

Damn it!

He logged into the Las Vegas property records and searched all her known aliases. Apparently, no one with those names owned property in the city or county during the past two years. Ditto for Karim and Firouz.

Strike three.

His phone rang. Davidson.

"Just checking. Everything still okay?" Davidson asked.

"Other than The Bitch is still out there on the loose? Everything else is wonderful."

The bell for the front-gate chimed on his phone. Chance gave an ominous growl.

"Opps, gotta go. Someone's at the gate."

"Wait! Do not hang up. Who is it?"

"Hold on, I'll take a look."

Arnold brought up the security camera.

Chapter 43

A HAWAIIAN-LOOKING guy in work clothes and clipboard in hand was peering in the gate. Parked at the curb was a panel truck with a Hawaiian Electric sign on the side.

"It's okay, just someone from the electric company."

"Good. But keep me on the phone until you know more."

Arnold quickly snapped pictures of the truck and the man, then hit the intercom button.

"Yes?"

"Afternoon, sir, Hawaiian Electric. I have to do an interconnection inspection. May I come in?"

"Hold on a minute, I just got out of the shower."

The technician made a show of checking his watch.

"Will do, but please don't take too long, I'm backed up this afternoon."

Then to Davidson, "I'm calling Fisher. Ping you later."

"Agent Fisher, Arnold Gold," he said, with a cautionary glance at the monitor.

His gut felt as if a bagful of gerbils was trying to escape. Chance had his nose to the crack between the front door and jamb, ears straight up, giving short occasional whines.

"A guy from Hawaiian Electric just showed up, claiming he needs to do an interconnection inspection."

"Say what?"

Uh-oh. Most people don't know solar panel terminology.

"For my solar panel system....the interconnection determines if I give or use power on the grid, depending on my needs."

"Is this type inspection normal?"

"Yeah, sorta...they do it couple times a year, but the thing is, it's only been three weeks since the last one, so I'm not due for a couple more months at the earliest."

"Think it's legit?"

"That's why I called..." The gerbils were scratching more fiercely now, his heart joining in on the race. The guy at the gate was showing signs of totally squirreling out on him. "It doesn't feel right to me...so I'm thinking...maybe he's, like, connected with Naseem? Or does that sound too paranoid?"

"Not at all! We're on our way."

"What should I do? Let him in?"

Scenarios flashed through his mind, some good, some not so good, most just flat-out horrible.

"Your dog there with you?"

"Yes!"

This calmed him...slightly...but the thought of putting Chance in harm's way....

"Here's what you do; let him in and keep him there long as possible to give us time to take control of the situation."

"Okay, that shouldn't be too hard." Unless, of course, the dude simply put a .357 magnum to his head and pulled the trigger the moment the door opened. "I just texted you a picture of him and the truck."

"Outstanding! We're all over it. Remember, stall as long as possible before you open that door. HPD should be there in two, three minutes."

Arnold watched the tech shifting from foot to foot, eyes darting between his watch and the van.

"Don't think I can stall too much long. He's rabid-bat anxious.

Looks like he's ready to do jackrabbit on me any second now."

"Alright then," Fisher said begrudgingly. "But do *not* disconnect this call. I want the call kept open so we can listen to everything that's happening."

Arnold opened the front door, allowing Chance to charge the security gate, growling softly, putting on a good show.

"Heel." Chance obeyed. "Good boy."

Arnold opened the gate.

"Sorry for making you wait."

The tech took one step back.

"Whoa! That dog under control?"

Now, face to face, the guy looked legitimate, right down to the small toolbox and blue HEC work shirt with a picture ID clipped to his left breast pocket. Then again, Arnold could forge one of those puppies in under two minutes. The man looked definitely native Hawaiian rather than Middle Eastern like Firouz and Karim, but so what? Asia and the South Pacific rim were overflowing with radical extremists.

Arnold ordered Chance to not growl. He obeyed, but didn't let up staring at the electrician.

"Him? Naw. He's a sweetheart. Protective, is all. Come on in." Arnold stepped aside allowing him to enter. "Where do you want to start?"

"I only need a quick check of the electrical panel," still eyeing Chance warily. "The records show it passed inspection three weeks ago, but some new regulations just kicked in, so we're required to double check a few things."

Sounded legit enough, but Arnold had bullshited his way past all sorts of human firewalls when actively hacking, so...

"In here."

Arnold showed him to the interconnection panel in the wall between a small pantry and kitchen.

The tech stepped into the pantry access.

"Go ahead with whatever you're doing and I'll give a shout when I finish," and set his toolbox on the floor. "Oh, before I start, is there a toilet I could use? Would appreciate it."

Arnold pointed, "Second door on the left," before perching on a stool at the kitchen counter, a spot that would allow him to watch both the powder room and pantry doors.

He opened an Internet search for window repair companies, jotted down the first five names, then began checking Yelp ratings. All five had excellent reviews, so he simply called the first one on the list as the technician walked from the bathroom to the pantry.

"ABC Glass and Mirrors."

"Do you repair glass sliders?" he asked with a glance at the broken glass.

Bursts of an electric drill were coming from the pantry as the tech began removing the panel cover.

"All the time, hon," the woman snorted.

He flashed on Rios's skull blowing away. A few measurements, fresh glass, and the window would be good as new. Not so with Rios. His life was over. The thought gut-punched him, stealing his breath, making the process of obtaining several bids seem emotionally overwhelming.

Fuck it. Ask this company do the job and this the hell over with.

Or...just hang up and deal with this sometime later?

What the hell's wrong with you? Rios died here. Deal with the consequences.

Silence.

He realized she was waiting for an answer.

"I need one repaired as soon as possible. When can someone come out?"

Don't even worry about getting a quote, just get it repaired.

"We need to take a look at the job and have you sign a quote before scheduling it. When are you available for Pete to come out?"

"Anytime today, if possible."

"Can't be today, hon."

"So, when *can* you do it?"

Jesus, just repair the goddamn thing.

"I need to put you on hold while I check."

Chance continued to stand just outside the pantry door, guarding. Arnold sat on the barstool, phone to his ear, waiting. He glanced across the ravine to the sniper spot and imagined the shooter stretched over the rock, centering the cross-hairs on his head just like he'd seen in movies.

How could he miss? Was it simply bad aim or was Rios the target? No, shooting Rios didn't make sense. Or did it? Did he have enemies? Maybe, but if that were the case, why shoot him here, instead of, say, at his own home? No…killing him made no sense.

Unless…it was intended to send a message.

Yeah? What would that be?

He couldn't think of one. No, hitting Rios had to be a mistake.

"Will someone there tomorrow afternoon?"

"Absolutely. What time?"

Just get rid of the fucking bullet hole, alright?

"Will one o'clock work?"

"Perfect. I'll be expecting you."

Taking the first step on this was a relief. Once that reminder was removed, a small part of his life would be return to normal; just one more step toward moving on with his life.

The tech came out of the pantry smiling and wiping his hands on a pale red cloth.

"All done."

Arnold held up his iPhone as if he was texting but was actually shooting a video of the guy.

"Everything good to go?"

The tech reached back into the pantry, grabbed the toolkit and headed for the front door, "It is," he called over his shoulder, clearly eager to leave.

Arnold caught up to him.

"Hey, before you go, show me what you look at during these inspections. The more I know about the system, the better I can keep an eye on things."

The tech pointedly checked his watch.

"Maybe another time. I'm seriously backed up this afternoon," and continued right out the door.

Arnold tried to come up with another delaying tactic but couldn't think of one, so just followed him to the gate, watched him climb into the van and drive away. There was no other vehicle in sight. Then he was back on the phone with Fisher.

"Where the hell are you guys? He just drove off."

"Calm down. We're on him."

"Expect a video of in your inbox in a few seconds."

"A video? Goddamn, Gold, outstanding!"

Chapter 44

LAST YEAR, WHEN Arnold brought Davidson to his house a day after Howie's murder, the lawyer used one of his counter-surveillance devices to scan for any bugs that might have been planted between the time the police left and before he was released from questioning.

At first, Arnold thought that owning a bug detector was, like, over-the-top-paranoid-insane. Then, after some serious reflection, reversed his opinion...especially when considering his own security requirements.

He was pleasantly surprised, and truthfully, a bit shocked at how easily he could obtain sophisticated equipment. Common retailers—Amazon and eBay, for example—offered a stunning variety of devices to detect just about any type of eavesdropping device out there, leaving him totally confused when it came to buying one.

After three hours of intensive on-line research, he boiled it down a few simple basics. He learned that all bugs essentially consisted of either a recorder or radio transmitter. Which, in turn, made a bug detector nothing more than a radio receiver. A hidden recorder was difficult to find because it transmitted no signal. A transmitter, on the other hand was relatively easy to sense and locate with a bug detector.

Shortly after moving into the house, he purchased one. His

rationale was simple; big corporations use sophisticated security to guard against sabotage, theft, and spying.

Why shouldn't he do likewise?

In spite of his efforts to maintain a low profile, he still risked having someone figure out he was winning more (well, way more) than the laws of probability allow. Making him live in constant in fear of discovery.

When developing his business model—if you could call it that—he programmed several safeguards into SAM to obscure his win/loss record. Primarily, he placed small bets across a wide number of sites under ten different identities.

In addition, SAM made sure his monthly win-rate did not exceed fifty-two percent across all sites combined. After all, two percent of one-hundred thousand dollars a month was twenty thousand; not chump change in anyone's book. Being greedy was a lightning rod for attention, especially since he had no way of knowing if the various sites were owned and monitored by the same organization. SAM was meticulously programmed to deal with these myriad details.

Having SAM do the tedious work freed him for more creative tasks, such as researching and refining the artificial intelligence engine. Like his hero, Nate Silver, Arnold could accurately predict the outcome of just about any event—elections, public opinions— for which data existed, making SAM invaluable.

Arnold turned on the bug detector and immediately heard two distinct signal whines. He swept the wand in a circle and learned they were coming from different locations. He walked the house listening to each signal getting louder or weaker until he located their source. Not surprisingly, one came from behind the guest bathroom electrical outlet. Had to give the tech due credit for popping that puppy in under two minutes. The second one—no surprise there either—came from behind the panel in the pantry.

Now what? Remove them?

The downside, of course, would be that this would tip Naseem (if she was behind this) that he knew of their existence. On the other hand, if he left them in place, could that be used to an advantage? Good question.

Hmmm...surely the terrorists anticipated he'd discover them, so why go to such an elaborate ruse for nothing?

Ahhh, okay...Naseem now knew his floorplan and exactly where the computers were.

Fuck! I hate that. Now what?

Well, for starters, talk it over with Fisher.

Arnold snatched his keys from the counter and bee-lined for the front door.

"Come on, boy, let's go for a walk."

Chapter 45

WITH CHANCE OFF doing his thing, Arnold sat on a park table to phone Fisher. He watched a bird hop along the ground hunting for food.

"Where are they?" Fisher asked.

"One's in the bathroom, the other's behind the electrical panel."

"You doped out their function yet? Voice? Data? What?"

"No, not yet. I wanted to run it by to you before I got near them. But if someone put a gun to my head and forced me to guess, I'd have to go with a keystroke recorder."

"Why's that?"

"Because I'm pretty confident they can't get past my firewall, so their best shot is to try to steal my password."

"Ah, gotcha." Fisher paused. "Thanks for the head's up. Give me maybe ten, fifteen minutes to discuss this with our techs, see if there's a way we can use this to our advantage."

"Good. Don't forget to point out a couple things; the guys who came up with these devices aren't just a couple sheep herders from Tora Bora. They're extremely sophisticated."

Arnold watched Chance chase the bird back into the air. Probably not as much fun as treeing a squirrel, but hey, you work with what you get.

"And they're pretty small to fit into the space."

"So? What's the point?"

"A small bug means small battery which means short life which means if they don't get my password in a day or two, they'll have to either find a way to enter the house again or move on to another tactic."

Arnold pulled a water bottle from his rucksack. He was sweating like crazy even though he wasn't in the sun. He and Chance both needed a drink the moment he finished the call.

"Ahh, I see where you're going with this. They'll break into your house when you're out. Sure, it'll trigger the alarm, but by already knowing exactly where to go, they'll be in and out of there before HPD can respond. Gutsy, but definitely doable."

"So, what do we do with them? Leave them or pull them?"

"Let me run this by our techies first. You okay with having the bugs in your house for a day or two?"

Getting them out was tempting, but capturing Naseem would make it worth any minor inconvenience.

"I'm good with leaving them, but what about the dude who installed them...what's going on with him?"

Another dog-walker came into view. Arnold was about to call Chance back when she released her Jack Russell from his leash. The dogs ran straight to each other and started sniffing butts. Arnold couldn't imagine the joy in that, especially if a dog's sense of smell is ten thousand times more sensitive than ours.

"We're still looking into it. The van's legit. We followed him across town and he's on a service call. Meanwhile, an agent's over at H-E doing a background check. We should have something concrete soon."

"What the hell you waiting for? He obviously works for them."

"Hey, cool it, Gold. I need to know more before tipping our hand. I want to know if he's really their employee and had a legitimate reason for the house call. Once I know those answers, we'll invite him to join us for a chat. In the meantime, you need to be here reviewing videos."

Oops. Forgot about those.

"No problem. Where do I go?"

"Good thing you asked. We've set a temporary command center at the Coast Guard station. Know where that is?"

Coast Guard station?

It took a moment to place it.

"That building on the pier?"

"That's the one."

"I'm on my way."

"This is bad, very bad," Akmar moaned with head bowed.

He, Naseem, and two other sympathizers sat in the office discussing next steps while Naseem remained stonily silent. She did not share their misgivings. Killing an infidel was to be glorified. Killing an agent of the infidel's government was even greater. Yes, the police would now make a much stronger effort to find them, but so what? They were already being hunted. What more did they have to lose? They might now even have an opportunity to strike an even mightier blow against Allah's enemies.

"Sister Naseem, you are being strangely quiet. You are thinking, yes?"

She turned to Akmar; "The road the Jew walks with his dog. This is relative isolated, yes?"

"The road to the view spot?"

She nodded.

"This is the perfect place to capture him."

"But we are not knowing when he goes there."

"This is true, but we must be patient. He will walk his dog there. And when he does, we'll be watching."

"But what if he is not going there? We cannot remain here forever."

"This is true too, and we will not. If we cannot capture the Jew on that road, we will capture him in his house."

"How will we do that?" one of the sympathizers asked. "The

police will come."

"Not if they are already busy with something bigger." With a smile, she addressed Habib. "Can you have the bomb finished in a week?"

"Yes."

"Excellent. If we cannot capture the Jew on that road, we will detonate the bomb during lunch hour when the most people are there. Then, when the police are dealing with that, we will enter the Jew's house to finish this."

Chapter 46

ARNOLD DROVE THE Pali Highway to where it funneled into
Bishop Street, then continued until it t-boned Ala Moana Blvd. The
US Coast Guard building was an old, two-story concrete structure
on Pier 4 that looked like a hold-over from the 1930s. A ten-foot
high cyclone fence topped with twin rows of concertina wire
encircled the entire pier. The front of the building contained no
windows, which struck Arnold as a bit weird. Why so much
security for a geriatric Coast Guard building?

Curb parking wasn't permitted on Ala Moana which left him
two options: park on the pier or search for a space blocks away. The
cyclone gate stood open.

Why not?

He drove onto the pier and angle parked in the first open spot.
All the surrounding vehicles had a similar colored numbered sticker
on their rear bumper, resembling a parking permit. The last thing
he wanted was to come out to find his car towed. Especially if he
were here for a just cause. He made a mental note to clear this up
with Fisher before becoming totally distracted. He clipped the leash
to Chance's collar, locked up the Mini, and headed for the only
door in sight. Locked. Not surprising, in view of all the other
obvious security. He knocked. A stocky female in crisp Coast
Guard whites opened the door, gave him a head to toe inspection.

"Can I help you?"

"I'm here to see Agent Fisher."

After verifying his name, she stepped aside, allowing him into a large, windowless rectangle of bare walls, cracked cement floor, and exposed ceiling beams. The only interior light came from computer monitors, a few LED desk lamps, and two rows of harsh overhead fluorescents.

The air was humid and smelled of warm electronics, dry rot, and a hint of moldy A/C. The door closed behind him, immediately exchanging street din for the hum of computer fans and muted conversations. The furniture consisted of mismatched government-issue rolling chairs and scarred gray metal desks. Atop several desks sat ultimately cool, state of the art computer equipment. Tower computers and laptops were ganged together with zip-tied bundles of thick, all-weather orange power cords in orderly lines between the workstation pods. Two massive side by side whiteboards covered a section of the far wall.

Fisher introduced Arnold to several team members while shepherding him to a battered Steelcase desk with twin 40-inch, high-def monitors in V-formation.

"We're screening all inbound flights to this island regardless of country of origin," Fisher explained. "Considering the large daily volume, it's a massive job. Our facial recognition software's fast but that doesn't make the job any less labor intensive. Every computer-generated hit requires a pair of human eyes to rule it in or out. Then, once we have an initial ID, we track that person's route from the arrival gate to the exit to extract every possible bit of information: Positive ID, who they travel with, flight of arrival, etc. All of it. And because you're the only one to actually be face to face with our target, you're the only one who can make a positive identification. Ready to start?"

"You bet!"

He was amped, in fact. Exhilarated to actually be assisting in a real investigation. Chance sat patiently on his haunches, beside Arnold's right leg, checking out the room. Arnold stowed his rucksack under the desk and then removed small aluminum bowl, set it carefully on the floor next to the desk and poured in some water.

"Probably best to move him behind you," Fisher suggested. "Agent Mays will sitting be on your right."

Arnold glanced around, but didn't see anyone. He moved Chance anyway.

"Water, coffee?" Fisher asked.

"No, I'm good, thanks."

He turned toward the clacking of a wheels rolling on cement and saw a thin African-American female walking his way, dragging an equally beat-up desk chair. After being introduced, she settled in on Arnold's right, Fisher standing to his left.

"Ready?" Mays asked.

Arnold nodded. She clicked the mouse beside his hand and the right-hand screen filled with a good quality color video of passengers exiting an arrival gate.

Fisher said, "We'll begin with deplaning passengers and if we don't come up with her there, move to the videos of the halls and baggage claim."

Arnold noted the time. He planned to take Chance for a bathroom break in an hour or so depending on how things went. At least the videos he'd review were pre-screened.

"Speak up if you want coffee," Fisher offered again. "Unless we get incredibly lucky, we're going to be here a long goddamn time."

Thirty minutes later Fisher's cell rang and he stepped away from their desk to take the call, leaving Mays and Arnold to their work. The videos were shot from ceiling mounted cameras approximately twenty feet from the gate and included a digital clock superimposed in the lower right corner.

Most passengers exiting the jetway turned to Arnold's right, but a few moved left or stepped to one side or the other to wait. Arnold watched intently as a woman exited the gate.

"Stop."

Arnold's heartrate accelerated.

Mays froze the image. Arnold pointed her out on the screen. "That one...she looks like her."

But a wide-brim hat made a positive ID impossible.

Mays slid a mouse to him with instructions for navigating the video; "Center the crosshairs on the suspect's head then right click."

She pulled another mouse into the work area.

Arnold followed her instruction as Mays opened the left-hand monitor and the screen filled with text.

She asked, "Why her? That hat hides her face."

"Nothing absolute...just...an impression, her body, her movements...they seem so familiar."

"Roger that. Good. We'll track her."

Mays continued the video at half speed, tracking the subject into the terminal. The woman glanced up once, as if looking for the baggage claim sign, appeared to catch herself before quickly lowering her head.

"Wait, go back."

Mays ran the video back and forth, frame by frame, until they could isolate the fullest facial image. Arnold studied it several seconds before his excitement crashed.

"No, not her."

Mays pointed to the second monitor. Arnold studied it a moment before realizing it was the computer-estimated probability of a match. Sixty-eight percent. Wow! Pretty impressive. Which immediately brought to mind a ton of questions about the software and system, but knew it'd just waste time from finding The Bitch.

A voice said, "We got him."

Arnold looked up to see Fisher was grinning.

"Huh?"

"The guy from Hawaiian Electric," Fisher explained. "Tanaka just brought him in for questioning. I'm going to run over there now."

Arnold pushed back his chair, all set to pack up. Fisher motioned for him to stay put.

"This is more important. Don't worry. I'll call if we need you for anything."

Arnold slowly settled back into the chair.

Why so disappointed?

He thought about that. Well, for one thing, he wanted more involvement in that part of the investigation. But knew Fisher was right. As tedious as this work might be, it needed doing. And for him to give it his best effort. The sooner he spotted her, the sooner they could track her down. Arnold paused to give Chance a few choobers before returning his attention to the task at hand.

"Where were we?"

Chapter 47

THEY WORKED INTO the second hour, Mays insisting on short breaks each fifteen minutes to stand, stretch their muscles, and perform eye exercises that she swore minimized boredom, fatigue, and eye strain. In spite of these, Arnold fought to keep from drifting off into daydreams of Rachael.

At the end of the second hour, he told Mays, "Chance needs a break. I'll take him out for, what, ten minutes?"

Back arched, she began to stretch out kinks.

"We could all use one." She called the other agents. "Anyone hungry? Y'all want to break for eats?"

A team member volunteered to make a sandwich run to a deli across town and took orders.

On the sidewalk, Arnold surveyed the immediate area for a place Chance could use. A wide median with a low hedge divided the six lanes of Ala Moana Boulevard, but was too dangerous and the sidewalk on this side had nothing but piers interspersed with sections of concrete balustrade.

He waited for the traffic light to change. On the other side of the street, a half block to their left, was a triangular patch of grass and trees so they headed there. As Chance sniffed for exactly the perfect spot to relieve himself, Arnold ran through a series of stretches, working out the leg stiffness from sitting so long.

Mays had a cup of freshly brewed coffee waiting for him when they returned to the desk ten minutes later. He paused to savor the strong flavor before resuming the boring work of video review.

Thirty minutes later, another passenger piqued Arnold's attention, snapping him from another daydream.

"Whoa, back up, back up."

Mays clicked the mouse.

"Tell me when to stop."

"Keep going…okay…stop." Arnold leaned closer to study the image, and pointed to one woman. "This one. Right there. Zoom in on her."

Mays typed the time and camera number into the computer and the right screen sectioned into four windows, displaying the same gate from different angles and distances. Arnold tapped the image that had the optimal viewing angle.

"Zoom in on here."

The four individual images blinked into one. Mays enlarged and sharpened it as Arnold watched.

"Okay, let's go back to the others."

Doubt began to creep into his first impression. This easy task was becoming more and more difficult. Simple as it was—just look at pictures until you recognize one, right? Can't be that tough—the endless stream of people began to play tricks with his memory, making everyone begin to look like everyone else, eroding his confidence. He closed his eyes and thought about the woman on the screen. Something about her felt so familiar….

"Well?" Mays asked.

He hesitated and looked more closely.

"There's definitely something there…definitely…let's check her out more closely."

"Roger that. Just for grins, how sure you on this one?"

"Oh, man…" He rubbed his eyes. "I want to say…seventy-five percent…maybe." And weighed that a moment. "Yeah, seventy-five feels about right. Go ahead, see what we come up with?"

"The whole enchilada?"

"Yeah. Go for it."

Mays typed a command.

"It'll take a few minutes to collate all the segments, but knowing arrival time will certainly speed things along. Plus, we got enough good angles, the software can provide us with a composite. It'll take a bit of time get it all together, so might as well take a twenty-minute break."

Arnold led Chance along Ala Moana to Aloha Tower Drive, past a row of office buildings to Irwin Park. With so many people around, he couldn't let Chance off leash, but the area was large and green and relative free of vehicular traffic so would serve the purpose. Arnold figured they weren't going to make it back in twenty minutes but that Mays might enjoy the longer break.

A half hour later he walked back inside to find Mays and Fisher intently inspecting the screen. Arnold came up behind them and glanced at it.

"Find something?"

Fisher nodded.

"You're not going to believe this, but the tech admitted to installing those bugs."

Arnold looked at Fisher blankly, before realizing what he was talking about.

"The bugs?"

"Yeah, admitted it right from the get go. I was expecting some half-assed bullshit story, but no, he flat-out gave it up." He stepped left. "Here's your seat."

Arnold remained standing, not sure exactly what the hell was going on, Chance in the heel position.

Fisher continued, "That's the good news. Bad news is, he denied knowing anything about anyone even remotely associated with Naseem or her group."

"That's bullshit! Start from the beginning. Tell me everything he said."

Fisher shrugged.

"Story goes he's packing up from another job when this stranger walk up, flashes identification, claims he's DEA. I asked him to describe the identification, but he says he was so shocked, he wasn't paying much attention. Said it all happened too fast. The supposed DEA agent tells him they're working a big case and need two listening devices planted in a target's house A-S-A-P. Yours, obviously. Claims he's their only hope of obtaining time-sensitive information. They offer a grand to do it. Cash. He figures it's legit, that he's helping law enforcement and it's easy money."

Arnold glanced from Fisher to Mays looking for any sign they're pranking him, but both appeared no-nonsense, dead-ass serious.

"Unbelievable! That's…fucking insane! How could anyone swallow such bullshit?"

Yeah? Well, how about the one in Vegas you swallowed hook, line, and sinker?

Fisher shrugged.

"What can I say? It's what he's saying and everything we checked out on him is righteous; has a flawless ten-year work history there and doesn't show up in any law enforcement databases. We're even checking into his social media posts, but if nothing shows up…" Fisher let it hang before adding, "To his credit, he's cooperating with us and hasn't made a peep about lawyering-up. Bottom line is my gut says he's giving us the truth."

Arnold's anger became first-clenching frustration.

"You're saying he's going to walk out?"

"Did I say that?" Fisher shot Mays a look of exaggerated shock. She shook her head, no. Then, back to Arnold. "We're not even close to being done with him and he's given no sign of wanting to leave. At the moment, he and a sketch artist are working on a composite. But yes, once we're done with our questioning, he's free to go."

Arnold stared at Fisher, then Mays, back and forth, struggling for words.

"He fucking aided and abetted terrorists."

Aided and abetted...a phrase he'd heard on TV. He liked the sound of that.

"Don't be going all Clarence Darrow on me, Gold. We don't have a choice in this matter. There's nothing to hold him on even if we were so inclined."

Chance stood rigid, ears back, canines bared, growling softly. Arnold grabbed his collar.

"Easy, boy."

With his free hand, he gave him behind-the-ear choobers, calming himself in the process.

Fisher poked a finger at Arnold's chest, "Calm your dog the fuck down," with a nervous glance at Chance.

Arnold patted the pooch's side. "We're good."

"Sure as fuck hope so." After a beat, "C'mon, we're wasting time. Let's get back on track and find these assholes."

Fisher had a point, even though giving the technician a pass seemed to be idiotic. He felt cheated. He was sure the tech was the key to locating Nasaam.

"That hat she's wearing," Mays tapped the monitor screen, bringing him back on task, "makes tracking her easier, but sure makes a clear face shot impossible. Probably the idea."

"This is the best I can do for now."

Mays showed him the software reconstruction from eight different images from as many angles. Arnold studied it carefully.

"Much better," he said. "I'd say ninety percent it's her."

"Excellent!"

Fisher, Mays, and Arnold slapped high-fives.

Arnold was totally amped now that they finally knew her

arrival time. But the island and city made for a pretty big haystack. Now they had to find her.

Fisher turned to Mays.

"The name on the ticket and her city of departure is good information to work with. I'll develop on that angle while you two track her through baggage claim and determine her mode of transportation. If she left in a taxi, work that up and find out where she was dropped off."

Mays said to Fisher, "It might go a bit faster if I work this solo. We done with him for now?" Then to Arnold. "No disrespect...don't want to burn you out, is all."

Fisher thought about it a moment, nodded.

"For now," and offered Arnold his hand. "Thanks for all the help, Gold. Trust me, we all feel your frustration."

Arnold was glad to get out of there. The stuffy dark interior had a time distorting effect on him. Evening was fast approaching and he needed to finish a ton of shit. He was forgetting something important...really important.

What the hell was it?

Had to do with SAM...and involved Naseem...*Arrrgggg!*

He stood, Chance automatically shifting to the heel position.

"Let me know soon as you get something. Hey, don't forget, you need anything more, anything at all, call," took one step away from the desk, paused, flashed Fisher a conspiratorial smile. "Remember, I can dig up all sorts of shit in a hurry. Soooo...."

"I bet you can." Fisher laughed. "But we need to do things by the book if it stands a chance of surfacing in court." He lowered his voice. "I'll be in touch."

Arnold clipped Chance's leash to his collar.

"Do me a favor?"

"If I can. What?"

"Text me her name and flight number."

The ticket was undoubtedly bought with a bogus card but would provide SAM with an additional bit of data to crunch. You never knew what might pop up...each new alias could potentially yield new information.

Fisher started to answer, seemed to reconsider, then gave a slight nod.

Chapter 48

ARNOLD PARKED AT the usual spot at their favorite recreational area. Evening was descending and all visitors were long gone. Perfect. Chance rocketed out of the backseat, hit the ground full throttle heading straight toward the foliage, and leaped in pure doggy bliss. Arnold started walking his usual path, ruminating about the woman in the airport video. Something was off, but he couldn't place exactly what.

Well, for one thing, she made a big deal of hiding her face from the cameras. Yeah? So what?

I would too if I were trying to hide.

Okay, point taken, but the thing was, there seemed to be a method in the way she played it. Yeah, playing…with the cameras, teasing them, showing *just* enough—but not quite enough—to reveal her face.

Making a game of it?

Yeah, that was it. Toying with them. No doubt about it.

For what purpose? Her act seemed more elaborate than a simple disguise. What?

Well, what about the obvious: an intentional deception, a deliberate way to attract attention to the wrong person? He tried find a reason to reject this conclusion, but couldn't think of what that might be. This was just too goddamned obvious. Or was he being influenced by the spy novels he loved to read? No, she had to be a decoy.

Call Fisher?

Would he take it the wrong way, think he was trying to tell him how to do his job? Maybe, maybe not, but was there any downside to voicing his concern?

Hey, screw it!

He dialed.

"That's crossed our minds, but it's all we have to work with, so can't ignore it. For the sake of argument, let's say you're right, it isn't her. We lose, at most, a couple hours. But...say it *is* her. In that case we're that much closer. Point is, we can't ignore her."

"Don't get me wrong. I'm not saying don't check it out. I'm just saying I think she's punking us."

"Believe me, we're not going be punked. No one's more paranoid than us when it comes to these assholes. Or, you saying you changed your mind, that it isn't a ninety percent match?"

"No, not at all...she looks like her, *but*...something's not right and it's bugging the shit out of me."

He paused, uneasy with asking the next question. Except for Howie, he preferred to work by himself rather than with others. He'd never joined in hobby clubs, chess groups, or after school activities. Not because he disliked the other kids, but it was difficult for him to collaborate—on anything, probably because he could solve problems quickly, making him impatient with others. He relied on linear deductive reason instead of intuition; a process beautifully suited for programing code.

But, tracking down Naseem would mostly likely result from a blend of deduction and intuition, just as it had in the hunt for Bin Laden. Now, for the first time, he longed to be included in the team, to enjoy the camaraderie of working shoulder to shoulder with Mays.

He swallowed.

"There anything I can do for you guys? I mean, you want me

back there? Anything at all?"

"Sure. We never turn down free help."

Fisher sounded amused.

"Fabulous! Hey, you guys eaten recently?"

Alright already, enough with the Jewish mother shtick.

"With all the alligators climbing up our asses we haven't had a chance. Why? You offering to bring food? 'Cause, if you are——"

"Name it."

"Hold on."

Arnold heard Fisher's muffled call to the group, then, a moment later.

"Yeah, we're ready for some eats."

"What would you like?"

"Dealer's choice."

While waiting for Chance to return to the car, he mulled over what to bring. Had to be something everybody liked, be easily shared, and tasty. Pizza? Was there anyone in the galaxy didn't like pizza?

Well...maybe vegans and few gluten-free nuts, but, hey, you can't please everyone.

He knew the best pizzeria on the island. Problem solved.

He came away from the counter with three large pies; one Italian sausage, one pepperoni, one triple-cheese in case a vegetarian was in the group. He threw in a side order of anchovies for those, like himself, who loved them. If this weren't enough, he'd go out again for a reup.

Before leaving the pizzeria, he stuffed a fistful of hot pepper packets and a to-go menu in his pocket. Just in case. Working for the team again—even as a gofer—whetted his appetite. Or was it just the greasy cheesy pizza smell filling the car? Did it make any difference? His mouth was already watering.

He was almost at the Coast Guard building when he realized he'd forgotten a few things, so doubled back to a nearby store to stock up on water, a can of dog food, a pack of paper plates and a roll of paper towels.

The pizzas were still warm when he carried them into the cavernous room. Everyone watched as he started to align the boxes side by side on an empty desk, but before he could finish setting out the plates and other supplies, slices began disappearing at an alarming rate. He served Chance dinner while the others ate and joked, clearly enjoying their dinner break. Now that the others were served, he loaded up on the last two slices of the double cheese. Everything else was gone.

"Bring me up to speed on what's happened," he said to Fisher.

Fisher tapped the side of his mouth and continued chewing, and, after a moment, swallowed.

"She appears to have been traveling with an unidentified male who could be the same one showed up at your place the other night. We haven't been able to obtain a usable facial shot on him either because he wore—surprise, surprise—a hat and made a big deal of not looking up."

Fisher paused for another bite.

Mays picked up the thread.

"They caught a cab outside baggage claim. Got an agent working up that angle in hopes we can determine their destination and method of payment. A hotel would be good, but they could just as likely be holed up with sympathizers. Metro's canvassing the major hotels for any check-ins fitting their descriptions. That's a long shot, I know, but it's all we have to work with at the present time."

"I need to ask…" Arnold said to Fisher. "The shot that killed Rios…were they shooting at me or him?"

Fisher shrugged.

"No way to possibly know but my guess is you."

Which wasn't the answer he wanted to hear.

"Why do you think that?"

"Because of the second shot. If Rios was the target, why hang around for the second one?"

Fisher paused to tongue a scrap of pizza from between his teeth. "A pro would've been long gone by the time Rios hit the deck."

Devastatingly clear logic. Too clear. Rios would be alive if he hadn't gone to Vegas.

How can I live with this?

Appetite now gone, he set his pizza on the paper plate.

"What's keeping them from another try?"

"Who knows? Could be anything. But I guarantee they're out there planning the next step. I can also guarantee they'll be more careful next time. Before they muffed that shot, they didn't know if we were here looking for them. They sure as hell know it now. I'm also sure they know they fucked up by killing one of ours. If I was her, I'd cool my heels before trying again. And while they wait, they'll try to find out as much possible about what we're doing. They probably think the longer they wait, the more likely we'll be forced to move on to another case. But I guarantee Naseem's not leaving this island until she leaves as our guest. Bet on it, Gold."

Fisher's cell rang. He stepped away to take it and a moment later flashed a thumbs up and returned.

"Our target's registered at the Hawaiian Village under the name Fakhira Khan."

"Both of them, or just her?"

"Only one on the register. A detective's heading there now."

After a stunned moment, the team began slapping high-fives. At last, something was working in their favor. But Arnold wasn't so confident. This was just way too easy, especially on top of his suspicion that Naseem wasn't the woman in the airport video. Fueling his concern was that he couldn't remember the important task he needed to do and it was driving him batshit. Had to get out of there and figure it out.

"Guys, I need to go take care of a few things...will check back later."

Chapter 49

BUTT PROPPED AGAINST the Mini, Arnold waited for Chance to finish. Frustrated at his inability to remember the crucial task, he was savoring thoughts of Rachael, of how different life would be if Naseem actually was at the hotel. It'd solve everything.

Rachael...despite all the confusion in his life, one thing remained obvious: he must end things with Loni. Seeing her for dinner now and then would be fine with him, but she'd never accept that. Besides, ending things was just one more step to becoming Arnold again.

Back home, he freshened Chance's water and dry food. Unlike dogs who scarfed down every morsel within seconds of it being put in front of them, he nibbled the dry food all day. With Chance taken care of, he turned his attention the hidden bugs.

What the hell was he accomplishing by leaving them in place?

Nada. He first pulled the one in the bathroom electrical outlet, followed by the one in the pantry.

He set them on the kitchen counter. They were identical. No identifying marks or distinguishing features. He snapped several pictures of them with his cell and checked to make sure they captured the few details he thought important.

Next, he wanted to find out what they were designed to do. With his bug detector next to them, he clapped his hands. No response. Meaning, they didn't record and transmit sound. He then typed a string of characters on his Bluetooth keyboard. Both bugs immediately transmitted signals.

"Gotcha!"

That settled it. As he suspected, this was Naseem's hail Mary attempt at stealing his password.

When he analyzed the bugs' signals on his computer he found they were identical. Electronic devices generate unique signals, or "envelopes" that can be sufficiently specific to identify the manufacturer. This is how NSA can identify an iPhone from a Samsung. Perfect! He knew an engineer who specialized in wireless device communication—complicated problems like being able to program a cardiac pacemaker through the skin, or having an iPhone read a Fitbit. He emailed a copy of the recordings to the dude asking if he could identify the manufacturer. Fisher would undoubtedly find this information useful.

One more item checked off the list.

He turned his attention to the video from the night Naseem scouted the house. In particular, he wanted to see if he could determine what she'd been carrying.

But, in spite of his arsenal of software, he couldn't penetrate the dense shadows obscuring the area of interest, so turned his attention to her face. By combining partial images from several different angles, he was able to build a clearer composite than the individual ones. No doubt about it, that was Naseem.

But, was she the same person in the airport video?

Key question.

Wearily, he pushed out of the chair. He needed sleep. Chance was already curled up in his bolstered bed, snoozing soundly. He stretched out on his own bed and tried to relax, but couldn't shake the unnerving knowledge he was forgetting to do something important.

Chapter 50

HIS CELL PHONE jolted him from ink-black sleep. He rolled over, grabbed it, squinted at the screen, but his grogginess combined with farsightedness made it difficult to read. He squinted more, extended the phone to arm's length; Fisher.

"Mr. Fisher, what can I do for you?"

"Got bad news for you. Naseem was never at the hotel."

Fisher's tone spoke of fatigue and concern, and perhaps a touch of frustration.

Arnold was now wide awake.

I knew it!

"Are you shitting me?"

"Fuck no. Gets worse: she hasn't set foot inside the place since check-in. We just finished interviewing the housekeeper for her room. She claims the room's never been touched."

He wasn't sure what to make of that.

"What about clothes?"

"That's the punch line. Seems that nothing was ever unpacked and the bed was never touched."

Arnold thought about that.

"What're you saying...that it's a diversion?"

"If it quacks like a pope and shits in the woods..."

Something about Fisher's tone made Arnold suspect he was holding back.

"Then what *are* you saying?"

Fisher hesitated, which only stoked Arnold's anxiety.

"We suspect it's nothing more than a trip-wire."

"What the hell's that supposed to mean?"

Chance was next to him now, staring up with his large brown eyes.

"Basic counterespionage technique. Say you come to town and want to know if you're being followed or spotted. What do you do? One option is to have someone skilled at counter surveillance keep eyes on your back. The downside to that is even someone highly trained can be thrown off now and then. Another option—and what I think we have here—is to set a trap that'll warn you if someone comes looking for you. If one of Naseem's sympathizers works at the hotel...a maid, floor supervisor, desk clerk...Naseem checks in and goes straight out the back door. The trap's set and you'll be notified the minute someone shows up looking for you."

"Wow. Cool!"

The strategy seemed elegantly simple.

"Hey, long as we're on the subject, there anything I can do for you this morning?"

A distraction from constantly worrying about Naseem's next attack would help...especially after hearing about the tripwire thing.

"What I'm going to say is completely off record. We clear on this?"

"I figure everything we discuss is off line."

"There *is* one thing...this is *not* intended to be construed as actionable and is for informational purposes only. Understood?"

Sounded like a classic cover-your-ass statement. If questioned under oath, he could testify to never making the next request.

"Got it."

"We wanted the basic details about her room reservation; reservation date, credit card used to hold it, and the credit card imprinted at check-in, but the management refuses to give that to us it without a court order and we can't get our hands on one for another twelve or more hours. Let's just say it'd expedite the investigation if we were to have that information sooner."

Arnold gave Chance more choobers.

"Interesting dilemma. Remind me again which hotel we're talking about?"

Fisher told him. "Hope to hear from you soon."

"Indeed."

Finally, he was all in, doing something substantial instead of some piss-ant Gunga Din shit. However, first things first.

After a quick shower, he drove Chance to the park for a short run. On the return he popped into Starbuck's for a classic breakfast sandwich and a triple-shot vente latte, both of which were a perfect temperature by the time he walked back in the house. While munching the sandwich, he pulled up the hotel website and jotted down the 800-reservation number. From there he worked back into their reservation system and eventually into the host computer.

Easy enough.

Thirty minutes later, after wiping residual grease from his fingers, he called Fisher.

"What room number she registered to?" Arnold asked.

"Eleven-oh-two."

"Hold on..." He found the room number. "Okay, got it. Ready?"

He'd briefly considered texting the information but decided a verbal message left no discoverable evidence. Particularly seeing how what he was doing was undoubtedly illegal. Not only that, but he remained seriously edgy from having the house bugged. And, for the first time, became worried about the penetrability of his security.

"I am."

"The room was reserved and imprinted with the same VISA card."

Arnold recited the number, security code, and expiration date.

"Same name as the airlines ticket; Fakhira Khan. I checked the address but suspect you'll be stunned to hear that it's bogus. I looked it up on Google Earth and it's five miles outside the Tucson city limits with nothing around but dirt and tumble weeds. That image might be a couple years old, so after we hang up, I'll double check the county property records to make sure there's been no recent development, but from the looks of it, it's seriously doubtful. I'll also backtrack the Hotmail address, see what I can dig up, but my money's on a throwaway. There anything else you want me to do?"

"Not for now. Thanks, this is good intel. I'll sic our financial guys on the card."

Fisher sounded genuinely grateful.

Arnold felt a broad grin creep over his face as he disconnected.

Just then, Chance gave a serious growl and ran to the front door as his iPhone pinged.

Who the hell was that?

He checked the security video.

Shit!

Chapter 51

A THIN, ANGULAR man, in dark blue pants and work shirt was peering through the gate, a panel truck at the curb with ABC Glass and Mirrors painted in red, white and blue on the side.

Why'd the name sound familiar?

Oh, of course! The slider.

Arnold hustled to the gate.

"Sorry to keep you waiting," and extended his hand, "Toby Taylor."

The name Gene was on the white plastic nametag above his left breast pocket and he was holding a rectangular aluminum box/clipboard. Arnold led him through house to the kitchen and the open slider where he pointed to the damage. A refreshing breeze was blowing into the kitchen.

Gene squatted, inspected the glass a moment, glanced up.

"A bullet hole?"

Fuck me, once again I have no explanation.

Of course! Who the hell has bullet holes in their house?

"Oh, is that what it is?"

Seriously? Is that the best you can do?

Gene eyed him a beat before turning back to the glass, inspecting it from various angles.

"Sure looks like one."

"Huh! When I got home yesterday there it was...I was so

pissed I didn't even think about to how it got there. Guess I just assumed some kid threw a rock or something," his babbling sounding lamer and lamer with each word.

Just shut up!

Gene stood, carefully placed the aluminum clipboard on the counter.

"I need to measure it. Someone from the office'll call you this afternoon with an estimate."

"Hey, just skip the estimate part and take care of it. I can't afford to delay on this."

Boy, that sounds desperate. Shut up, for Christssake.

"No estimate?" A shrug. "Whatever."

Gene paused to look around the kitchen, as if assessing the interior.

Arnold wiped his palms on his shorts.

Chill, dude.

"Okay, look, my bad...you're absolutely right...have someone call with the estimate. But, like I just said, I need it taken care of...the sooner the better because, ah...my mom and dad are coming back in about a week and, ah, well..." letting his words die.

With a sympathetic nod, Gene opened the aluminum clipboard and removed a sheet of multilayered carbon paper.

"Okay to use the counter?"

"No problem."

Gene pulled a measuring tape from his wide leather belt and began to measure dimensions which he duly recorded on the form.

"Where're your folks?" he asked offhandedly.

"On a cruise in South East Asia," he said, trying for a ring of authenticity.

Minutes later, Gene packed up, collected his measuring tape and pen. "Diane'll call this afternoon with the estimate."

"Thanks. But just go ahead and schedule it for the next possible opening. I'm really in a bind here...my parents will kill me if..."

"See, the problem is," now taking the tone of a grade school teacher, "this being a custom job, we don't have the panel in stock, so the glass needs to be cut to spec, so the turnaround might take upwards of two weeks."

Two weeks? He wanted—no, *needed*—the remnants of Rios' murder out of his life soon as possible. The constant reminder was becoming unbelievably depressing.

"What would be the repair time if I agree to a surcharge?"

Nothing like throwing money at a problem.

Gene's expression brightened considerably.

"I'm sure something can be arranged."

With Gene gone, Arnold returned to his desk for a deep dive into the Hotmail account used to reserve the hotel room. As suspected, the account was used for only that purpose. The search, however, wasn't a total waste of time. The originating computer, he learned, was a Dell Inspiron. Taken alone, this trivial bit of information was worthless, yet it might prove to be of future forensic importance. He filed it away.

Skype rang. Rachael? He glanced at the app. Nope, his friend—the expert in wireless device communication. He double-checked to make sure he would answer in audio only. He allowed no one but Rachael to see either his face or the interior of the house.

"I have the information you want, but before we get onto that, I need to ask how the heck you got your hands on that shit?"

"Some asshole planted them in my place. Why?"

"Because we ain't talking the level of the crap you pick up at SpyStore dot com. We're talking serious-ass, government-level shit here."

Arnold recoiled.

"For real? Like, intelligence agency shit?"

"For real. We're talking A-N-T level shit for the T-A-O," referring to the Tailored Access Operations division of National

Security Agency.

When a spook needed specialized equipment to infiltrate a computer or network, they tap ANT, their in-house geeks. Arnold wasn't sure exactly what the initials stood for, but rumor had it that it stood for Advanced Network Technology, the super geeks who develop the seriously sick James Bond gadgets.

Interesting.

How the hell did sophisticated spy equipment end up in his house?

Call finished, Arnold took the bugs to the kitchen, dropped them in a glass of water and watched a few tiny bubbles come popping out, took the glass out to the deck, set it next to the balustrade for anyone with a good pair of binoculars to see. Hopefully they cost those assholes some serious coin.

He settled into a chaise, called Fisher, explained what he just found out about them.

After a few silent seconds, Fisher said, "I assume you have a punch line to this little story?"

"Indeed. According to him, they're CIA level technology."

"How sure are you of this?"

"Personally? I don't have a clue. I'm just repeating what my friend said. But I trust him because he's a champ at this sort of thing. I'll give you one if you want, but I'm keeping the other."

"I'll send someone to pick them *both* up. They're evidence, Gold." Pause. "Nice work. To tell the truth, I forgot all about them with everything else going on."

Call finished, Arnold closed his eyes to grapple with the unrelenting conviction of forgetting something important. A flicker of it had flashed into his mind during the call, but vanished before he had time to write it down.

What the hell is it?

He brewed an espresso, carried it back to the desk to cool. In times like this, his best strategy was to concentrate on an entirely different task, something of relatively little importance. He checked his bets on the weekend games, noticed that it was only an hour until the kickoff of Thursday Night Football, but none of the players were on his Fantasy Football roster. Next, he reviewed his Bitcoin and PayPal balances. Everything appeared in order, which, under any other circumstance would've been calming, but now only fueled more anxiety.

What was he forgetting to do?

"Arrrrgggggggg!"

Alright, already, time for a serious break. He loaded Chance into the car and headed for the park.

With Chance running freely, Arnold meandered the dirt path, wracking his brain for a new slant on Naseem. In spite of kicking over every stone he could think of, he knew he forgot to do something important. What? Part of the problem was with so many things bombarding his brain in such a bam-bam-bam, rapid-fire sequence, it was forcing him to play defense, which increased the odds of really screwing up.

What could he do to put Naseem on defense?

Give up, think of something pleasant.

Rachael.

He paused to relish the memory of their brief encounter last week in Seattle. She looked beautiful, exactly how he remembered, maybe even better. How did she feel about him? Was there any chance...oh, crap, what time was it?

Time to head home.

He was meeting Loni for dinner in an hour—a meeting he was dreading.

Chapter 52

ARNOLD CURLED UP for a quick nap and immediately fell asleep, then awoke fifteen minutes later, fully refreshed. Cat napping was a skill he'd honed during coding marathons that would last days on end. Now, at the ripe age of twenty-four, he no longer pushed himself as hard. Besides, his days now included Chance, and doggies were creatures of habit who thrived on routine-structured lives. Truth be told, he also favored this more ordered existence to his previous free-range days.

He ran electric razor over his face, showered, dressed in olive cargos, blue floral aloha shirt, and Nikes sans socks, inspected himself in the mirror, decided he was presentable.

Wallet? Check.

Keys? Check.

Fly zipped? Check. Good to go.

Chance clung to his side from shower to final inspection, exhibiting his best hang-dog persona, obviously aware he wasn't included this evening. Flaps down, head lowered, he trailed Arnold into the carport. Arnold shook his head, dropped to his haunches, took the pooch's head in his hands.

"You're worse than a Jewish mother. Know that?"

Chance threw himself on the concrete, rolled onto his back. Thump-thump-thump.

"Alright, already. Stop with the guilt trip, okay?"

Thump-thump-thump.

Arnold gave him one final dose of choobers, threw in a few rabber-d-jabbers for good measure, leaned down, kissed his nose.

"Daddy goes. Chance stays. Daddy will be back."

Chance wagged his tail: okay dad.

The drive downtown was easy with rush hour now tapering off. His first pass through the restaurant neighborhood yielded nothing in the way of street parking, so he opted for the Sheraton garage in spite of the outrageous cost.

He exited through the rear of the parking lot into the alley, turned left onto Kalia Road, hung a right past the Halekulani onto Lewers Street, the whole time mentally rehearsing his strategy and the words he planned to use.

She was a great girl, and all, but...

A group of chatting Chinese tourists, four abreast, were approaching from the opposite direction, bogarting the entire sidewalk, coming straight toward him, ignoring everyone else, and eventually forcing him to step into the street to avoid being trampled. He turned and watched as they continued hogging the sidewalk, either oblivious to the chaos they were causing others or simply not giving a rat's ass. It was a time of evening the streets typically overflowed with tourists enjoying the warm tropical salt water air scented with coconut suntan lotion and car exhaust.

Ah, life in a tourist city...

He arrived at Taormina a few minutes before his reservation. Their table—his favorite—was empty, a reserved sign centered on the white tablecloth. He preferred the two tables beside the front window because of the street view. The hostess led him there straightaway. He waved away the offered menu, having memorized it months ago. Typically, he ordered the catch of the day, partly out of love of seafood, partly because he believed a diet rich in fish helped maintain good brain function. The smell of garlic oil whetted his appetite.

Loni appeared five minutes later, stunning as usual, in a sleeveless, knee-length business suit as black as her ponytail. Then again, she'd undoubtedly look spectacular in waif rags. He assumed she came straight from a meeting or showing. His nervousness spiked. Dinner was going to be a bitch.

"Have you ordered drinks yet?" she asked, eyeing him curiously.

He averted his eyes and wiped his palms on his shorts.

"No, just got here."

Right on cue, the waiter materialized.

"Something to drink while you decide on dinner?"

Loni nodded to Arnold, signaling she wanted the usual.

"We'll both have a glass of Chianti."

"Excellent choice, Mister Taylor."

She studied him with a curious, almost clinical, expression.

She knows something's up.

He began fiddling with the flatware. The restaurant noise grew more intense.

She waited.

He sucked a deep breath.

"So, how was your day?"

"What's up, Toby? You look...upset," and cocked her head.

Aw man...

He glanced out the window at the foot traffic and carefree tourists enjoying another evening in paradise.

Come on you pussy, cowboy up.

Loni waited.

He replaced the fork, smoothed the tablecloth, sighed.

"We need to talk."

"I can see that."

He swallowed, resisting the urge to play with the fork again.

"Here's the deal. I think we need to stop seeing each other."

There! The words were out. He felt a rush of relief for getting that part over with.

"You *think?* It sounds like you've already decided."

Her eyes hardened into granite nuggets.

He began to study his fingernails.

"Does it make any difference? The point is, our relationship is over."

After an exaggerated show of glancing around the immediate area, Loni's flamethrower eyes blazed into him. Slowly, precisely, she set one hand atop the other, perfectly equidistant from her knife and fork and stayed motionless for several incredibly looooong seconds. Tick-tick-tick....

"Why?"

One syllable. One word. Exploding with inquisition, accusation, acceptance, disappointment.

How does she manage to pull that shit off so effectively?

There was only person in the world who just might've been able to exceed such monosyllabic intimidation: his mother. (Bless her soul). Her eyes continued to burrow into him like a fucking optic nerve roto-rooter.

Mercifully, the waiter materialized with two glasses of dark ruby wine.

"Ready to order or do you need a few more minutes?"

"A few more minutes, please," Arnold croaked before gulping a sip of wine to wet his throat.

Like a mariachi band showing up tableside at the crux of an important conversation, the waiter—who didn't take the obvious hint to leave—launched into his canned speech, "Just so you know our specials this evening..." and continued on describing a pasta dish, the catch of the day, and a vegetarian medley.

Finally finished, he floated away.

Arnold seized the opportunity to inspect his wine. Admittedly, a wimpy diversion, but what else could you do when scrambling to get your shit together? The discussion was turning way, way more difficult than anticipated. Probably, because he'd never broken off a relationship with anyone, much less a female. Loni being his first real…what? Girlfriend?

Girlfriend? Really? Dude, that sounds so…high school.

"Why?" she asked at last, still skewering him with her glare.

For one insane sick crazy inappropriate moment, he imagined a cartoon conversation bubble floating over his head…totally and completely blank.

"Because…" he blurted. "I'm in love with someone else."

Another wave of relief swept over him. He inhaled, sat back, met her stare, and nodded.

There! It was done.

She recoiled as if physically slapped, but quickly recovered, sat back and crossed her arms defiantly.

"*That* girl in the picture?"

He started to ask, "What picture?" realized how goddamn lame it'd sound—especially on account of Rachael's picture being the target of several barbed comments from Loni—and because each time she raised the issue, he'd adroitly dodged any response.

Time to fess up.

"Yes."

She shook her head, eyes continuing to blaze contempt.

"Why did you lie to me all this time? Why didn't you tell me the truth when I asked? Why lead me on?" her voice growing louder with each syllable, to the point the couple on his left were now staring, no longer making any attempt to be discreet.

No way in hell could he explain things without going into his past, including such incriminating tidbits as terrorists and murder. Yeah, sure, given enough time, he might be able to shuck and jive his way through a plausible-enough tale. But he always tried to not spin fabrications because they were, well, just too much effort to keep straight and would eventually be a road straight into a pit of quicksand. He raised both palms in a what-can-I-say gesture.

"I don't want to discuss this any further. I'm sorry things have to end like this."

This only intensified her scorn, a feat that he'd sworn was

impossible two seconds earlier.

"Why tell me *now*? Why didn't you say something when you started *sleeping* with me?"

By now her voice was only barely below a shout.

Don't get sucked into this, because it's heading straight into a pile of dog shit.

"Look, Loni, I'm sorry. I don't know what more to say."

"No shit, you lying motherfucker!"

The chair legs screeched over concrete as she pushed back her chair. She threw her balled up napkin on the table and stormed out of the restaurant.

Chapter 53

HE FIGURED BY now every eye in the universe—well, certainly, in the restaurant—was beaming condemnation at him. Too embarrassed to look anywhere but out the window, he stared at the passing cars and people.

Just slink out?

You can't. You need to pay for the wine.

He stared at Loni's crumpled napkin, acutely aware of the eyes watching and waiting for his reaction. Ignore them long enough and they'll turn their attention to other more productive things. Their knee-jerk assumption would undoubtedly be to assume he was a complete jerk who took advantage of that poor girl.

Okay, so what? What difference did it make?

They couldn't possibly know the whole story, so how could they judge? But he knew damn well they would; without knowing the facts, people tend to side with the woman because our culture seems to demand it. Realistically, in the greater scheme of life, what the hell difference did it make? Except for the waitstaff—all of whom had previously benefited from his generous tips—he'd never see any of them again, so their fleeting ill thoughts of him meant nothing. Regardless, mortifying embarrassment tingled his face. His only relief, he knew, would come from walking out the door.

He glanced at the wine, his glass still half full, Loni's untouched. Would it be bad form to chug them both? The alcohol certainly was inviting. Especially after what just happened. Besides, he hated to see good wine go to waste. But downing both of them? That might seem...a bit tacky.

Just slink out as soon as possible, dude.

Hold on. Do they have doggy bags for wine?

Man, how totally absurd!

But the thought caused a snigger.

Oh, shit, Dude, don't start laughing now...not with everyone looking at you.

But struggling to keep the laugh corked only intensified the ridiculousness of the thought, making it funnier and funnier...until the whole frigging wine doggie bag thing just snowballed. He clamped his mouth shut with his hand and fought the brewing volcano...until...it just fucking exploded through his nose in a muffled strangled cough of wine and snot.

He could feel the stare of slack-jawed diners and discreetly tried to wipe his hand with his napkin, not daring to laugh or show his face to the audience in spite of the huge relief over the end result...as unpleasant as it was for both of them.

Life gets just so frigging complicated at times.

Five minutes later, wine finished, emotions finally in check, he waved his credit card at the waiter, who wasted no time running it through a card reader.

Arnold added an overly generous tip to the charge, partly out of fondness for the waiter, but mostly to assuage his guilt for occupying a prime table for a mere two glasses of wine. In a small place like this with slow turnover, seating was a premium. They lost business tonight because of him, but he'd make it up to them in the future.

Hopefully with Rachael.

Out on the sidewalk, leaning against the wall, he wondered how he might've handled the situation better. Well, for starters, he should've cut things off when she first showed signs of being more interested in his finances than him. And now, looking back at their relationship more objectively, he knew after their second dinner that they were never going be more than intimate friends. Well, okay, their sex was terrific, but it certainly hadn't been selfish or one sided.

His flexible schedule and lack of social entanglements made him wonderfully available for spontaneous bootie calls any time of day. Like any normal female, she had needs and wasn't too thrilled at the prospect of banging a customer or colleague. *But*, he asked himself, was he guilty of sending the wrong message? Was he the cold-hearted, selfish sonofabitch she claimed? *He* didn't think so, but knew he probably wasn't the most objective person to answer that.

Well, that relationship was finished. A relief, really. Still, he wished he might've dropped The Bomb with a bit more finesse. Hell, a lot more finesse.

Regardless of the post-game analysis, he was satisfied with the final score. Breaking up was the right thing to do. Plus, he'd no longer feel guilty about their sexual liaisons. A guilt fueled by his intense feelings toward Rachael...as if he were being unfaithful to her. How stupid was that? Seeing how they didn't even have a relationship. Yet.

A quick look at his watch. Now what? He didn't feel like going home just yet, despite knowing Chance was waiting. He felt at odds, in need of a walk, a distraction to help clear his head. Besides, being out here on the crowded sidewalks seemed to be a balm for his acute loneliness now that Loni was gone from his life.

He started along Lewers, past Don Ho Street toward Kalakaua Avenue. He loved to window-shop this stretch of main drag, checking out all the high-end stores: Furla, Bulgari, Salvatore Ferragamo, and the king of them all, Apple.

Although he could afford to splurge on a luxury item now and then, he never did. In part because he couldn't bear to throw money away over such stuff. That's what all those expensive accoutrements were: unnecessary *stuff*. He preferred to invest any extra funds in stocks and pay down the mortgage. He didn't plan to remain a gambler forever and was recently toying with the concept of returning to school.

Besides, what good did fancy shoes or high-end Swiss watches do for you other than make you feel good about yourself and, perhaps, a bit superior to those who couldn't afford the same luxury? He believed that true contentment boiled down to having those things you value most.

Future security and financial stability were at the top of his list.

He did, however, enjoy seeing how others—especially people with wealth—chose to spend money. The most over-the-top extravagant excess he'd ever seen first-hand was the luxury yacht, *A*. A year and a half-year ago he watched her cruise into Elliot Bay for a refueling stop at Pier 90. The mega-yacht's design seemed so startling and unusual that he immediately Googled it.

Up it popped in Wikipedia.

The boat was built in Kiel, Germany, for a rumored three-hundred million bucks! At three-hundred and ninety feet long, it ranked as one of the world's largest private yachts, boasting twenty-four thousand square-feet of interior space. He shook his head at the sheer excess. Who the hell had that kind of money to throw around?

Apparently, the Russian billionaire who owned it.

He stopped at the Furla window to admire the handbags, the sight triggering bitter sweet memories of his ill-fated Vegas trip, when Breeze sat him down in the mall to explain the concept of trophy purses. Looking back on the experience, the paradox was that he owed her a great deal for helping him transition to his present stage of life. *But*, he quickly reminded himself, like most valuable lessons, the tuition turned out to be extremely expensive. And, in fact, he was still paying the price.

By now, his appetite had returned, so he stopped by McDonalds for a quarter pounder with cheese and an order of fries, which he ate while meandering back to the car. He paid for the parking and headed home to take Chance on his evening walk. Yes, breaking up with Loni was now felt...liberating.

Liberating.

He had mixed feeling about that word...it sorta fit...in a Doctor Philish way, but also made him feel like celebrating. What? Hmmm...how about texting Rachael, to ask if she'd like to go with him in Maui? Excellent!

Really? What if she's already involved with someone? What if she's serious about the guy?

His gut did a back flip, his imagination running wild with that.

Reality check, dude. These are all the things that need to be settled as you start forging your new life.

On second thought, might be better to hold off messaging until he'd spent time to wordsmith a message for just the right tone. Then again, maybe perfect wording wasn't the objective.

Maybe it came down to one simple thing: did he have any sort of a chance with her?

When Arnold walked out of the garage, Chance was in the courtyard, tail going like sixty. Which was unusual. On most evenings if he spent time outside, he was curled up on the pavers or the garage concrete instead of in his doggy bed.

After a doggy kiss and a few choobers, Chance whined an unusual tone and trotted to the front gate. This warranted a look. Something was up. Chance barked once.

Arnold could barely make out a lump on a paver six inches from Chance's front paws. Using the iPhone flashlight, he kneeled for a closer look, saw what appeared to be close to a half-pound of raw hamburger. Apparently untouched by Chance. A sickening sensation flooded his gut.

"Good boy! Good boy!"

He hugged the pooch. Thank God he followed his training to not eat food from a stranger. He decided to call Fisher to tell him about it, but before dialing, just to make sure Chance didn't erroneously think the meat was okay to eat, he waved him away with a "no."

"Smart dog," Fisher said. "Hope you reward him appropriately. You touch it?"

"No, I'm afraid to. That's my next question; what should I do with it?"

"Don't touch it. We'll send someone to pick it up, have the lab run toxicology on it, see what shakes out. You never know, this could turn into something. Hang on while I make arrangements."

A moment later Fisher was back; "HPD's sending an officer. In the meantime, you reviewed your security video?"

"Not yet. I just got back. I'll do it soon as I get off this call."

"Excellent. Let me know what you come up with."

"Wait, before you go, how long you think before the police get here?"

Chance needed to be taken for a walk.

"An officer is in route. Unless there is a major diversion, they should be there in ten, fifteen minutes."

Chapter 54

ARNOLD WANTED TO be home when the car arrived, so only walked Chance to the end of the block and back. Soon as the cop picked up the hamburger, he planned on driving Chance to the park for some quality time.

They had just about reached the front gate when an HPD cruiser rolled up and a female officer stepped out and introduced herself. Arnold showed her the meat.

She squatted down, used an LED flashlight to inspect it, stood up, shook her head, muttered something unintelligible, then, "Be right back."

She returned from the patrol car wearing blue latex gloves and holding a Ziploc bag, bagged the meat, sealed the plastic, stripped her gloves, nodded at the ground.

"Better hose that area down real good to wash away any residual."

Good suggestion, hadn't thought of it. Made perfect sense.

"I'll do it right now."

Sometimes good intentions never quite pan out because Arnold ended up short-changing Chance's evening walk. Too many important jobs were still left to do before he hit the sack. In particular, he wanted to find the video of the asshole who tossed the hamburger into the courtyard.

After freshening the pooch's food and water, he rewarded him with two Wet Noses special peanut butter doggie cookies.

But before starting work on the video, he whipped up a hot chocolate by stirring a large dollop of Hershey's syrup into a mug of milk, microwaving it to temperature, then brought the mug to computer room. This task required the twenty-seven inch hi-def monitors instead of the Surface.

He began with the front gate camera starting from the time he left to meet Loni on through when he returned home. The recordings were motion activated instead of continuous, so he took the extra time to review them at normal speed instead of fast-forward to decrease the risk of missing a very brief event.

Thirty minutes later, he found the segment he was searching for, backed it up, and watched again at half speed. The asshole approached the gate by sticking next to the wall, using it as a shield from the camera. Arnold interpreted this to indicate they knew where his cameras were located. The act of tossing the hamburger was only a blur, making the video worthless for anything other than pinpointing the time: 8:03 PM.

He switched to footage from the wide-angle at the corner of the house, started the video at 8:00 PM. A car pulled to the curb in front of the neighbor's property. Arnold isolated, then enlarged the best frame of the vehicle, but streetlamp glare on the windshield plus with the vehicle's dark interior made it impossible to make out who was inside. He assumed the dashboard lights were purposely turned off.

He resumed the video at half speed, saw the passenger door open and a hooded figure step to the sidewalk and dart to the wall. He played the segment back and forth frame by frame until he isolated the best image. Big surprise, a hoodie hid his face.

His? Why did he think the thrower was a guy? Mulled that one over. Well, their walk for one thing. And then there was the throw; definitely a guy throw. But, he quickly admitted, this was only an impression with no objective proof.

Okay, anything else?

No, not really.

Clothes? Cargo shorts, Converse tennis shoes, muscular legs. Okay, the legs...another reason to think male. He sat back, sipped the hot chocolate, mulled it over some more, replayed the segment five additional times but didn't find anything new.

Okay, what about the car? A Honda? Gray or silver—the exact color difficult to determine with the hue of the mercury vapor light. Metallic paint, for sure. No fancy rims, decals, or distinguishing features other than a sticker on the front bumper to indicate a rental.

He couldn't make out the rental agency sticker.

The license plate?

Unfortunately, a palm frond obscured most of it, but he did make out two digits. Enough, he believed, for Fisher to work with. He enlarged, cropped, and sharpened the images of the vehicle and license plate, then texted them to Fisher. Did the same with the pictures of the hamburger thrower, figuring that although the face was obscured by shadows, wall, and hoodie, the FBI techs could estimate his height and weight by comparing the image to surrounding objects.

For the sake of completeness, he reviewed the recordings from the other cameras during the same time period, but they supplied nothing additional. He phoned Fisher to explain what he just sent him. The man sounded flat-line dog-dead tired.

"Plan on getting any sleep tonight?" Arnold asked.

"If I can. Why?"

"Because you sound too tired to even think straight."

"Matter of fact," Fisher added. "I was just turning off the lights. What up?"

Arnold explained the reason for the call.

He opened all the sliders to allow the trade winds to blow through the house.

Now what?

Too amped to sleep in spite of being tired as hell, but even if he couldn't sleep, it'd do him good to simply go horizontal and relax. Nothing was super urgent at the moment, so he stretched out on the bed flat on his back, closed his eyes, tried to relax but couldn't, not as long as he knew he was forgetting something important.

Shit!

Chapter 55

ARNOLD ROLLED OVER and grabbed his phone before it could ring again and realized he'd been dead asleep. Squinting, he made out Fisher's name.

Jesus, does the man ever sleep?

"Good morning," Arnold croaked, his mouth as dry as the Mojave Desert.

"Sorry to wake you but we finally caught a break. Naseem was picked up thirty minutes ago."

Arnold sat bolt upright, wide awake.

"No shit?"

Could it possibly be true?

Naw, can't possibly be.

He scratched his head and ran his tongue over his teeth.

"How'd that happen?"

"Nothing fancy. Dumb luck, actually...good ol' boots on the ground police work. A cop on routine patrol spotted her exiting an ABC store and detained her on the spot. He brought her in ten minutes ago."

Fabulous. But was that a slight tinge of doubt in Fisher's voice?

"But?"

"She claims to be Fakhira Khan, a Pakistani national here on vacation."

And there it was.

"Same as the airline ticket and the hotel reservation?"

"That is affirmatory."

Wow, definitely fucked up.

A bad feeling blossomed in his gut.

"And you believe her?"

"At the moment, I'm not sure what to believe. Sure looks like the person in the airport video—what we could see of her—and also our file picture of Naseem Farhad. Her Pakistani passport is issued to Fakhira Khan and so far, that squares with ICE. There's nothing to suggest it's not legit."

"What're you saying? She's not Naseem?"

"No. I'm just giving you the facts as we know them. For now. We're not finished with her yet...not by any stretch. I still want to run down several lines of inquiry...including those little dramas at the airport and hotel room. I have two agents working up her identity. The reason I'm calling is, we need you here ASAP. You're the only one who's seen Naseem up close and personal. How soon before you get here?"

Arnold's mind began racing..."Let's see...how does fifteen minutes sound?" Quickly reconsidered. "Where are you?"

"Thanks for asking...in the Police Commission building on Richards. Upon entering the building, identify yourself to the desk sergeant and tell him you're there to see Tanaka. We'll make sure he knows you're coming."

Arnold recalculated.

"Make that more like...forty-five minutes. I need to shower and feed Chance...." then, factoring in the maddening morning traffic, "Aw, man, don't hold me to anything...I'll be there soon as I can."

"Sooner the better. She's lawyering up, so we can't ask her anything at the moment. That's why it's urgent to nail down her identity."

Arnold dumped a can of Chance's favorite food in his dish before hitting the shower. He decided to shave in the car. He threw on a pair of sun-faded cargos, a well-worn vintage 2010 DefCon tee, black and white Nikes, and slung his rucksack over his shoulder. By then Chance was finished, so they jumped in the Mini for a quick stop at the park long enough for Chance to take his morning dump. Next came Starbucks where he grabbed a breakfast sandwich and vente latte, figuring if that wasn't sufficient caffeine, the cops had more. He scarfed the sandwich while driving.

Miraculously, he scored curb parking on Richards Street, a half block from the front of the four-story police building. With Chance on a short leash and latte in hand, he bounded up the steps and through the glass doors.

Moments later, an officer escorted him through security to a darkened stark room. The far wall featured a large rectangular window into a brightly lit interrogation room with one table and two metal chairs. The woman sat in a chair with her back to the window, making it impossible to see her face. Tanaka and Fisher appeared to be having a serious discussion. They motioned him over.

He stood at the window studying her for familiar details. Same black hair, same general build, but so what? She sat perfectly still, breathing slowly, perhaps meditating. He opened his iPhone camera to take a picture or two the moment she turned enough to catch part of her face. He'd run whatever pictures he got through SAM's facial recognition software for an objective analysis. He waited and watched.

A minute ticked slowly past.

Finally, Fisher whispered, "Her lawyer can't make it for another hour, so we just got a temporary reprieve. If you identify her as Naseem, she becomes a terrorist suspect and the whole game changes. Otherwise, we don't have diddly squat." Several more seconds slowly ticked past. "Oh, and before I forget...that hamburger? That shit was loaded with enough strychnine to kill your friend ten times over."

Arnold reached down, thumped Chance's side.

Good dog.

Training had saved his life. Soon as he had a chance, he'd email the trainer about what happened.

Without warning, the woman turned, stared directly at him as if able to see through the mirrored glass. Sent a fucking an ice cube slithering down his spine but he maintained enough presence of mind to snap three pictures before she returned to her previous position.

"Well?" Fisher asked. "What's the verdict?"

Chapter 56

ARNOLD WAS STUDYING the pictures closely. The face was close, very close, but...

"Something's not right...can't say for sure exactly what, but that's not her."

Fisher flinched as if gut-punched, but remained silent. Tanaka remained inscrutably poker-faced, silently staring.

Arnold wondered why he wasn't disappointed? Probably because he'd known it couldn't be this goddamn easy. He shook his head.

"She's messing with us. No different than that fucking charade at the airport."

"We need tangible information, Gold. Why that isn't her? Sure as hell looks like our file pictures."

Good question.

He had no a snap answer.

What was it, exactly?

Eyes closed, he concentrated on the subtle minutiae of Breeze's face, memorized during their time together. The arch of her eyebrow, the curve of her upper lip, small imperfections in complexion...was that oval black mole on her left cheek? And now, thinking about it, the more uncertain he became. Then again, maybe that's reason...the mole.

"I'm not a hundred percent on this but...that mole on her face is different. Naseem has one, yeah, just in a different location. Check your file."

Jaws clenched, knuckles blanched, Fisher glared at the ceiling tiles.

"How close to a hundred percent are you?"

"It's been a year since you last saw her, hasn't it?" Tanaka asked hopefully.

"Hundred percent? Never. Death's the only hundred percent thing I know of. I'm just saying that woman *isn't* her."

"No doubt at all on that?" Fisher asked, a vein on his right temple bulging.

Arnold shook his head.

"I'd put money on it. Believe me, no one in this room's more bummed about this than me. Something's different about her...I can't say for sure exactly...the mole is one thing..." An idea hit: "She doesn't have an identical twin, does she? Seriously...I mean, because that woman's that close."

"Look, Gary, we can't afford to fuck this one up," Tanaka said.

Fisher nodded. "Yeah, yeah...copy that." Then to Arnold, "Before we call it quits, I want you to step in there, get in her face, see if that changes your mind. Do that and I'll accept your answer. You onboard with that?"

Yeah, he'd do it, but knew it was unnecessary, that it wouldn't change his mind.

"Yeah, I'm good...so long as long as I can keep from bitch-slapping that smug smirk off her face."

"Seriously, Gold?"

"Just...no, I'm good...got it totally under control. I'm just saying..."

Fisher studied him a moment longer, turned to Tanaka.

"I want this recorded. Every fucking second."

Tanaka nodded.

"Locked and loaded."

Arnold kneeled down to Chance. "Daddy goes. Chance stays."

They were outside the door, Fisher's hand on the knob, rehearsing exactly how he wanted this to play.

"Soon as I open the door, you step in. Don't say a word. Just look her in the eye. I'll be watching over your shoulder." Fisher turned to Tanaka, "Ready?"

The detective nodded. "We're rolling."

"Alright then, let's do this."

Fisher opened the door and stepped aside for Arnold to enter.

The woman looked at him, smiled.

"Hello, Arnold. It's been a long time."

The air was suddenly gone from his lungs, making the room swirl around him. He turned, reached for the door jamb, fighting to stand long enough to get the hell out of there. He finally stumbled back into the hall. Fisher slammed the door behind him. He bent over, hands on knees, gasping for air.

Fisher put his hand on Arnold's shoulder.

"You okay?"

"God*damnit!*" Tanaka slammed his fist against into his palm, again and again, *smack-smack-smack*, the three of them back in the observation room, Arnold's left hand against the wall for support, still working on filling his lungs. Fisher was at the window, hands in pockets, silently glowering.

Chance whimpered and licked his hand. Arnold bent down to massage his neck, comforting them both.

"Oh, man, she's close!" Arnold said to no one in particular. "I mean, *really, really* close," his index finger a half inch from his thumb for emphasis. "But that voice…that's not Naseem."

"No doubt at all?" Fisher asked.

"Ninety-nine-point nine percent. She's not in that room."

Silence. Fisher continued staring as Tanaka did a slow burn, clenching and unclenching his fists, eyes riveted to the concrete floor. Arnold fought to keep from bolting from the building, just putting as much distance as he could between himself and this fucked-up situation.

"Naseem's probably laughed herself sick by now. Shit!"

Fisher nodded.

"This's not the first time I've seen this shit happen. Three years ago, DEA was on to a dealer in Tijuana. Piece of shit did pretty much the same."

Tanaka, appeared on the verge of popping a coronary, continued studying the floor.

"I don't get it," Arnold said.

"Get what?" Fisher snapped.

"How's she knows it's me? She called me Arnold, not Toby...my real name, dude! How's she know that?"

Fisher fired back.

"Seriously?"

Took a moment, before it clicked.

"Okay...wasn't thinking, is all..."

Fisher blew a slow breath, raked his fingers through his hair.

"Not your fault, Gold. It's just..."

He shook his head, unable to finish.

"She's well coached, probably shown a couple pictures," Arnold said to no one in particular. "Meaning, of course, she's either been in contact with Naseem or someone close to her. Right?"

"You think?" Tanaka thumped his forehead. "Wow! How the hell didn't I think of that!"

Fisher signaled time-out.

"Hey, no use beating up on each other. We've got a situation, is all. Let's deal with it."

Tanaka gave a disgusted snort before turning to the window.

"So, tell me," Arnold said to Fisher. "How's this supposed to work?"

"She's a decoy. While we're here jerking off," with a nod toward the interrogation room, "Naseem's out there gathering intel. Think about it; in a matter of days she knows several things.

She knows you're alive, where you live, that you're working with us...and, far as she goes," pointing at Naseem's double, "maybe she hopes to get lucky and we'll take the bait and stop looking for her. You have to admit, she's damn near perfect."

"I buy that," said Tanaka. "Thing I don't get is shooting Rios. What'd that get them?"

"That," Fisher replied, "was a mistake. Nothing else makes sense."

"And the hamburger?" Tanaka asked. "How's that work?"

Arnold was wondering the same thing.

Fisher said, "Naseem knows the dog's guarding the house, so that's a damn good reason to neutralize him. Plus, she gets some revenge if it succeeds. And even if Gold finds it, that causes fear. After all, she's a terrorist. Creating terror is what they do for a living."

Arnold agreed with that.

Yet...

"There must be some useful information you can get off her."

"We'll try, but with her lawyering up there's not a lot we *can* do. She'll be out of here two minutes once her lawyer arrives."

Arnold's head felt ready to explode. He wanted to scream.

"No, hold on...there's no way this is just coincidence. The timing doesn't fit."

"What are you talking about?" Fisher asked.

"Think about it; this took planning, right? She recognized me, right?"

"Yes." Fisher said.

"That means she's seen a picture of me."

"And your point is?"

"That woman landed two days *after* Davidson did. That means Naseem had to set it up *before* the Al Jazeera story came out."

"New flash, Gold. I get it. I agree. But what you don't seem to understand is we have nothing to hold her on."

Shaking his head, Arnold took Chance's leash.

"You need anything more from me or can we go now?"

Fisher raised a questioning eyebrow at Tanaka—who shook his head.

Fisher said, "Make sure your phone's on. You'll need to come back sooner or later, but yeah, we're done for now."

Tanaka walked them to the front door and into the bright humid air.

They were almost at the car when he realized he forgot to tell Fisher about Davidson's devices being hacked.

Go back, tell him?

He thought about it. Something was holding him back.

What?

Well, for one thing, if Fisher thought the devices were bugged, he'd have the Bureau's techs all over it and Arnold wasn't willing to relinquish that part just yet.

Chapter 57

ARNOLD HEADED STRAIGHT home in spite of feeling guilty for neglecting Chance's walk, but rationalized it by planning on a longer one later, after he learned everything he could about Khan. He dumped the car at the curb rather than waste the time waiting for the gate to open. Chance peeled off for the garage instead of going inside with him.

Arnold began by running the pictures of Fakhira Khan through SAM's facial recognition. Along with that processing, he Googled her name, but it coughed up more hits than anyone could reasonably handle. Narrowing the list down to the right person turned out to be more difficult than expected, especially with Khan such a common name.

He took a quick break to the kitchen for an espresso and when he returned, SAM had an answer. Small problem: the articles were in Punjabi. He started churning them through Google Translate. Ten minutes later he knew Khan's identity. He dialed Fisher.

"I dug up good info on Khan," he told Fisher. "Guess what?"

"She's a Bollywood actress from Mumbai. That it?"

He was stunned. "How'd you find out?"

"Extraordinarily canny police work. I interviewed her. She's extremely forthcoming, even gave us her website. You checked that out yet?"

Earth to Arnold: there were sources other than the Internet to obtain information. Thank God Fisher couldn't see his face.

He gulped the dregs of the bitter espresso.

"Glad to know she's cooperating. She didn't happen to mention who put her up to this, did she?"

"Nope. But we're far from wrapping up this interview. Both she and her lawyer have no problem cooperating. Here's the Cliff Notes version: an unidentified person initially contacted her by courier. Since then everything else's been transacted anomalously over the Internet. She claims to have never laid eyes on the person or people she works for."

"Internet? We're talking email?" Jesus, if there was any chance….."Can you send me copies?"

"Don't see a reason not to...*after* our tech's finished with them. At the moment, our biggest concern's the chain of evidence in case any of this turns out to be worthwhile. Our tech rattled off some mumble jumble about triggering an alarm in the account, so she's taking extreme caution."

Excellent.

He agreed with being careful, but did the tech really know how to sidestep *all* the potential traps? Yeah, probably. The Bureau's geeks were no slouches.

"What about the timing thing?"

Fisher hesitated before saying, "What?"

"This whole look-alike double thing. If Naseem didn't know I was alive until ten days ago, how the hell did they dig up a double, prep her and get her here so quickly?"

"That, Gold, was one of our first questions. Very simple: this ain't her first rodeo with them. She's stared in four other bit parts here in the States and Europe over the past year."

Fuck me!

His brilliant question sounded idiotic.

"Who's *them?*" he snapped. "Sorry. Didn't mean to sound like that."

"No offense, because that, sir, is the mother of all questions and is exactly what we intend to find out. That said, as much I enjoy chitchatting…I have more pressing matters to deal with."

"Wait. One more thing: you got someone working the money angle, right?"

"You mean, how she's paid? No, we're not there yet."

"Send me anything—anything at all—you want researched."

The FBI geeks were good, but also very busy, and there were only so many hours in a day.

"Roger that."

He called Davidson, brought him up to speed on Naseem's double and the ongoing interrogation.

Who gave a shit if his phones were monitored and Naseem knew about the call?

"She must know something that will help find her," Davidson said.

"One would think. I have a hard time believing she's a total dead end."

"Fisher is correct about one thing. They have nothing to charge her with. We should be happy she is cooperating."

Call finished, Arnold grabbed Chance's leash, headed for the door, realized he was forgetting something, backtracked to the kitchen, stuffed four special peanut butter doggy biscuits in his rucksack, headed back out to the car determined to compensate for shortchanging Chance that morning.

Chapter 58

ARNOLD WORKED HIS way through thick traffic toward Puu Ualakaa State Park, one of Chance's favorites. He loved the place for the spectacular city views. The only reason they didn't visit it daily was the pain-in-the ass traffic, which he swore was worse than Seattle's. If that could be even remotely possible.

Two blocks from the freeway underpass he stopped to pick up a ham and cheese on rye, two bottles of chilled Evian, and a lunch-size bag of Maui chips. Minutes later, they were tooling up Round Top Drive to Nutridge Street, then along the narrow, curving asphalt to the viewpoint parking lot. The road ended at three concrete posts, beyond which a winding dirt path led to a pergola with a spectacular view of Honolulu and Diamondhead. He parked at the end to the lot, far as possible from tourists. Their usual walk was to stroll back along the road for a mile or so before turning around to return to the car.

He packed the water bottles, sandwich, and doggy biscuits into the rucksack, locked up, paused to savor the drop-dead perfect weather. Eighty degrees, a refreshing salt air breeze, puffy white clouds shot-gunning an azure sky.

What could be more perfect?

As they strolled the narrow two-lane blacktop driven up just moments ago, Chance sprinted ahead, darting in and out of thick clumps of Bana grass and lush palms, sniffing shrubs and leaving strategic markers. Soft humid air scented with the fragrance of tropical flowers, produced a lovely refreshing contrast to the ever-pervasive downtown odor of rotting garbage and car exhaust.

Although he missed so many facets of Seattle, Honolulu's tropical climate surpassed the fall and winter months of Seattle's ever-present, gray, bone-chilling overcast. If things worked out as hoped, he'd be able to merge both lifestyles; winter here, summer in Seattle. Not at all complicated. If—and this was huge—he could reclaim his old life, he could afford to live both places. What an ideal arrangement. Too ideal. Ideal situations happened to other people, not to him. Still...he'd give it his best shot.

Would Rachael want to live both places?

She'd love it. Probably.

Assuming, of course...

He pulled out his phone. Go ahead, dial. No, wait. Wait until....

I hate this shit!

A biblical irony seemed in control of his life: his greatest asset, SAM, was also greatest liability, a lightning rod for this present clusterfucked life. None of this would've happened if he hadn't shot off his mouth in Vegas. For him, what happened in Vegas sure as hell didn't stay in Vegas. Why had he been so stupid? What insecurity compelled him to prove to Breeze that he possessed more skill than an ability to sign Visa slips? It was flat-out embarrassing. Worse yet, he was still paying through the nose. If he could reverse the clock fourteen months....

On the other hand, if, through some time-warp miracle, he could change the past and not make that trip to Sin City, where would he be now? No telling. Certainly not here. Every action produces unique consequences. There would be, however, major differences: Howie would still be alive. Meaning, his funeral never would've occurred, meaning he never would've wrapped his arms around Rachael, meaning....

Alright already! Enough!

He continued along the road, allowing Chance ample time to enjoy himself while he wracked his brain for some way to find Naseem for Fisher before could she nailed his ass. Sooner or later the FBI, CIA, or Homeland Security would run her down, but that might just be too late for him. There had to be something he could do but couldn't think of what that might be.

The sound of a car engine approaching broke his train of thought. He stepped off the narrow asphalt.

"Heel."

Chance obediently trotted over, tongue out, tail wagging, then abruptly turned and growled. Arnold rested a hand on the pooch's head as the engine accelerated, growing louder, coming fast from around the curve ahead. Strange...most vehicles slowed for that curve. He looked to see if they could step further off into the shoulder of the road. Not really, the thick vegetation made it almost impossible.

Suddenly a black Ford Escape squealed around the bend, barreling straight for him.

Don't they see us?

Arnold waved frantically at the oncoming SUV but it accelerated.

"Come!"

Arnold plunged into the dense foliage, Chance at his heels.

Mother fucker!

He started to flash the driver the finger when the vehicle screeched to a stop.

He did a double take.

Shit, it's them!

An adrenaline surge hit, focusing the image with hyperintensity. Time froze, cars doors slammed, a command was shouted.

"Come!"

Arnold wheeled around, started running away from the road, crashing through thick knee-high grass, Chance at his heels, not barking. He saw a narrow dirt trail ahead and bolted for it, as footsteps crashed through the jungle behind them, followed by a muttered curse.

Shit, they're gaining.

Arnold forced his legs to pump harder. He wasn't a runner, yet was putting every ounce of energy and willpower into each step as hard as he could. The path continued to curve up the side of the ravine, melding into steeper terrain ahead, his legs straining beyond anything imaginable, moving him steadily up the slope in spite of occasional slip-sliding in the volcanic scree. He sprinted another fifty yards, slowed to glance behind them.

Goddamnit! They're still there, coming fast.

He sped up again, rucksack pounding his back with each step, making balance tricky. Out of habit, he'd slung the pack over only one shoulder and it was now killing him, but there was no time to adjust it.

Just toss it?

No. They would need the water if they ever managed to get out of this mess.

Fat drops of sweat flew from his face as others slithered down his body, his lungs pleading for oxygen. The path forked and Arnold continued on the uphill climb, hoping—no, praying—they'd turn downhill.

Yeah, until it dawned them...

The incline steepened; the foliage now sparser in rocky volcanic dirt. He could hear them scrambling up the trail behind him and caught a glimpse of a dense group of palms surrounded by a thick clump of low vegetation. He dove for it, Chance following. He rolled to his feet, scurried behind a palm tree, crouched, cautiously peeked around the trunk and now could barely see the trail through the foliage. Good. They were hidden.

Well, maybe not so good.

If he could see any part of the trail, they could see him too...maybe...but only if they looked very closely. The vegetation might just hide him.

At least now he wasn't on the open trail. He remained in a crouch, muscles tensed, ready to bolt again. Chance was panting loudly.

He placed a reassuring hand on his neck and whispered, "No bark."

Chance understood but just to be sure, Arnold flashed the hand-signal to him.

His breaths were coming in hard, ragged, sucking gulps, his lungs fighting to repay the oxygen his muscles were screaming for. This short break might just work to his advantage if those assholes continued past...until they realized...at least it was giving him an opportunity to catch his breath.

It dawned on him just how loud their breathing sounded, so he covered his mouth with his hand but didn't dare risk doing the same with Chance for fear of freaking him. To his amazement, Chance pushed his muzzle into Arnold's armpit, muffling his pants too. Arnold wanted to hug and praise him but instead just nuzzled him. They stayed very still, listening for movement and scanning the thick jungle at the trail, Chance's ears scanning side to side. He heard only the rustle of palm fronds and bird calls.

Where the hell are they?

Suddenly, came a harsh hushed whisper—just two staccato words, a command maybe—from off to his right. Followed by a second whisper, further away, from a different location. They probably separated at the fork in the trail instead of committing to only one path.

He strained for other sounds but heard nothing new.

There! Two distinct whispers. Closer now.

How many people were inside when the SUV screeched around the curve? Had no idea. He was too fixated on the driver's determined eyes.

Silence. Another birdcall. The breeze gusted, palms swayed, then the crunch of gravel underfoot. Closer still.

Chance tensed. Slowly, gently, Arnold squeezed his neck reassuringly. They were pack. They'd protect each other no matter what.

Another whisper. Closer still. Arnold's eyes searched the vegetation. Nothing. A gruffer voice whispered back, louder still.

Silence.

Then...one more footstep.

Jesus, how much closer could they get without running smack into us?

A shadow flickered past a tall clump of grass directly ahead. Two seconds later a second a second shadow passed the same spot.

They're trying to follow my footsteps.

He waited.

Silence. Another curt, muffled whisper.

What the hell language was that?

Clearly, one person was in charge.

Shit, shit, shit. They figured it out.

A twig broke.

Did they split up again?

Thank God his breathing was quieter now, almost back to normal yet every muscle in his body was burning in pain. Chance raised his snout, sniffing, tracking scents...giving a soft growl. Arnold tapped his head.

Stop it.

Silence.

A shadow fell across the trail again.

Could they see him? Maybe. Maybe, not.

Make a break for it? And go where? Bushwhacking through this shit would be crazy noisy, slow, and too easy to follow. Yeah, but what other choice was there? Stay here and be found? It sounded like they were heading straight for him. Besides, it was too late now. His only option would be to wait it out, see what happened, and pray they missed him.

The crunch of brush underfoot...then another.

A man suddenly filled the small clearing dead ahead and

Arnold was staring straight into his face. Malaysian?

What the fuck do I know? Filipino, Chinese, Thai. Could he tell a difference?

The Asian cocked his head, listening.

Jesus, the fucker must be able to hear my thoughts.

Don't be ridiculous.

Arnold held his breath. Slowly, the man made another tentative step toward him. Now Arnold could see all of him—including the chrome-plated pistol in his hand.

I know him...and flashed on the airport video, the man with Naseem's double. He hadn't caught a clear view at his face in the video, so this feeling of recognition was nothing more than Gestalt.

A second man suddenly appeared behind the first, muttering something. The leader turned and exchanged whispers. Then, to Arnold's horror, the leader turned toward him again and swept the gun in an arc from right to left.

I'm fucking toast! Should've run when I had the chance. Too late now.

He fought an almost overwhelming urge to bolt, to just make a break for it. Take his chances.

Don't dare move. Not now, not with that asshole breathing down your neck, pointing a gun at you.

The leader took another slow cautious step forward, the second man falling in behind, both sets of eyes searching the jungle ahead.

The leader stopped so close that Arnold was peering straight into his eyes.

Why doesn't he see me?

The man turned, whispered. The other one nodded, moved to Arnold's right.

Arnold motioned Chance to get ready, but the shepherd's leg muscles were already quivering with tension, his teeth bared and glistening. Suddenly, the tall clump of Bana grass directly in front of Arnold's face swept aside. The attacker's eyes widened in surprise.

Chapter 59

CHANCE WAS ALREADY airborne, lunging for the man's wrist before Arnold could spring. The shepherd's jaws ripped into flesh and bone as eighty pounds of hurtling muscle slammed his chest, the impact sending him flailing backwards onto razor-sharp Bana grass. Growling viciously, jaws clamped to his wrist, Chance flung his head from side to side.

The screaming Malaysian tried to wrench his arm from Chance's bone crushing jaws, but this only made matters worse, for Chance was on all fours now, whipping his head back and forth with deeply ingrained strength and fierceness. Enraged, Arnold dropped knees first into the man's face, producing a nauseating crunch of bones. The gun fell from the man's hand. Arnold dove, scooping it up.

Chance gave one last savage jerk, creating a sickening snap as bone and skin tore. Just then, the second man came crashing through jungle toward them. Arnold pointed the gun in the general direction and squeezed off a deafening bang.

Then they were bounding full-out down the same trail they'd climbed moments ago, heading for paths he knew intimately, not bothering to glance behind them for fear it'd slow them, scrambling as fast as possible without stumbling or sliding on loose dirt. Then they were streaking past the black Ford and cut right, jogging the road for another fifty feet before picking up a trail he knew would lead into another ravine and eventually out into a familiar neighborhood.

He ran flat-out another hundred feet before stopping to catch his breath and to listen for footsteps. He seriously doubted they'd follow, especially considering how badly injured the first man must be. He could hear only his own raspy breathing, Chance's panting, and more rustle of vegetation in the breeze. He glanced at the chrome-plated gun in his right hand and became acutely aware of how heavy it felt. He knew absolutely zip about guns, so didn't have an idea of the make or caliber, but the cops would, so decided to keep it for Fisher and Tanaka.

He shrugged off the rucksack, uncapped a water bottle, sucked down two long pulls before letting Chance lap the remainder from his cupped palm. Then he carefully placed the gun in the pack, made sure it was secure, and this time, slipped both straps over his shoulders.

With his attackers apparently not following, he paused to check the signal on his cell, but as suspected, it didn't even register one bar of strength in this ravine. A little less afraid now, he rested for three more minutes to allow their hearts and lungs to recuperate. Finally, he started walking again, but at a more relaxed pace. In spite of the brief rest, his nerves felt like high voltage wires and his hands were shaking and his legs wobbling, so progress was now slow and stumbly, making him marveled at having made it this far downhill without going ass over teakettle.

By the time the dirt path leveled out into a residential street the cell strength was up to two bars, so he sat on the sun-baked dirt to call Fisher.

"The man on the airport video?" He blurted between gasps, his words coming faster than his thoughts, "The one with Naseem?" adrenalin still zinging his nerves and causing his hands to shake, thumping the iPhone against his ear, "just tried to kill me."

It took him three more jumbled tries to get the story out,

complete with the location of the black Ford SUV. But he was pretty damn sure that by now, there was little to no hope of the police catching those fuckers anywhere within miles of the park, but they now knew the description of the vehicle, so....

"Hang on." A moment later Fisher was back. "HPD's got cars on the way there now, but chances are they're long gone. Guess how far depends on just how bad their injuries are. The one Chance took care of...he alive when you ran?"

Good question.

"Far as I know, but he's hurt bad. Chance was totally serious once he got his teeth into him. For sure his arm's broken and his face...shit that's got to be a mess...probably a ton of broken bones...but far as I know, the other one's not injured."

He neglected any mention of taking a pot shot in his general direction. He'd be surprised if the bullet got anywhere close to twenty feet of him.

"Hold on."

He could hear Fisher pass on the information, probably to Tanaka, then was back, "What was the make and color of the vehicle?"

Arnold described it as a black Ford SUV, remembered the surfboards on top, so threw in that detail. Problem was, the island was crawling with gazillions of similar vehicles, surfboards included.

"Where're you now?"

He told Fisher the street.

"Stay there, don't move, we'll send a car to pick you up. In the meantime, we'll alert the clinics for a man with facial and wrist injuries. Say again which arm?"

"Right wrist."

He cringed at the memory of Chance's jaw tearing into it.

"If it's as bad as you say, he's in need of some serious medical attention. Hey, Gold, this could be break we need to break this open."

Chapter 60

AFTER DISCONNECTING FROM Fisher, Arnold continued to sit on the warm dirt and tried to calm down, knowing it'd be difficult to stand again with his legs so shaky. His muscles ached and his hands wouldn't stop trembling, so instead he sat there and hugged his knees and tried to concentrate on slow, deep breaths, but couldn't get the sight of the chrome pistol aimed him out of his head.

He hugged Chance and kissed his forehead, repeating, "Good boy!" before rewarding him with a barrage of behind-the-ears choobers and finally, two peanut butter cookies.

Chance understood "good boy," but more than the words, he could read Arnold's emotions uncannily. The two of them were pack and would protect each other without question. Arnold shared the last bottle of water with him before giving him the two remaining biscuits.

Finally calm enough to attempt to stand, he wiped his palms across the chest of his sodden t-shirt, then wearily shouldered the rucksack. For a moment after getting up, he remained still, waiting for the initial dizziness to subside before starting down the final stretch of trail. Thirty seconds later they entered the familiar neighborhood. Except for a smattering of cars along the curb, the street remained empty. He slowly walked the sidewalk toward the corner.

Two minutes later a patrol car crept down the street toward him so he stepped into the road and waved. The car pulled alongside and the driver side window whirred down.

"You Taylor?"

"I am."

"Get in. I'm to drive you downtown."

"Tell you what…take me up to the view spot instead. My car's there."

Arnold and Chance climbed into the back seat which smelled vaguely of stale vomit, urine, and sweat.

They pulled into the parking lot where two police cars were already parked with their misery lights flashing and two officers talking to four touristy looking people. Arnold and Chance climbed out of the car and thanked the driver for the ride. His Mini appeared exactly as he left it.

On the drive back to town, it dawned on him that he'd no idea where Fisher was, so phoned him. Fisher gave instructions to come to the FBI Field Office.

Field office? Where the hell is that?

"Siri, where's the Honolulu FBI building?"

Google Maps popped up with the route diagramed.

The field office—a fortress containing enough reinforced concrete to withstand a direct nuclear missile hit—looked like a huge rock island floating in a sea of asphalt, the building and humongous parking lot bordered by cyclone fence topped with parallel rows of concertina wire. He pulled up to the guard house and gate, lowered his window.

A stern-faced dude in a black uniform leaned in, eying him and the interior.

"Sir, state your business here, please."

"I'm meeting Special Agent Fisher."

The guard leaned back to give the Mini a visual once-over.
"Name?"

Good question.

Did Fisher tell them to expect Arnold Gold?

Arnold swallowed.

"Toby Taylor," since that's the name on his driver's license.

Good thing, too, because the guard held out his hand.

"Identification."

He passed him his license. After comparing him to the picture, the guard returned it.

"Park in the lot to your left," with a vague wave in the general direction of expansive sweltering asphalt only slightly smaller than Lake Huron.

Arnold and Chance crossed over sun baked asphalt to sun-baked concrete on to the front door and another uniformed officer who verified his name and nature of business. Apparently satisfied, the guard pointed to a row of molded plastic chairs.

"Have a seat. I'll call up."

While waiting, he checked his email and texts. Nothing needed an immediate answer, so he pocketed the phone and shut his eyes in another useless attempt to release the tension still zinging him. But without a distraction the memory of the close call remained a vivid endless loop.

Shit!

Out came the phone again. He opened the CNN app but couldn't concentrate.

Fisher finally materialized, had Arnold sign in and submit to an optical fingerprint scan before being handed visitor badges for both Chance and himself complete with a stern warning to keep them clearly displayed at all times and to surrender them before being allowed to exit the building. While slipping off the rucksack at the security scanner it dawned on him....

Holy shit!

Hands in the air, pack on the floor, he backed away from the conveyer belt.

"Agent Fisher?"

Fisher circled back through the checkpoint scanners.

"What?"

"The gun's in here," with a nod at the rucksack.

"Gun? What gun?"

"The Malaysian's...the guy Chance attacked."

Fisher grimaced.

"In there?"

"Yes."

His face radiating heat.

"Loaded?"

With a shrug, "Yeah...I guess...thing went off," and discretely neglected any mention of being the one to pull the trigger.

"Keep your hands up like that and take three steps back. Do *not* make any attempt to reach for it."

Twenty minutes later, the handgun was now in an evidence bag on its way to the lab, Arnold and Chance finally made it through the security, Arnold keeping Chance close. They rode an elevator to a third-floor office where Tanaka waited at a small oval table, working on a laptop.

Once all were seated, Fisher asked Arnold to take them through the encounter. During the narration, he kneaded Chance's neck, occasionally pausing to praise him.

"Why do you say Malaysian?" Fisher asked.

Good question.

He finger-combed his hair and thought about it.

"Nothing in particular, I guess...just came to mind..." A shrug. "Looks like a dude I know from there...did I mention he resembles the one at the airport? With Naseem?"

Fisher made a note on a legal pad. Arnold slipped out of the chair, knelt beside Chance and began to pet him.

Tanaka's phone rang.

The detective glanced from the screen to Fisher, "Excuse me, I better take this. Could be something," and hurried from the room, closing the door behind him. Fisher asked another question about the Malaysian.

Tanaka returned with a broad smile. Fisher stopped in mid-sentence.

"What up?"

"A couple hikers just called in body off the John Burns Freeway. The responding officer says it's a match for the Malaysian."

Fisher's eyebrows shot up.

"A body? As in dead?"

He began collecting his cell, keys, and pen from the table.

Tanaka shut the laptop.

"Seriously dead. Face stove in, just like the kid said. Severe gash on the right wrist. The officer says the hand looks almost ripped clean off." Then to Arnold; "The two of you must've put a real hurt on that piece of shit." To Fisher, "I'm running out there now. Want to tag along or finish up?"

Fisher turned to Arnold, "We'll finish up later. Right now, you need to vacate the building with us. Your car here?" and finished stuffing his items back in his pockets.

"Why don't I come?" Then quickly added, "I need to identify the body anyway, right? Confirm he's our guy?"

Fisher turned to Tanaka; "Your call." Then, as a side note to Arnold, "Until it's confirmed as a terrorist, it's their show."

Tanaka shrugged.

"Kid's got a valid point...we need to settle that issue right off the bat."

Fisher was herding Arnold and Chance into the hall now, on toward the stairs.

"Stay out the way unless instructed differently. Do *not* touch anything. Just stay out the way. I'm serious as a Fukhshima meltdown." Then to Tanaka, "The kids can ride in back."

Tanaka blasted through the stairwell door without waiting for the elevator.

"What's the story on how they found him?" Fisher asked as they were pulling away from the parking lot security gate, Tanaka at the wheel of an unmarked motor pool car.

"Pretty straightforward. Couple hikers see what looks like a body, walk over for a better look, realize what they're seeing, called 911."

Arnold was leaning forward trying to make out their words over the cacophony of road noise and full blast A/C, Fisher's back wedged between in the seat and passenger door, half turned toward Tanaka.

"And the noted cause of death?"

Tanaka—focused more on driving than chatting—was steadily accelerating through traffic, in route to freeway H1 Arnold suspected, the speedometer passing seventy now. Once they settled into the appropriate lane, he settled into the seat.

"That's the interesting thing. Officer thinks there's a small caliber entrance wound to the back of the head. Says there wasn't any doubt about the vic being deceased, so didn't mess with the body...but that's the way it looks to him."

"Executed, huh." Fisher shook his head slowly. "Must've needed more than a bandage. His good buddies probably assumed we had the clinics on alert, so decided to take care of the problem themselves. Man, sure is cold!"

Arnold was holding tight to Chance's collar to keep him from sliding around the slick upholstery. Tanaka toggled on the siren and strobes as they flew past Pearl Harbor.

"Sounds about right."

Tanaka took the ramp up over H1 to H3—the John Burns Freeway—that transects the island in between volcanoes.

"Place we're going's an undeveloped off-ramp," Tanaka

explained. "A real pain in the ass to reach from this direction because it's off the oncoming lanes," with a nod toward the road. "No way to cross over until you're almost on the other side of the valley, which is just about the other side of the island...makes for a long haul out but a chip shot return."

Eventually, Tanaka exited onto what might someday be an operable off-ramp, but for now dead-ended at a wall of four end-to-end concrete barriers two hundred feet off the freeway. Three patrol cars were scattered haphazardly at the end of the road, lights flashing as a cop was setting up a line of dayglow pink cones to keep vehicles out of the area. Two news choppers were hovering overhead and Arnold saw a cameraman aiming a huge lens out a side window.

Fisher unclicked his seatbelt and said, "Stay here until we call you over. Got it?"

"No problem."

Arnold was happy just to be out of the goddamn backseat. He bet Chance agreed.

He paced beside the right fender, craning for a glimpse of the body, but the view was blocked by cops milling around. He realized he couldn't remember what the asshole was wearing but, then again, clothes hadn't been the focus of his attention. He realized he couldn't see anything so walked Chance to the side of the off-ramp for some quality shrubbery sniffing. Chance was already panting in the heat so Arnold opened bottle of water for them.

"Yo, Gold!"

He glanced toward the voice, saw Fisher wave him over to the cop cluster, shortened Chance's leash, trotted over. The body was on its back, face turned away from the freeway, insects buzzing around it, a thick pool of blackened dried blood on the concrete.

Arnold dropped to his haunches for a closer look and was momentarily shocked by the pallor and trauma, the face barely recognizable. Still, there was no doubt this was the asshole. A strange emotional brew boiled up; relief, sorrow, and joy from knowing the person who wanted him dead was, instead, the one to die. But also realized that one more person had been wasted because of him.

What was the total now?

Four? Howie, Karim, Rios, and now him. He felt as if a weird gravitational death field surrounded him. He hated that.

Huh?

Tanaka just asked a question.

Arnold stood up.

"Yeah, that's him."

"No doubt at all?" Tanaka asked, obviously surprised by Arnold's conviction.

"No doubt at all." Chance growled softly. "He agrees," with a nod in the pooch's direction.

The cops laughed.

"In that case, you're done here. Thanks," Tanaka said. "Wait by the car and I'll find someone to take you back. We'll finish up your statement later. Thanks for your help."

Arnold meandered back to the car as Chance returned to investigating shrubbery. He settled down on the cracked, weedy cement in the shade of the fender, leaned his back against the warm metal, closed his eyes, tried to think of something positive and pleasant...like Rachael, but couldn't stop the constant memory loop; the Ford barreling straight for him, the gun aiming at his head.

Would he ever forget? No, probably not.

The mind doesn't toss out memories of such pivotal life events. And, for the first time, he realized the difference between pain and suffering; pain stops the moment a noxious stimulus is removed whereas suffering remains for the life of a memory. Howie's murder taught him the horror of PTSD.

On top of everything else there floated the knowledge of forgetting to do something important.

What?

It flickered vaguely into consciousness then vanished...then returned...

Holy shit! The license plate.

The color...white. There's more. Before another distraction wiped it out again, he dictated it into his iPhone.

Okay, what else?

Ahhh, yes, the first two letters: HG.

He jumped up, yelled, "Hey, Agent Fisher! Just remembered something."

Fisher passed the license plate information to Tanaka, who got The Big Blue machine rolling on it.

Fifteen minutes Tanaka brought over a beefy uniformed officer.

"Fisher and I need to stay and wrap this up, so Kalua'll run you back. Appreciate all your help on this. As of five minutes ago, every swinging dick on the island's looking for that Ford."

He shook Arnold's hand.

"You'll call if something breaks?"

Although anxious to get back to work, he wanted to make certain of remaining in the loop.

Tanaka grinned.

"Count on it."

Chapter 61

HE ENTERED THE house expecting it to be calming, but it didn't help at all. He stood at entrance to the great room fighting an almost overwhelming urge to scream or throw something or...wasn't quite sure what...just do *something* to release the pressure cooker in his head. He dropped into a living room chair, but immediately needed to stand, so walked to the deck to gaze at Diamondhead.

Shit!

This didn't do a thing for him either. And knowing he forgot to do something important was like acid eating away at his brain.

Do something to relax, dude. Yeah? Like what?

Back in the kitchen, he looked around. A beer?

Hell, why not?

He settled into the deck chaise with a beer. Five minutes later, nerves still high-voltage power lines, he tried to meditate. Didn't work. The stillness shrouding the house—usually soothing—only amped his edginess. He sucked down a long pull of beer, shut his eyes, and tried a relaxation exercise, but the fucking black Ford continued to sabotage his brain.

At the fridge again, he grabbed a second beer.

And stood at the balustrade to stare at the view. Sit? Stand? Pace? What? His eyes wandered over the ravine to the sniper spot. Goddamnit, do something—anything—just stop these damn flashbacks.

A shower wasn't any help either. In the mirror a worn, haggard face stared back. When would this circle jerk end? It sure as hell couldn't continue. Either he or Naseem had to die. There was no other way out of this.

He wandered to the kitchen again, noticed the unfinished beer on the counter, carried it to the computer room.

"Good evening, SAM."

"Good evening, Arnold. How was your day?"

"Ah, man, sucked! Totally, totally sucked. Had a few problems, but they're taken care of."

Sorta.

"How about you?"

"We're up to date on Week Four." Referring to the NFL season. "All bets go live at one AM unless otherwise instructed."

Hold on…SAM's words jarred loose a vague memory…the forgotten elusive task…something to do with SAM? Yeah, maybe. What? It was SAM, goddammit…the night Naseem showed up at the gate…he began running through the events of that night…he came in here to look at the monitors….

Holy shit, he'd given SAM the "initiate cellphone scan" instruction that activated his StingRay, a cell phone surveillance device originally developed by the military and intelligence community but was now commonly used by law enforcement to record unique identifying data from any cellphone within range.

When on, all cell phones continuously communicate with the strongest cell signal available. This allows some apps—Google Maps for example—to continually track a phone's location. If Naseem was carrying a cellphone that night, StingRay should've captured its unique ID. If so, SAM might be able to locate her now.

Holiest of holy shit!

Assuming, of course, she her phone was with her that night instead of a disposable burner. Big assumption.

Oh, God, please…

271

Turned out StingRay had captured two phones, making it very likely they were the terrorists'. He fed the data into an on-line database and learned that one was a Samsung and the other was an iPhone. The good news was that neither one was likely a throwaway. The bad news was that a phone's unique identity is programmed on a SIM card that can be swapped out.

He learned that both phones were on the Verizon network. Having previously hacked into those servers, he was scrolling through their database within minutes. The account was under the name Malik Khan. He made a note of that. The iPhone was last used in downtown Honolulu four hours ago but only briefly before being turned off again. He printed out a list of all calls made in the past three days, then repeated this process for the Samsung. That phone was registered to Hazig Yang, a name that meant nothing to him. It too was either turned off or out of cell tower range.

He called Fisher with the information.

"Goddamn, Gold, outstanding!"

Fisher's uncharacteristic enthusiasm buoyed his spirits.

"Anything else I can do for you in the way of, ah...research?"

He hoped not. His burst of exhilaration was rapidly fading into heavy fatigue. He needed sleep.

"No, we're good. Man, you really outdid yourself this time. Get some rest and we'll touch base in the morning."

Before turning in, he asked SAM to monitor both accounts and notify him immediately if either phone was turned on.

He downed the dregs of the beer before climbing into bed.

Chapter 62

HIS PHONE WOKE him at 6:43 AM. He rolled onto his side, squinted at the bedside clock.

Aw man...can't be good.

"Hey, you da man!" Fisher. "Your half-ass impression turned out to be bang on. Your friend Hazig Yang is—oh, I suppose it's grammatically more better to say *was*—Malaysian. Turns out he's known to run with a group of Islamic fundamentalist shitheads with ties to what's left of ISIL. Homeland Security is all over this now."

Arnold was sitting on the side of the bed, running his toes through Chance's soft fur. Thump-thump-thump.

Fisher asked, "You up for breakfast?"

Arnold, still waiting for his brain to reboot, was sufficiently awake to be aware of primitive hunger pangs in his stomach.

"Does the Pope shit in the woods? Where?"

"Dealer's choice."

Arnold knuckled a granule of sand from his right eye. "Just woke up...how about Starbucks on Auahi Street? Say, forty-five minutes?"

He freshened Chance's water and dog food before jumping in the shower. Ten minutes later, dressed in beige cargo shorts, a bright blue Google t-shirt and gray Nikes, he walked out the front door.

When he and Chance entered Starbucks, Fisher—still in

yesterday's clothes—was at a bistro table, intently studying a laptop, face displaying a day's worth of stubble and darkly ringed eyes, both jarringly out of character.

"Jesus, Fisher, you look like dog shit."

Ignoring the snarky comment, Fisher picked up his coffee.

"Had any sleep at all in the past twenty-four hours?" Arnold asked.

Fisher yawned, stretched his back.

"Fornicate thyself, Mr. Gold." He paused to glance once again at the screen, "Grab some breakfast and we'll talk."

A moment later Fisher glanced back up to see Arnold still standing there, waved him away again.

"Go! I have some things to finish before we discuss anything. And before you ask, no, we haven't learned anything more about our friend."

Arnold still didn't move. Fisher stared.

"How is it conceivable I didn't make myself clear? Go!"

Arnold dropped into the chair directly across from Fisher, set a triple-shot Grande latte and beloved breakfast sandwich on the table. Fisher was now place-kicking donut crumbs off a grease-stained white paper plate, one at a time. Arnold waited a beat before unwrapping his sandwich to cool.

"Well?"

Fisher kept up the suspense another few seconds before saying, "We got a potential break early this morning," and let it hang.

Fucking Fisher!

"C'mon, man!"

Silence.

Arnold decided two could play the same game, so, busied him by gingerly poking the contents of the steaming sandwich back into place. Fisher would tell him. Eventually.

Fisher watched.

Fuck him, I'm hungry.

He bit into the sandwich. Big goddamn mistake. A glob of red-hot cheese welded itself to the roof of his mouth, burrowing in like a charcoal ember. He immediately tried to dislodge the sucker with the tip of his tongue, but the smoldering glob wouldn't budge. He sucked a mouthful of air and fanatically glanced around for a cold drink. The lump fell dropped off, leaving burning pain.

"Something wrong?" Fisher asked with feigned innocent bemusement.

Fuck you.

Arnold gingerly probed the burn margins with the tip of his tongue and knew that spot would be sore as hell for at least four or five days.

"Sorry, missed that, what'd you say?"

Ignoring the pain would be impossible.

"The black Ford SUV with the surfboards?"

"Uh-huh."

Arnold sucked another open-mouth breath but no help.

Fisher continued to grin as if knowing exactly what just happened.

"A city cop spotted it in a parking lot off Alakawa Street."

Alakawa Street? Huh! Sounded familiar. Where the hell was it?

He lifted the top of the sandwich to release more steam, then glanced up.

"Go on, I'm listening."

Where was Fisher headed with this?

Fisher casually sipped his coffee.

Alright, already!

"I don't get it. What are you not telling me? Is it a stolen vehicle? Who owns it? You obviously don't have the driver in custody, right?"

"The plates are off a Lexus sedan reported stolen four weeks ago. HPD's running the vehicle's VIN and working up that part of the investigation but what I need from you is an eyeball confirmation that it's the vehicle that attempted to run you down.

As for the driver…we've no idea where he is."

Fisher yawned.

Arnold began to rewrap the sandwich.

"Well, hell, what're we doing here? Let's get going."

They piled into Fisher's car, Arnold slouched low in the back seat, eyes barely above window level, peering out, Chance up front with Fisher, nose out the side window.

When they were two blocks from the lot, Fisher explained, "The vehicle of interest will be to your right. I'll drive by but won't stop unless there's a good reason. Ready?"

"Roger that."

By now, the sandwich was finished and he was sucking scraps from between his teeth.

They turned onto Alakawa Street, doing twenty-five, staying in the flow of traffic. Arnold recognized the nondescript street as one used for trips to Costco. He just hadn't bothered to register the name.

"We're coming up on the block now," as Fisher prepared to turn into the lot.

He glanced around as if looking for a parking spot. Neither man spoke.

Arnold recognized the vehicle immediately, the surfboards bungee-corded to the roof rack. As they slowly passed, he scanned the vehicle's headlights, grill, and bumper.

"Yeah, that's it. No doubt. Right, right down to those shitty headlight protectors and paint chips in the right front fender. There's no doubt at all."

Strange, how so many small details came flooding back soon the moment he saw the vehicle.

The dog growled.

"Chance agrees."

"Good enough for me."

Fisher continued out the opposite end of the lot onto Alakawa, turned toward the piers.

"What now?" Arnold asked, wiping sandwich grease from his fingers with a paper napkin.

Should've bought a second one. It'd be a perfect eating temperature by now.

"I'll drop you at your car so you can get on with your day."

Seemed ridiculous to stay scrunched down in the seat so he sat up.

"No, I mean, now that I identified the SUV, what happens next?"

Fisher appeared to weigh an answer.

"We need to determine if it's abandoned or only parked temporarily. For now, that means keeping it under surveillance and wait for something to happen. In the meantime, HPD's tracking down the owner."

"That's *it?*" What Fisher just outlined seemed...totally unsatisfactory. Based on a wealth of watching true-crime shows on *Dateline*, he figured the vehicle must be a treasure trove of forensic information. Then again, Fisher seemed to know what he was doing, so decided there must be a good reason for their decision. He leaned over the seat, scratched Chance on the neck. "Is someone watching it now?"

He hadn't noticed anyone, but then again, that was undoubtedly the point. Besides, he hadn't been looking at anything but the Ford.

"Of course."

"So, like, maybe I should stick around?" Arnold asked hopefully.

Fisher laughed.

"Oh, so they can spot you? News flash, Arnold. You're their target."

"I could, like, disguise myself."

"And your dog? No, trust me, you don't want to stick around even if we allowed it. Watching that vehicle's a job that's guaranteed to be a pain in the ass for whoever's given the assignment. If that vehicle's abandoned, we could be mashing hemorrhoids for days."

"True, but they could also show up two minutes from now."

Fisher braked for a light.

"In that the case, we'll be extremely lucky."

Fisher was correct. There were more productive jobs to do. What, exactly those might be, wasn't entirely clear, but he'd figure it out.

"Make you a deal."

Fisher shot him a sideways glance.

"I'll check back later. Don't forget, it's not like I don't have skin in this game."

Fisher shrugged.

"Suit yourself, Gold, but more likely than not, we'll be sitting on our hands waiting for the driver to show or the owner to give us something useful. In the meantime, we're taking a hard look at every business in the immediate area. Could be the vehicle was dumped, but it could also be that the driver is somewhere nearby."

Arnold checked to see if SAM had an update on either of the terrorist's phones but unfortunately, there was nothing, which only stoked his nervousness. He couldn't just sit around, waiting for something to happen. It seemed like they were so close to finding Naseem...he had to come up with a way to aid the investigation. With or without Fisher. But first, Chance needed to be cared for.

Arnold decided to hike to the Puu Ualakaa State Park trail for an hour, partly to exercise Chance and partly to give himself time to think. Sitting at home simply wasn't going to cut it. Before leaving downtown, he stopped by a convenience store for bottled water, a sandwich, and bag of Maui chips. A long walk was exactly what he needed.

Fifteen minutes later, he parked off of Tantalus Drive, slung his rucksack over a shoulder, stuffed the leash in his pocket, and led

Chance across the narrow asphalt onto a dry dusty trail. Dark, sodden rain clouds threatened but with the temperature a lovely 82 degrees, it hardly mattered. In fact, a shower might feel refreshing. He planned on hiking two miles before turning back. They started up the trail, Chance bounding ahead as usual, familiar with the route.

Fifteen minutes later it hit him. He stopped, ran through it again.

Yes!

"Come!" and took off jogging to the car just as the downpour broke loose, soaking him in seconds, but with his mind zinging along at rabid-bat speed, being wet didn't even register, Chance running alongside, glancing up now and then, aware of Arnold's excitement.

By the time they piled into the car, the sun was back out and steam was rippling off the black asphalt. Arnold lowered all the windows, gunned the engine and calculated the fastest route to the house.

Chapter 63

ARNOLD MADE A bee-line to SAM and opened Google Earth. He quickly zeroed in on the Alakawa street parking lot where the SUV was discovered. Some quick research disclosed the lot was owned by TransPacific Storage Inc, a warehouse.

A little more digging gave him the names of the properties along the both sides of the street for the entire block, most of which were also warehouses. Excellent. Most storage facilities maintain tight security, which of course, meant video surveillance.

Fifteen minutes later, he was inside TransPacific's security system. Two minutes after that he located the video recording of the parking lot. He began reviewing the first one at 2X reverse speed starting from the time the police officer called in the Black Ford.

Took twenty to find the key segment: the vehicle pulled into the lot at 4:37 AM. The driver locked up and hurriedly walked away. The recording was too grainy for a clear image of the driver's face so he enlarged the best shot to the point of pixilating and then applied smoothing and sharpening software.

Although the image still didn't have great detail, it was sufficient to identify the driver as the dead attacker's accomplice. He knew that for a litany of reasons his copy of the video wouldn't be admissible in court; however, the information would be crucial to Fisher. Now, knowing about it, the FBI or Homeland Security could figure out a legal reason to obtain the recordings legitimately as evidence. Before he called, he decided to see if there was any more information he could uncover, so resumed working.

After leaving the vehicle, the driver headed east in the direction of Costco. Perfect. Costco undoubtedly housed some insanely sick security, which, if luck held, would include views of the sidewalk in front of the building. Fifteen minutes later, he was sorting through six cameras, searching for the best views.

He found two.

Within minutes he was reviewing another video of the terrorist. He noted the time and camera number to pass on to Fisher. Mentally in the zone, he used the same the strategy for neighboring buildings and bit by bit reconstructed the asshole's route.

Until the guy simply vanished.

Arnold replayed the video immediately preceding the disappearance.

What was he missing? Where did the man go? One moment he's walking along the sidewalk, the next moment he's gone.

Must've entered one of three buildings on that street.

By switching between videos from the three surrounding buildings, he narrowed the choice to one stretch of sidewalk. Leaving two possibilities: the corner building or the immediate neighbor on the south side of the street.

Back to Google Earth.

A quick trip to the Honolulu property records showed the corner building was a tool and die shop and the other an import/export company.

An import company?

How fucking perfect was that?

That just had to be *the One.*

He called Fisher.

Chapter 64

"ANY DOUBT ABOUT this? Any doubt at all?" Fisher asked with a hint of cautious optimism, as if Arnold's conclusion was too good to be true.

Arnold checked the satellite view on Google Earth again.

"A hundred percent? Never. But what other choices are there? He didn't simply teleport to Katmandu. He's got to be in one of those two buildings...and my money's on the import place."

"I guarantee you're correct about Katmandu, but will reserve judgment on the other bet." Pause. "Tanaka needs to be brought up to speed," he muttered. "Hang on a sec."

Arnold heard a muffled conversation and wondered....

What was so complicated? Knock on the doors, find out who's inside. Simple process of elimination.

"We're pulling it up on Google Earth," Fisher said. "Standby one."

"We're looking at the satellite image now. Interesting. Only three blocks from the lot."

"So? Go take a look. What's the issue?"

"No, Gold, we only get one shot at this. When we knock on a door, I want to be able to go in and take a look around. That means we need a warrant, and to get one, we need to show probable cause. Legally. At the moment we don't have anything close."

Arnold was clicking his mouse, *click-click-click*, his anxiety ratcheting up with each second ticking away.

What was to keep those assholes from disappearing again while Fisher and Tanaka dealt with the red tape?

"Can't you simply knock on the door and *ask* who's inside? Won't that tell you something?"

"Sure. We can do that. But if those shitheads are inside there's no way we can legally enter and then, by the time we get a warrant, they *will* be in Katmandu."

"What if you could look inside the buildings *without* going in?"

Fisher let several beats pass.

"The hell are you suggesting?"

"I have this totally awesome drone. What if I go there and accidently on purpose peek through a few windows? There's got to be a couple windows...and we know from the satellite view that both those building have skylights. That's better than nothing, right?"

Dead silence for several seconds, then, "Hang on, I'm putting you on speaker...okay, Tanaka's on, so for the record, I am *not* requesting you to fly your drone anywhere near the warehouse district...however, if, however, *you*, as a private citizen, wish to fly your drone—which is an established hobby of yours—in that particular area of the city, there's no law prohibiting you from doing so provided you abide by federal regulations."

Arnold was already forming a mental list of items to pack.

"Understood! We'll be there soon as humanly possible."

Fisher told him where to meet.

Arnold pulled into a corner parking two blocks from the buildings of interest and four blocks from the lot where the Ford was parked. He parked in the stall next to a non-descript beige van next where Fisher and Tanaka stood. Several SWAT members were milling around two black SUVs. Both Fisher and Tanaka wore Bluetooth earphones and throat mikes which Arnold suspected they were communication links to SWAT control. Arnold clipped a leash to Chance's collar and walked over.

"The paperwork to execute this legally is in the works," Fisher said. "But we have no idea how soon that'll take to be approved. We referred to you as a confidential informant, which allows us to withhold your name for now. The official story is you saw the Ford being parked when you just happened to be walking the same direction as the driver. I realize how lame that sounds, but it's all we could come up with on such short notice. How soon before you can take a look?"

Arnold popped the back door of the Mini, hauled out five pieces of equipment which he quickly assembled into one large device that resembled a five-point star with propellers and a set of landing skids underneath.

"The control system is my own design," Arnold explained proudly. "An on-board computer has built in AI and is totally way more superior to anything you can buy. I named him RAID…for Robotic Artificial Intelligence Drone. He's a pretty amazing dude actually, which I say in all modesty."

He carefully removed a transmitter from a Pelican case and connected a length of coax to a directional Yagi antenna. By now Chance was off sniffing at the tires of other vehicles.

Arnold unwrapped the controller, a heavy glove designed to be worn on his right hand and swapped out his regular glasses for a modified VR headset.

"His motors are so silent it's spooky." Arnold removed a special Microsoft Surface from a padded carrying case. "All set. Where do you want me to work?"

Fisher pointed to a white van parked alongside a SWAT SUV.

"How's that look?"

Arnold worried that the metal walls might partially shield the signal. He needed control of RAID to be flawless.

"Those top vents open up?"

"They do," Tanaka answered.

Then why the hell are they closed in this heat?

"Good. Open them. I'll try to snake my antenna through one. The straighter the path, the better the communication. If that won't work, we'll find a better spot, but it'll be best if we're in shade so you can watch the view from onboard camera on the tablet."

Arnold took a moment to study the surrounding buildings. Trucks and trailers were parked in loading zones and parking lots along the streets but vehicular traffic was minimal. It dawned on him that the cops probably had the streets closed off.

All the neighboring buildings were one-story affairs, with one squat rectangular structure only partially obstructing his line of sight to the target, making the flight path relatively straight forward. Three buildings—in particular the one of interest—had peaked corrugated metal roofs of varying pitches while the rest were simple flat tar surfaces. The place he was betting on had four flanged ventilation ducts along the peak with a large rectangular skylight on each side that kissed at the apex.

Perfect.

The interior was sweltering, cramped, stuffy, and reeking of perspiration and sour milk. He set the Surface on a small aluminum shelf on the left wall so Fisher and Tanaka could see what he was viewing in the VR headset. He pushed the antenna through an open vent, aimed it toward the roof, then, satisfied with the angle, duct-taped it solidly in place. The coax was long enough to reach the shelf where he set the transmitter.

Finally, he duct-taped the coax securely to make sure it didn't dislodge under its own weight when RAID was airborne. As a failsafe, after setting everything up, he climbed back on the chair to double check the antenna position, tugged the coax slightly, made two more minor adjustments and was set.

"Is it okay for Chance to sit in the front seat?"

He didn't want him in his car even with the windows down.

"No problem," one SWAT member said.

Arnold stood at the back of the van for a moment, studying the surrounding buildings one final time, mentally rehearsing his flight path. Then he placed RAID on Mini's roof, checked its stability with the motors running, and stepped back into the van.

Fisher followed him inside and closed the door. The temperature immediately skyrocketed. He was sweating and his heart was galloping faster than American Pharaoh. He paused to flex and extend his fingers and mentally got ready for the most important drone flight of his life. Until now, he'd only flown RAID for fun or an occasional security patrol around the house.

Would his robot provide the cops with the information they urgently needed?

He dried his palm on his cargo shorts before sliding on the control glove that he secured with a Velcro strap.

One last minute minor adjustment, then, "Okay. Let's see what we have. Going live...."

A close-up of the Mini's roof appeared on the Surface and his headset.

"You're seeing a live feed from RAID," he muttered, as if Tanaka and Fisher hadn't already figured that out.

He slowly raised the glove index finger.

"Houston, we have...liftoff."

The image Mini's roof grew smaller on the screen as RAID gained altitude. With the drone now airborne, Arnold angled the lens from straight down to straight ahead. An ultra-high-def image of the peaked roof appeared on the screen.

The left side of the target building directly abutted the neighboring machine shop whereas the right side was separated from its neighbor by a space perhaps only two feet wide. The entire property was enclosed by a ten-foot high cyclone fence. A small concrete loading area took up the space between the fence and the front of the building.

As RAID approached the target, they could see an unobstructed view of the street and loading area.

"No one's outside the building," Arnold said. "Unless someone sees us from that window, we're good."

His narrative was irrelevant, he realized, because Tanaka's men would advise them of at any sign of activity outside either building, but verbalizing his thoughts helped relieve tension.

Arnold rotated RAID's camera in a complete circle, looking for anyone watching. No one appeared to pay the drone any attention.

Lucky.

"I'll bring him down."

With RAID three feet above the front peak of the target, Arnold scanned the building but saw nothing remarkable. The corrugated-metal front wall contained one large roll-up loading door, a small pedestrian door, and a small square window five feet below the peak of the roof. The lack of windows was another reason this building seemed such an ideal place for a hideout.

"Can't risk going any closer to that window," Arnold said.

"Why's that?" asked Fisher.

"Don't want anyone to notice us."

"Yeah?" Tananka said with a chuckle. "What're they going to do about it?"

"Take your time," Fisher said reassuringly. "Use your judgment."

Arnold jockeyed RAID over the right skylight, inches from the glass. He sensed Tanaka and Fisher tense as his own heart galloped and his fingers became slick with sweat. He adjusted the lens for a clearer view into the warehouse.

A stout steel I-beam ran the length of the building, perhaps six to seven feet below the peak of the roof, partially obscuring their view. To compensate, Arnold moved RAID from side to side, varying the viewing angle. There was nothing but the cement floor below.

"No second floor."

"This all helps...you're doing good," Fisher said.

Tanaka grunted.

"Haven't seen any movement or sign of anyone."

"You recording this?" Fisher asked.

"No...thought that on account of you not being able to legally use this, I shouldn't. That wrong?"

"Hell, don't see what we have to lose at this point...might as well go for broke. Record it."

"Roger that." He started the camera rolling. "We've seen all we can from this side. I'm going to the other one now."

Because the skylights abutted each other in the middle of the roof, he figured that by viewing the interior from each side along various angles, he'd see just about all of the floor.

RAID was performing so well that he began to relax and actually enjoy showing off and finally being of some tangible assistance to the investigation.

He was just about to reposition RAID when a figure darted from the front to the back of the building.

"Catch that?"

"I did," Fisher answered.

Tanaka grunted agreement.

Shit! The only way to see to all the way to the rear of the floor would be to look through front window just below the peak of the roof.

But before doing that, he wanted to know, "What's the back of the building like?"

"We don't know much about that," Tanaka replied. "An alley divides the block. We walked it. The back of the property's enclosed with the same cyclone fence, but the inside's covered with sheets of plywood, so you can't see a goddamn thing back there."

"You have a helicopter or drone on this?" Arnold asked, thinking either HPD or Homeland Security would have one deployed by now.

"No. We don't want the rotor noise attracting any attention until we're all set, and that includes the paperwork. Our drone's on loan to Maui PD for the day. One thing I can say for sure is, there's not much space back there, so we might as well have a look now."

Arnold flew RAID over the peak of the roof to the rear of the building. Just as Tanaka described, a boarded-up cyclone fence blocked a ground-level view of the enclosure, which turned out to be nothing more than a small cement patch stacked with weathered wood pallets and flattened cardboard. A tiny, rectangular, corrugated metal roof protected a square of weathered wood porch.

Like the front of the building, the rear wall housed a rectangular window six feet below the peak of the roof, but seventy-five percent of it was occupied by a rust-streaked ventilation fan. Arnold jockeyed RAID as close as possible to the pane of glass.

"See anything of interest?" he asked them.

"Hard to see shit through the dirt," Fisher answered. "Might as well go back to the front and try for a view of the back from there."

Arnold's gut knotted.

"No problem," he lied. "By the way…you guys look into who owns the buildings?"

He was jockeying RAID back along the peak of the roof.

"Not yet. Why?" Tanaka asked.

"Because the same person owns both."

"No shit? A machine shop and export company?" Fisher said. "Just the properties or the actual businesses?"

"Both. I shit you not."

"Remember the name, by any chance?"

"No. But it wasn't anything familiar."

"I'll see who's working on it," Fisher said.

"Reason I even bother to bring it up is the possibility the two are connected…through a door, I mean."

"We're all over it," Fisher said.

RAID was hovering just above the front peak now.

"The problem with what this next move…" Arnold muttered to no one in particular, "…is being seen from inside."

"Think it makes a goddamn bit of difference at this point?" Fisher replied. "I guarantee they sure as hell know we're here by now."

Arnold swallowed hard and decided to minimize the risk by spending as little time as possible at the window. Besides, this could be the wrong building and he might be getting wrapped around the axle for nothing. Maybe Fisher was right, maybe it didn't make a damn bit of difference if Naseem's group spotted them. Or maybe Naseem's group wasn't within a five-mile radius.

Or maybe they were watching us watch them?

"Ready?"

"As ever," Fisher replied.

Tanaka grunted agreement.

Arnold lowered RAID to the window. The tricky part was to move close enough to maximize the view yet not clip a propeller. Sweat was streaming off his face and chest, intensifying his thirst. The image autofocused and suddenly he could clearly see the entire length of the poorly lit interior, all the way to an unpainted plywood wall—probably ten feet high—with a small door to what would logically be an office.

"See that? Someone's in that doorway." Arnold said, pointing to the figure.

Light from the office was haloing the person's head making it impossible to discern their face.

"I do," Fisher said. "Can you get a better look at their face?"

Arnold zoomed in, refocused, snapped a picture.

"A picture's coming your way," he told Fisher.

"Nice!" Tanaka patted his shoulder.

"Can you get a closer look?" Fisher asked.

"To the window?"

"Window, zoom, whatever, just get us a better image of their face...something to work with."

Ah, Christ! He was already pushing his limits.

"Man, I don't know...."

"Would infrared help?"

"Hell, got nothing to lose." Switching to infrared, he snapped off two stills. "They're on the way."

He sent copies to SAM before sending them to Fisher. SAM could merge the infrared and the normal shots for more detail. By now, his nerves were totally fried and his muscles fatigued.

"I need a quick break, sorry."

Neither Tanaka or Fisher protested. With RAID now on autopilot safely above the front roof, he leaned back, sucked down several slow measured breaths and dangled both arms loosely at his side.

"I'm looking at them now," Fisher said. "Nice work. I'll forward these to the office, get one of our techs on it."

"I still need to know what's in the area immediately behind the front door," Tanaka said. "It's the only area other than the back room we haven't seen. Any chance you could give the back window another try, see if we can see anything in front?"

Arnold took a deep breath, wiped his face with a towel, gulped a long pull from his water bottle, then drained it.

Could he peek through that without trashing RAID? Was it possible? Yeah. But probable? No.

For many reasons: the closer the window, the stronger fan turbulence, and strong turbulence increased the risk of clipping the glass and destroying the drone. Then again...was the fan even moving? Besides, RAID could be repaired.

What the hell difference did it make?

A high-pitched beeping caught his attention. The low-battery indicator was now flashing red.

"Aw, shit, batteries are dying...I have a back-up pack in the trunk."

If he stood any chance at all of getting away with the back-window maneuver, he'd need all available juice.

"We may not have that much time, Gold."

"Sorry...but the battery..."

Fisher pressed his ear bud and turned away from them, mumbled into his comm set, nodded, turned to Tanaka.

"Received tentative confirmation on the picture: looks like it's Akmal, Naseem's traveling companion." He flashed Arnold a thumbs up. "You got'em, dude. Well done!"

Fuck a battery change, this was turning into some serious shit.

"I'll get you that look through the window."

"Outstanding!"

Fisher slapped Arnold's shoulder.

RAID flew over to the rear peak of the roof, then lowered to window level. Arnold's muscle fatigue was making his fine finger movements herky-jerky and he was now resigned himself to destroying the drone. Then he noticed that the fan blades weren't moving. Just another problem he didn't have to worry about.

"Okay, here we go." He held RAID inches from window, focused the camera and now they could see the length of the interior to the front door. "Yo, look!"

Through the dim light, they could barely make out a man peering through a narrow gap between one side of the loading door and the jamb. He was holding what looked suspiciously like an AK-47.

"Shit! That's just fucking wonderful," Fisher said. "They're armed and know we're out here."

He quickly sent the word out on his com set.

The RAID controller was beeping faster now, warning of impending power failure.

"Uh-oh. RAID's running on empty..."

Crap, was there enough power to make it back?

"Keep on station, Gold. We're going tactical." Fisher ordered.

The battery light flickered a moment, then went out.

Chapter 65

ARNOLD HAD RAID barreling straight back toward the parking lot, low, over buildings, coming fast. Shouldering past Fisher and Tanaka, he jumped from the van as RAID thumped onto the asphalt, bounced once, the motor stone-cold dead.

With RAID safely on the ground, he turned his attention to Chance. He kept the car stocked with a dish and bottled water, and as soon as Chance was drinking, he chugged an entire bottle himself. A bit less thirsty now, he swapped out RAID's battery pack before returning to the command van. Tanaka—face grim—was in hushed conversation on his phone. Fisher's face appeared to be equally grim.

"What up?" Arnold asked.

"Nothing. That's the problem." Fisher nodded in the general direction of the warehouse. "Until the surrounding structures are completely evacuated, we're in a holding pattern."

He started to massage his temples.

Although Arnold was pretty sure what the answer was, he asked anyway.

"Then what?"

Fisher's look drilled him. "Now's not the time, Gold."

"Would an eye in the sky be of any help?"

Fisher squeezed the bridge of his nose, blinked darkly rimmed eyes, muttered, "Goddamn it!" checked his watch, then turned to

Arnold. "Sure. Always good to have as much intel as possible. HPD's chopper should be on station in two minutes."

After swapping out the battery pack, Arnold flew RAID to the warehouse front window for the best view of the office, no longer concerned about being discovered, and saw a figure run into the office and shut the door.

"You catch that?"

"Sure did," said Fisher.

He caught more movement.

"Looks like there's at least two people in there."

Arnold estimated the plywood wall of the office to be about ten-feet high with the peak of the roof closer to twenty, making it possible for there to be a loft area over the office. The warehouse interior was illuminated by only the light filtering through the small dirt-caked windows and equally grimy skylights, leaving the loft in dark shadows.

"See that loft over the office? And that ladder attached to the wall to the left of the door? I swear I just made out some movement up there."

Fisher asked, "Can you zoom in on it?"

He jockeyed RAID as close as possible to the window, the camera panning side to side, searching for the best possible angle, saw the office door open and a figure step out.

"Whoa! Check it out."

He tweaked the focus, zoomed in, snapped three shots, *click-click-click*, but didn't have time to view the images before the person ducked into the office. He backed RAID off to a safe distance from the window, flipped control to autopilot, rocked his neck side to side to loosen up before checking the pictures.

"Let's see what we got."

But before he had a chance to look, his iPhone rang a special ringtone; SAM had an urgent message. He gave it a glance, then a double take.

"Holy shit! Naseem's cell just came on...she's texting."

"I'll put our phone guy on it," Fisher said.

"Don't bother, it's off again. Wait...sweet! I got the GPS coordinates. Lemme see what pops up on Google Maps...holy shit! It was right there," pointing to the target warehouse. "She...well, at least her phone's right there."

Chapter 66

WHILE FISHER AND Tanaka coordinated with SWAT, Arnold took Chance around the block, staying well away from the target building. By now the parking lot was teaming with vehicles and officers in full SWAT gear. After a brief debate, during which Arnold pointed out to Tanaka just how much he'd been involved the investigation, he was granted a special permission to observe the unfolding drama from the periphery, on the stipulation that he stay behind protection and out of everyone's hair.

Arnold freshened Chance's water dish and set it in the shade of a fender. Then, as Chance lapped noisily, he chugged another full bottle of water before packing his equipment back in the car. Finished, he approached Fisher, who, at this point, was taking a back seat to HPD.

"What's the plan?"

He'd never seen Fisher so stressed and disheveled; shirt sleeves rolled up above the elbows, collar open, wadded tie stuffed in the breast pocket.

"SWAT's good to go but HPD's still clearing the area. They figure...ten more minutes until showtime, but hey, nobody's leaving that warehouse at this point."

Arnold heard *whump-whump-whump,* looked up, saw a police chopper take up position about a hundred feet above the building, heard a series of rapid squawks from a police radio. He made small talk as Fisher stole nervous glances at his watch, then raised a finger to silence him, pressed his ear bud, nodded twice, said something into his throat mic.

Then to Arnold, said, "SWAT's ready to roll. Remember your instructions. Stay the fuck behind the tank. It starts to move, move your ass to another vehicle."

"Yes, mom."

Fisher flashed him serious dose of cop-eye.

"Follow those instructions, Gold. This type of situation can turn into a real shitstorm before you have time to blink."

Arnold moved Chance an additional half-block back, behind the mini-tank. Peering around the tank, he could see the warehouse shimmering through heat waves rising from baking asphalt. He double-wrapped Chance's leash around his hand in case the dog bolted at a loud noise, watched as the SWAT team leader walked to the cyclone fence and raise a bullhorn to his mouth.

"Honolulu Police. Open the door and exit the building with hands above your head."

Silence.

The SWAT leader repeated the instructions. Suddenly the warehouse front window exploded. Something pinged two feet above Arnold's head.

Holy shit!

Arnold dropped into a crouch, hugged Chance by the neck and was happy to use the tank as a shield. SWAT opened up, pouring rounds into the warehouse for what seemed like minutes instead of seconds. The firing stopped abruptly, leaving only the rhythmic *whoomph-whoomph-whoomph* of the overhead helicopter. Police began calling to one another, making sure everyone was okay.

Seconds dragged with no response. The SWAT leader—crouched behind a vehicle—repeated his instructions.

Still no response.

Arnold watched two SWATs—armed with automatic weapons—crouch-run to new positions behind a large green

Dempsey dumpster, closer to the warehouse door but still outside the cyclone fence, one carrying an industrial looking bolt cutter. That's when Arnold noticed a heavy-duty chain and padlock securing the gate.

With four SWAT members behind the dumpster, the leader signaled the one with bolt cutter. He sprinted toward the gate. A burst from automatic weapon opened up from the warehouse window, the officer stutter-stepped, went down, and then began crawling toward a blue metal recycle bin. The other officers let loose with suppressing fire as a SWAT cop leaned out from behind the dumpster and fired a grenade launcher at the blown-out window. The explosion was tremendous. The officer calmly reloaded, fired again, then once more. By now plumes of white gas were billowing from the blown-out window.

Silence.

A hand slapped Arnold's shoulder. "Move!"

Arnold and Chance ran across the street to a new position behind a beat-up Chevy. Crouching behind the rear fender, he watched the armored vehicle roll down the street, turn left, run over and squash the cyclone fence without any resistance from inside the building. The vehicle stopped three feet from the front door and five SWAT team members scurried into new positions behind its protective armor. Once in position, one leaned out from the left side of the vehicle and emptied a full clip into the window and adjacent wall. This move was repeated by two other team members.

Still no reply.

Seconds later, the SWAT leader raised the bullhorn and ordered the occupants to open the door and come out.

Still no response.

Arnold watched six officers move cautiously forward, one carrying a steel battering ram to smash in the pedestrian door. Preparations complete, the team broke open the door and swarmed into the building.

Chapter 67

"COME ON IN." Arnold opened the gate for Fisher with Chance at his side wagging his tail. "Can I get you a water?"

"No thanks. I'm catching a Seattle flight, so this'll be very quick." Fisher paused in the courtyard, to give Chance his own brand of choobers and in return, received two sloppy doggy kisses. Greetings done, Fisher said, "The home office thinks I've been kicking it too long in the sun and surf so want me back in them fields tote'n them bales."

"So soon? It's only been, what, twenty-four hours?"

Arnold waved him inside where the sliders were open allowing a soft breeze to circulate.

"The local office can finish the leftover paperwork. In the meantime, since arriving here, my Seattle work's been piling up nonstop." Fisher paused in the foyer to survey the interior while Chance sniffed his leg. "Wow, sure is one killer view, Gold. Damn shame I'm on my way to the airport or I'd take you up on the offer," this being Fisher's first time in his house.

"At least sit down and tell me what's so important that you had to say it in person...but before we do that, what about of the officer, the one who was hit in the shootout. How's he doing?"

"Doing well, I'm happy to report. Was wearing his Kevlar, so just came away with a nasty bruise and a couple cracked ribs." Paused a beat, added, "Don't mean to trivialize it...I'm just saying it could've been worse." Fisher checked his watch. "Look, I need to make this short." He stepped into the great room, glanced around once more, still scoping out the interior, before locking eyes with Arnold. "You need to know a few things. First, thanks for all your help. You supplied crucial intel at a crucial time, so I speak for both myself and the Bureau when I say your help was greatly appreciated."

"Thank you."

"What I'm now about to say is for your ears only."

Arnold nodded.

Fisher inhaled deeply and glanced away.

"Only two bodies were recovered from the warehouse. The first, a male, apparently died from a single head wound. The other—also male—died of multiple bullet wounds. We're working up their identities now but have a very interesting autopsy finding: the head wound is of particular interest because evidence indicates it was inflicted by one of their rounds."

A sick feeling flooded Arnold's gut. "You're saying—"

"—Naseem wasn't one of the victims."

Stunned, Arnold stared at Fisher for several seconds.

"But we clearly saw three people in there, maybe more. What happened?"

Fisher glanced away.

"That's another thing you had right...there *is* a door between the warehouse and machine shop. We suspect they initiated the firefight to cause a diversion...to make it easier for Naseem to slip out the other building. Apparently, when the first shots were fired, the team members covering the neighboring building ran over to assist...meaning, no one was paying attention to a side door around the corner. We think she simply walked away."

He stepped toward the door.

Arnold pressed his palms against his temples and shut his eyes.

"Fuck...you're telling me she's still out there!"

"Afraid so, Gold," Fisher said with unmistakable

disappointment.

With a whimper, Chance nuzzled Arnold's thigh.

"But I have good news for you," Fisher added. "The witness protection program's still on the table. It'd solve some problems for you." Fisher raised a questioning eyebrow but Arnold turned to stare at the bullet hole waiting to be repaired. "Did Rios have family?"

Fisher nodded. "A wife."

Fighting back tears, head bowed, both palms pressed to his eyes. "That's all on me...it's my fault."

Fisher took a step towards him.

"Not true at all," in an uncharacteristically sympathetic tone.

"No one anticipated a sniper...certainly not Rios...and it was his responsibility to assess the situational security. If anything, that puts it on us, not you."

Arnold opened his mouth to explain but no words came.

Fisher glanced at his watch. "Look, Gold, I don't mean to appear insensitive...I can see how upset you are, but I really have to catch the flight. Just promise me you'll think it over before making a final decision."

The frog in Arnold's throat was rapidly becoming anger.

"Think about what? Nothing's changed from last year! I don't trust being a case file. Not even with the FBI. Shit like that leaks all the damn time."

Fisher backed up a step, hands raised.

"I disagree but will spare you a lecture. Just do me one favor."

Arnold shook his head, disgusted and frustration.

"What?"

Fisher stepped toward the door again.

"Give some time for this to settle in before you make any decision, one way or the other...just give it more thought. You know how to reach me." Fisher paused for a final glance at the living room and distant view. "I understand why you don't want to leave this," then was out the front door.

"Wait," Arnold called, hurrying to catch up. "You need to hear this."

Another impatient glance at his watch.

"I'll make it short. I didn't mention this before...not with all that was going on...but, I got a call from a real estate agent...a guy wants to buy the house...all cash offer, no inspection, a fourteen-day close..."

Fisher motioned for him to hurry up, get to the point.

"I didn't think I'd do it, but you know...if she's still out there...there's no reason not to, right? Oh, shit, almost forgot...what about my trip? Where are we with the arrangements?"

"Thanks for reminding me," Fisher said with a mischievous grin. "Everything's set. You're booked into the Hyatt on Ka'anapali Beach."

Arnold blushed.

"Two rooms?"

He wasn't about to presume Rachael's reaction to arranging only one room. In spite of their frequent texts and phone calls, neither of them broached the subject of mutual feelings.

Assuming a single room would work for them was be premature.

"Yes, two rooms. She'll be traveling under a false identity and we've made arrangement for an Air Marshall to be on both flights."

Wow, big surprise.

"She okay with the Air Marshall thing?"

"No. That part's classified, so keep it secret."

Arnold nodded agreement.

"Just as well."

Fisher offered his hand. "Hope this means I won't see you again...if you know what I mean. Regardless, thanks again for your help."

"You're welcome."

Chance watched the two men shake hands.

Fisher was almost out the gate when Arnold called out, "Wait!"

He was unable to bear the guilt a moment longer.

Time to confess.

"What?" Fisher said with obvious impatience.

"Stop searching for the leak."

The thought of an innocent person being under suspicion haunted him.

Fisher's brow furrowed. "The leak?"

"The Al Jazeera story?"

"Yeah? What about it?"

Arnold swallowed to steel his resolve.

"There wasn't one. *I* sent the reporter the information. I knew on account of what happened to Firouz and Karim, that Naseem would just keep digging and digging until she figured out where I was. Hell, Davidson did it, so why not her? I wanted to settle it...just get it over with."

He stopped.

What more could he say?

Apparently stunned, Fisher just stared.

"And guess what?" Arnold continued. "My plan almost worked...it put her in your crosshairs...but then...for Rios...Christ, I never dreamed that someone..." Tears flooded his eyes. "I am *so* sorry. I can't tell you how sorry I am."

Chapter 68

WITH FISHER GONE and his emotions back under control, Arnold dialed Palmer Davidson's back line. Busy. He left a message to call back soon as possible, then dialed Loni. They hadn't spoken since their disastrous dinner at the Italian restaurant, so he had a few nagging worries about offering her the transaction. But, having already mentioned the potential sale, he felt obliged to give her the right of first refusal. If she declined, fine. It'd be a slam dunk finding another agent.

She answered on the fourth ring and Arnold got straight to the point.

"Remember I mentioned someone might be interested in buying my place?"

"Yes."

Curt, factual, none of the prior emotional connection.

"Well, I decided to sell and am wondering if you'd like to represent me...if you're okay with it."

After a brief hesitation, "Why me?"

Uh-oh. Last thing he needed right now—if ever—was another confrontation. This sounded like her typical prelude.

"Sorry, should I ask someone else?"

"Arnold! Don't be such a dick. I ask every client the same thing. Why do you want me to sell your house?"

He was tempted to correct her, to say she wouldn't be *selling* it. It was a done-deal. She wouldn't incur marketing cost and wouldn't need to be bothered with all the pain-in-the-ass showings. She needed to do only a trivial amount of paperwork before pocketing a handsome commission. Her surliness, he suspected, was circumstantial.

"A couple reasons, actually...you sold it to me, so I feel indebted." Sorta. "And, as I said, I mentioned it to you, so it's only fair. That's it."

He neglected to mention that her easy commission would help sooth his conscience over prolonging their relationship.

Did that make him a pig?

Another long pause.

"Where will you go?"

"I have no idea."

Oh, bullshit. How can you live with yourself?

Seconds ticked away.

"How soon...I mean, what's your timeline?"

"We can start the paperwork today."

"You're totally committed to this...I mean, absolutely? I thought you loved it there."

I do, but my life has changed.

"Yeah, I'm good. Thanks for asking."

His phone beeped. Davidson.

"Oops, got an important call coming in. Call you back soon as I take care of it."

After ending her call and taking Davidson's, he heard the man say, "To whom am I speaking? Mr. Taylor or Mr. Gold?"

Arnold laughed while walking through the kitchen to the deck, cell to ear.

"Your choice. I have a proposition for you. Is this a good time to talk?"

Standing at the railing now, he gazed past the distant city to Diamondhead, a view he dearly loved.

"It is. However, before I forget—which seems to be

happening with disturbing frequency these days—thank you so much for the lovely case of Leonetti. You did not need have done that."

Arnold smiled, only mildly satisfied with his choice. He'd hoped to come up with something more special than wine, but knew Davidson well enough to recognize sincerity in his voice.

"I'm pleased you like it. Hey, look, I know you're busy, so I'll make this brief. The reason I called..." He brought Davidson up to speed on the terrorists, the firefight, and Fisher's concerns about Naseem. "It all boils down to this: I'm going to disappear again and need your help. You okay with that?"

"That all depends on what you want me to do."

"Nothing illegal, if you're worried about that. Okay, here's the plan..."

When Arnold finished explaining, Davidson chuckled.

"Know what? That is just crazy enough to work. You say the buyer lives in Dubai?"

"His permanent residence is Munster, Germany but his business dealings are in Dubai."

Arnold watched a JAL 787 on final approach into Honolulu International.

"And a local real estate agent will represent you as the seller?"

"Yes."

Davidson snorted.

"Shall I fly over? I assume you know that I am not a member of the Hawaiian Bar and have no expertise in real estate."

"Is that necessary to handle the buyer's end?"

"Just to be clear, I simply serve as the buyer's legal representative. Is this correct?"

"Correct."

Chance barked at something in the ravine, but not his alarming bark. Probably nothing more than giving a bird a load of crap for having the nerve to invade his territory.

"You know I never pass up an opportunity to visit Honolulu. I will arrange my schedule and book a flight. I have nothing pressing at the moment that cannot be put on hold. Fact is, as a result of our heart to heart, I decided to lighten my practice. And, as long as I will be over there, I plan to take a look at a few condos."

"I should be in Maui by the time you arrive but will be available on my cell and Surface to sign the documents electronically. I'll send you the agent's contact info soon as I hang up. Loni Lee's her name."

"The woman with whom you had a relationship?"

"Uh-huh."

Davidson laughed. "You never cease to amaze me." A brief pause, then, "You realize, of course, you cannot hide forever, that you always risk discovery. I simply want you to be realistic."

"I just hope Homeland Security will nail Naseem's ass before she finds me again."

"I agree. At least moving again will provide you breathing room."

Arnold moved on to a cheerier subject.

"I'll handle your reservation and expenses. You want your room at the High Colonic, right?"

Davidson chuckled again.

"Please make that the *Halekulani*," and told him the number of his favorite room. "Oh, and one more thing before we disconnect."

Arnold glanced at the ravine again. "Yes?"

"Have you explained things to Rachel yet?"

A wave of nausea hit.

"I take your silence to indicate your answer is no," Davidson said.

Arnold exhaled and nodded. "Correct."

"Son, if you wish to build a significant relationship, you must be honest with her. Keep in mind; she *will* eventually learn the truth. Something as significant as this just cannot remain hidden. What will happen *when* she learns you lied?"

"But see…I haven't really lied exactly…I just haven't disclosed everything."

"There is a difference? Willfully withholding—"

Arnold interrupted.

"—yeah, I know, I know…"

"Just think about it. It will be difficult, but I have faith in you to do the right thing."

Chapter 69

ARNOLD WAS BOUNCING foot to foot, waiting in the arrivals lounge of Kahului Airport, having already secured the rental at Hertz and locked his luggage in the trunk. He was glancing nervously back and forth from the arrival board to the map of the island. Their route to the hotel cut across the waist of the dumbbell-shaped volcanic island, wound along the north coast through Lahaina, then along the coast for a few miles, a drive he estimated at an hour, maybe more, depending on traffic.

How would Rachael feel about him after being together more than ten minutes? Separation breeds desire, he knew. Sometimes unrealistic desire. What would it be like to touch her skin and talk face to face? To maybe put his arms around her...their only physical contacts had been at Howie's funeral and in the lobby of her apartment building, both too hurried and distorted by stress to give any clue as to how things might play out once they could relax and totally be themselves. Would she still seem amazingly beautiful? Had the relationship with Loni tainted him? Most importantly; how did Rachael feel about him? Good questions. Scary questions. All in need of answers. Especially, if he intended to move forward with regaining his life.

Each passing second stoked his anxiety. So many answers would come in the next few hours, yet the anticipation of this impending in-the-face reality was, in itself, terrifying. Especially his fear of disappointment. Had he built up his expectations unrealistically? Would anything less than a best-case scenario turn out to be a severe disappointment?

Best-case scenario? Shit, best case scenarios never happened with Arnold Gold. Not even close.

"Alaska Airlines Flight 27 from Seattle is now landing."

That's her!

Relieved at the distraction, he glanced up in time to see the massive black tires of the white 777 kiss the runway, puffing little clouds of gray smoke and, in the process, releasing another crate of butterflies into his gut and steal air from his lungs.

He was terrified at what the next thirty minutes might bring.

He waited nervously in the humid tropical air of baggage claim. Did she check her luggage or bring just a carry-on? Underwear, bathing suit, blouses, shorts were all she really needed, but he suspected she ignored his advice. Breeze taught him that women prefer to travel with more clothes than they can possibly wear.

*Breeze...a*mazing how well he compartmentalized Breeze, the teacher from Naseem the terrorist, and it irritated him to realize that a small part of him still felt some gratitude toward the woman who got him over the hump.

So to speak.

Stop it!

He caught sight of Rachael cutting through the clot of deplaning passengers flooding the tarmac, heading toward the building where the stationary carousels and conveyer belts awaited a frenzy of hands.

"Rachael!"

He jogged toward her, waving. She saw him and stopped. He threw his arms around her and hugged, the smell of her hair suddenly very real and startling familiar. She hugged back.

Eyes closed, he inhaled her scent deeply, and held her with surprising fierceness for a long delicious moment. She gently pushed away to study his face, which triggered his space-heater impersonation. Which accomplished nothing more than fuel embarrassment over his embarrassment. She laughed at that and pulled him back into her arms for another tight hug.

Arnold cleared his throat.

"You, ah, have any baggage to claim?"

"No, just this wheelie, like you suggested," she beamed.

Taking the handle from her, he started leading her toward the exit.

"Our rental's in the lot. I think it's a bit of a drive to the hotel...there's water in the car for us," and realized he was blathering like a meth-head chipmunk.

"Lead on."

"Checking in?" asked the boney Hawaiian male clerk with a Hyatt name-tag pinned to the breast of his blue and white aloha shirt while eying Arnold over the top of a black Dell monitor.

"Reservations for Toby Taylor and Sarah Stein."

Arnold glanced at Rachael, waiting with their bags several feet away. The clerk typed for several moments, frowned, started typing again, leaving Arnold with even more apprehension.

Had Fisher not made the reservation? What if the hotel was full?

Another thirty seconds of typing and frowning.

"I see you'll be with us twelve nights and that the room charge has been prepaid. Is this correct?"

"Yes." Arnold muttered, his nervousness escalating.

The clerk held out his hand.

"I'll take an imprint of your credit card to cover the cost of incidentals."

Arnold handed over the card. The clerk swiped it, started typing again.

"We have you down for two non-smoking king-sized rooms, correct?"

"Yes."

Hopefully one might be smoking.

His face immediately reddened at the thought.

"I'd like to make a copy of a photo ID...a driver license or passport card will do."

Arnold passed him his driver's license.

With check-in finished, the clerk returned the driver license, credit card, along with two room cards.

"Would you like the bellman take your luggage?"

"That's not necessary." And felt the need to justify this. "We only have carry-on."

The clerk nodded.

"Your rooms are on the seventh floor. The elevator is through the alcove straight ahead."

He pointed to Arnold's left.

As the elevator ascended, Arnold held out Rachael's room key.

"Here you go."

She looked at it questioningly.

"What's that?"

"The key to your room."

"*My* room?" sending him a suspicious look. "We're in *separate* rooms?"

"I..." Arnold's face started in on the space heater thing again.

The elevator dinged. The doors slid apart. Rachael stepped out, Arnold following. She held out her hand.

"Where's *your* key?"

"Right here."

"Let's see..." She snatched it away. "Follow me," and headed down the hall pulling her black Tumi. "I didn't come all this way to stay in a room by myself. What were you *thinking*, Arnold Gold?"

Arnold's heart exploded.

That evening they sat in the hotel restaurant enjoying a leisurely glass of cabernet before ordering dinner. They'd been chattering non-stop the entire hour since being seated, neither one in any hurry to order or do anything to shatter the enchanting glow.

God, I missed her.

They turned to watch a hazy, glowing horizon swallow the blood-red ball, dimming the dining room to only candlelight and soft overheads. Strategically placed floods cast long shadows out over the sandy beach as white-capped waves pounded sand and rocks. Hawaiian music played softly in the background. Arnold reached across the table and took her hand in his.

Unfuckingbelievable, Rachael Weinstein sitting across the table at a hotel restaurant in Maui. Was he dreaming? Would he awaken to find himself alone in bed with his beloved pooch curled up on the floor next to him? Guilt tapped his heart for boarding Chance yet again, but took comfort in knowing how well the staff cared for him. Also, Chance didn't seem to mind his last temporary stay there. In fact, he probably enjoyed the added company of other pets. The vet jokingly called him Head Nurse because he was the only pet allowed to roam the clinic during office hours. Chance also made it his mission to sit patiently at the kennel doors of pets (cats included) recovering from anesthesia. The vet believed that his presence soothed their post-op recovery.

"Don't take this the wrong way," Rachael said, "but being with you makes me feel closer to Howie. The two of you were so tight, such good friends." She shook her head and blotted a tear from her eyes with the corner of her napkin. "I miss him so much."

Arnold's heart turned to lead.

"Rachael, I'm so sorry," and slowly withdrew his hand from hers.

My fault.

"I know..." She swallowed. "Sorry...didn't mean to break up your story. Go on...then what happened?"

Arnold was finally explaining—in a somewhat abridged and strategically edited version—the story of Las Vegas and how his gambling had caught the attention of the Jahandars. He omitted any reference to Breeze's carnal services. Maybe some other time. More likely never. However, if he ever *did* explain that part, he'd certainly not admit to paying for the sex and companionship. Even after a year, he felt slimy about it, and wished he could permanently delete the memory.

"The gas exploded and the house went up in flames. I was just lucky to get out."

Davidson's advice—his warning, really—reverberated through his mind.

You need to tell her and you need to do it now.

"But…you're holding something back, aren't you?"

Rachael's large brown eyes continued to scan his face. Arnold sucked a deep breath and nodded.

"Yes."

"Well?"

He swallowed again.

Why does this have to be so fucking hard?

"I triggered the explosion. On purpose."

Her eyes flashed confusion.

"Why, for god's sake?"

"So they'd think I was dead. That's the only way I could possibly escape."

She seemed to consider this.

"Why didn't the FBI do something? Why didn't they intervene?"

"Because they were using me to find the others."

She studied his eyes a moment longer.

"That's not all, is it."

A statement, not a question.

He wanted to deny it, but Davidson was right; he had to tell her all of it.

"The one guarding me…Karim? He was still inside the house when I escaped."

She stared, poker faced, giving him no hint as to how she was processing the news.

Disappointment? Yeah, probably.

Regardless, he needed to set the record straight. If he lost her in the process, well, at least he was taking another step toward regaining his real life.

"On purpose?" she repeated.

He lowered his gaze in shame. "Yes."

"Know what? Given those circumstances, I probably would've done the same thing. After all, he was going to kill you."

It took several seconds for her words to sink in, but when they did, he felt overwhelming relief. Davidson was right again; telling her needed to be done and now there was nothing more to hide. Well, except for screwing Naseem....

"I still don't understand why you weren't the least bit concerned about the effect your vanishing act might have on others. Me, for example."

"Oh, Rachael, that's not true." Shaking his head. "I did care. I just couldn't see any other alternative. Not then, not now. If I could've come up with a way to tell you without putting you at risk, I would've. But I couldn't."

An existential part of him hovered over the table, peering down, reminding him of all the dinners he shared with Breeze in Vegas. Had it not been for those, he wouldn't have the confidence to be chatting with Rachael now.

Funny, the paradoxes life generated.

"You folks ready to order?"

Arnold glanced from Rachael to the waitress.

"Yes," then to Rachael, "we have eleven more days to catch up and I'm starved."

Her eyes warned that this particular topic was far from being finished.

She turned and smiled at the waitress.

"I am famished, too."

Chapter 70

TEN DAYS INTO their vacation, while hiking a trail in the Kula Forest Reserve, Arnold paused, wiped his brow with the back of his hand, pulled a water bottle from his rucksack, and offered it to Rachael. After she drank her fill, he finished it off and stuffed the empty into the pack.

"Sit down for a moment, we need to talk about something."

"Really? Can there actually be another revelation? I don't know if I can handle any more after what I've already heard."

He laughed, but it came out nerd-nervous-hollow-lame instead of the cool, unflustered Davidson knockoff he wished he could manage. That degree of cool could never be him. He chose a flat chunk of volcanic rock for them to sit on.

"More sunscreen?" he offered as a delaying tactic.

For days he'd been mentally rehearsing this little speech and now, with their vacation about to end, he would man-up and deliver it.

She accepted the sunscreen.

"Probably could use a bit more. Boy, sun's sure bright here."

He watched her work the thick white paste into her tanning face. Finished, she returned the tube. He stalled by applying another coat to his forehead and nose in spite of the *Wired* ballcap he was wearing.

Alright already, out with it.

"I've been thinking a lot…about us." He took her hand in his. "I love being with you," then paused, self-conscious at spewing such sophomoric drivel.

"I like being with you too, Arnold."

"I want to find a way for us to see each other more."

She glanced down at their joined hands.

"What exactly are you saying?"

"What would you think about moving to Honolulu?"

Oopppsss.

"I mean…being a nurse and all, you could probably find a job here, easy…and if you rented an apartment it'd be no problem returning to Seattle if…"

She cupped his head in her hands, leaned in for a long, deep kiss before backing away to lock eyes with him.

"I'd love that, Arnold…*but* there are huge problems…too many problems for that to work."

A granite boulder grew in the back of his throat. He tried to swallow but the damn thing was lodged too tightly….

"Problems?" he croaked.

She dropped her arms to her side, shook her head slowly side to side.

"Oh, Arnold, how can you be so surprised? We've discussed this too many times now."

His limbs began tingling, his heart galloping.

"I'll do anything to change…whatever you want. I just don't want…I can't bear to lose you again."

"Arnold, please…listen to me. *Carefully.* You need to understand this. It's too important." Her eyes were pleading. "I want to be with you, too. I have since I was twelve. I'm happy being here now. *But*…anything more than this…vacation…is just not going to work." She glanced away. "I want to be with Arnold Gold, not Toby Taylor or whatever persona you're using to hide from people who want to rob and kill you. Now that I know what actually happened, I'm terrified…absolutely terrified. I'm afraid for you, Arnold. I'm afraid for me. I couldn't handle this fear day in and day out all my life. I'm not as strong as you. It'd be too much to bear. It would destroy any feelings I have for you. I just can't live like that...I refuse live like that."

Well, at least the problem wasn't him per se. These other problems could be resolved.

"I get it, I really, really do," his mind now frantically searching for a solution. "The thing I didn't mention is I've already started to change things. I sold the house and altered my identity again. I'm starting fresh. This time it'll work, I know it will."

She frowned.

"Didn't you just hear what I said? That *is* the problem, Arnold. In a nutshell. I *can't* live like that. I *refuse to* live like that."

He was losing her and it hurt to his core. He started scrambling for the tiniest ray of hope.

"Look, Rachael, I can't change what happened. I can only try to change what *will* happen. I didn't ask to be thrown into this nightmare. It just...evolved."

On account of shooting off your mouth in Vegas, you putz.

"Oh, Arnold...there's something else too."

Oh, shit.

"What?"

She turned away.

He wrapped his arms around her and hugged her tightly.

"Just tell me. There's nothing that I can't change. I'll do anything to be with you."

She pushed away.

"It's the gambling."

"Oh." He thought about that a moment. "I'm not sure what that has to do with *us*?"

"Oh, for god's sake, Arnold, don't be ridiculous," flashing a frown of exasperation. "That's what landed you in this mess. If you continue to gamble, what's to say these situations won't happen again? It seems simple: you're a gambler and gambling attracts criminals. Not only that, but winners attract attention. You're treading on very thin ice and I'm not going to put myself in a position to have to constantly worry what'll happen to you...to us!"

She did have a point. This wasn't the first time he'd worried about the same thing. It was the primary reason for setting up such elaborate security. He got an idea, raised a just-a-minute finger and thought about it.

Yes, he could stop gambling. Tomorrow, maybe.

The only issue was how to support himself.

Well, cross that bridge tomorrow. Do what most people do. Find a job. His spirit brightened.

"Hey, I can change this. How would you feel about us if I got a job?"

"That'd definitely help," she said with a tinge of suspicion. "But that wouldn't change the fact there those people still want you dead."

True.

"Promise me one thing...you'll think about it? When you get home, think about it, okay. In the meantime, I'll figure a way out of this. Believe me I will. Just think it over, okay?"

Her eyes softened.

"I'll *think* about it because I care so much for you. But you need to think about it too...carefully. You're smart. If there's any way to get rid of all this...danger—and I mean forever and ever— and you can live as the Arnold Gold I knew in Seattle, I'll consider moving here on a trial basis. But *only* if I'm absolutely convinced the threats are gone for good. It's not negotiable, Arnold. I mean it."

Chapter 71

ARNOLD SET THE perspiring long-neck pale ale in its usual spot on the end table alongside the TV remote and settled into the couch. Chance circled three times before dropping to the floor at his feet, sighed, nestled his snout between his paws, and closed his eyes. Arnold leaned over to give him a serious dose of behind-the-ear choobers.

The Sunday Night Football halftime report was on; three talking heads critiquing the first half of play. Twenty-thousand dollars—split among ten online sites—riding on the game. So far, SAM was bang-on. Not only that, but several of the night's impact players also starred on his Fantasy Football team. This would be the final bet of his gambling career.

Yes, his sports gambling would cease, but that didn't mean SAM's talents would be put out to pasture anytime soon. Arnold was transitioning his system's uncanny skills from gambling to stock selection, and so far, was doing very well at it. To Rachael's credit, his retirement from the on-line sports gambling gig was turning out to be a significant improvement in his quality of life. He was convinced that SAM could help parlay his modest nest egg into significant nest egg. In the meantime, he had applications in the in-boxes of the two major cybersecurity companies, FireEye and Palo Alto Networks.

Life was good.

Well, except for Rachael.

She still needed to be convinced of his conversion.

Two months had passed since Davidson sold his beloved Honolulu house to Hans Weiser, a wealthy businessman from Munster, Germany. Herr Weiser, a man with substantial bank holdings in Dubai, paid the full asking price of two and a half million dollars. And because Loni Lee only needed to shuffle a few papers in the transaction, she'd agreed to a deeply-discounted broker's fee of one-half percent. In spite of the discount, she'd scored a sizeable chunk of coin for a trivial amount of work.

So...as far as anyone knew—not that anyone was asking—Toby Taylor had simply disappeared from the face of the earth. Where Mr. Taylor had gone was anyone's guess. And, as far as SAM's bots were concerned, no one seemed to be interested in searching for him.

He raised the beer in a silent toast to Palmer Davidson. How fortunate to have such a talented lawyer. Especially considering the alacrity with which he completed the house sale knowing full well that Hans Weiser was just another false identity in Arnold Gold's large arsenal. Arnold would be the first to admit that selling the house to himself had cost the commission, but chalked up that expense to the cost of Toby Taylor's disappearing act. Besides, staying in his beloved Honolulu home meant avoiding the myriad hassles and expense of an actual move: packing, relocating, unpacking, all the various pain-in-the-ass details such as changing address or locating a dentist...on and on.

For him, life was exactly as it had been since moving in a little over a year ago. Best of all, Chance didn't need to acclimate to a new environment. They slept in their same beds, walked their favorite paths. This was, after all, a house he still loved dearly. And, as far as Fisher and the FBI were concerned, who gave a rat's ass about Hans Weiser?

The end of month two of Rachael's six-month trial period would finish tomorrow morning. If the next four months remained as drama-free as these past two, she planned to join him in Honolulu. They had not yet discussed where she'd live when that happened, but he figured they'd cross that bridge closer to the time.

Live together?

That was his preference.

Get married?

Even better. But Rachael was proceeding with extreme caution, holding fast to her demands of no terrorism, Internet gambling, and other high-drama components of Toby Taylor's life. Actually, he agreed with her. Life *was* more enjoyable this way.

And if perchance he bumped into Loni? Well, hell, he never said he intended to leave the city. But he seriously doubted their paths would cross.

Yes, life was good. His gaze wandered from the TV to his beloved view and hoped Rachael would love the house as much as he did. He'd posted several pictures of the interior and view in their shared Dropbox folder, but knew that two-dimensional photographs never capture the three-dimensional magic of sight. At least it gave her a feel for the place.

The phone rang.

He glanced at the caller ID.

Restricted.

Only telemarketers used that ploy.

Another ring.

Arnold replaced the phone on the table.

A third ring.

Shit.

He picked up, fully prepared to give the caller an earful.

"Hello."

"Arnold?"

An iceberg formed in his gut as his mouth opened in shock.

"Don't tell me you've forgotten me already? After all of our good times together in Vegas?"

ACKNOWLEGEMENTS

Thanks to the following people for information, help, and inspiration in writing this story.

Detective James Laing (Ret.), King County Police Department
Kent Lyde
Dmitry Kaplan
Simone Frazer
Nancy Evans
Karen Davis, Esq.